LIFE'S A BEACH

PORTIA MACINTOSH

B

Boldwood

First published in Great Britain in 2021 by Boldwood Books Ltd.

Copyright © Portia MacIntosh, 2021

Cover Design by Debbie Clement Design

Cover Photography: Shutterstock

A CIP catalogue record for this book is available from the British Library.

Paperback ISBN 978-1-80048-754-3

Large Print ISBN 978-1-80048-750-5

Hardback ISBN 978-1-80162-898-3

Ebook ISBN 978-1-80048-748-2

Kindle ISBN 978-1-80048-749-9

Audio CD ISBN 978-1-80048-755-0

MP3 CD ISBN 978-1-80048-752-9

Digital audio download ISBN 978-1-80048-747-5

Boldwood Books Ltd
23 Bowerdean Street
London SW6 3TN
www.boldwoodbooks.com

For my husband Joe & my amazing family

For my husband Joe J and amazing family

1

Your wedding day is easily supposed to be one of the happiest days of your life – but if you want to make absolutely sure it is, you can always spend £2,500 on a horse-drawn Cinderella-style carriage.

'It's top of the range,' the hotel wedding coordinator assures me. 'It's a gorgeous ivory fairy-tale pumpkin carriage, with a stunning white upholstery interior – it even has a little crown on top. It's always in incredibly high demand.'

'It sounds beautiful,' I reply.

'If you do decide to have your wedding here, we can make arrangements to suit your big day – whether you want picking up from home, taking to the church, or here if you would prefer one of our non-religious ceremonies, which I highly recommend. Churches can be so drab. Of course, there is an additional cost per mile, but we can get down to things like that later. Shall we head inside?'

Annette is the wedding coordinator at The Chadwick Hotel in York. We're currently standing outside the five-star hotel, admiring the Grade II-listed building from the gravel pathway that leads up to it.

It's a gorgeously warm sunny day. The kind where you can comfortably get away with wearing a strappy sundress, but not quite hot enough to leave you looking a mess – a few degrees hotter than this and my long, straight blonde hair would be half frizzy, half stuck to the sides of my face hair instead. Today is just perfect though, so it's sundresses, sandals, straight hair and smear-free make-up.

'Yes,' I reply excitedly. 'Let's do it.'

'So, the hotel has actually been open for more than a century. As you can see, it boasts an ornate terracotta façade, typical of high Victorian architecture, and the stone cupola makes for a stunning backdrop for outside photos.'

I smile and nod because, if I'm being honest, I have no idea what any of that means. It is a gorgeous old building though, surrounded by large gardens full of flowers, huge ponds with grand fountains at their heart, and trees in all directions. It's hard to believe we're so close to the city, and impossible not to get carried away, thinking about pulling up in front of the huge doors, having my photo taken with my dad, and then coming back out here after tying the knot to take gigabytes worth of photos with my future husband and everyone we love.

'Beautiful,' I say simply. There's just no other word for it.

Once inside the large lobby, Annette picks up a wedding pack that's waiting for me at reception, before leading me past the grand wooden staircase that sits in the centre of the room. I marvel at the spectacular light that hangs at the centre of the atrium, a large double drum chandelier suspended high above, captivating me so powerfully I nearly bump into a hotel employee coming the other way.

'Oh my gosh, I'm so sorry,' I blurt. 'I was mesmerised.'

'No worries,' he says with a laugh.

Annette laughs gently.

'You'd be surprised how often that happens,' she reassures me. 'Come, let me show you the function room.'

'The function room' sounds like a rather bland concept. Well, many places have a function room, from restaurants to town halls, so the only real expectation I have is space for tables. But this function room surely deserves a grander title, because it is *everything*. It's maybe three times the height of a regular room, with enormous arch-shaped windows that flood the place with the most beautiful natural light.

'Ah, Lady Penelope, I see the windows have caught your eye,' she says before she laughs to herself quietly. 'Do people ever call you Lady Penelope?'

Only *all the time*, that's why I usually go by my nickname, Peach. Otherwise I get Lady Penelope from *Thunderbirds* or Penelope Pitstop from *Wacky Races*. I thought I was in the clear by the time I reached uni but then that movie called *Penelope* (about the girl with the pig snout) came out, and one lad caught on and teased me about it. I never thought I'd reach my thirties and still be dealing with it.

'You're the first,' I reply, hovering in the middle ground between a polite lie and raging sarcasm.

'That's so funny,' she says. 'Anyway, the windows, if I just push a few buttons...'

Annette taps her tablet screen a few times before blackout blinds descend, plunging us into darkness, but only for a split second before the ceiling comes to life with delicate little fairy lights, like a dark night sky full of twinkling stars. A few more illuminate the ivory tulle curtains that adorn the walls in different colours.

'Disco mode,' she says with a smile. 'For the evening party.

We recommend our in-house DJ, who previously had a residency at... Gosh, one of those hip holiday destinations, I'm certainly not cool enough to know what it was. I do hear he's very good though, so you can request him for an additional cost.'

'Oh wow,' I say, still staring up at the ceiling. It's about all I can say, with my mouth hanging open like this.

I've visited a lot of wedding venues recently, but this one is by far the most beautiful. It's just a cut above the rest.

'If you want to take a peep at your brochure,' she suggests. 'We can look at packages, see what works for you. Let's take a seat at one of the tables.'

The packages are named Silver, Gold and Platinum. That's why this place is a cut above the rest, because they don't even have a lowly 'Bronze' package, and they don't actually have their prices in the brochure – that's when you know something is *expensive*.

'We can cater to all dietary requirements,' she says. 'And we're quite flexible. For an additional fee.'

She keeps saying 'for an additional fee', and I can see this wedding getting more and more expensive by the moment.

'You were thinking sixty guests for the wedding breakfast and one hundred in the evening?' she double-checks.

'That's right,' I reply.

'That's not a problem. Over the page you'll find our prosecco packages—' Annette wrinkles her nose with disgust '—but most of our guests opt for champagne – for an additional fee,' she adds. 'But it's totally worth rejigging the budget for.'

'Money isn't going to be an issue,' I say casually. 'You only do this sort of thing once, right?'

'That's the plan,' she replies with a smile. 'I'd be lying if I said I hadn't had some repeat customers though.'

Annette drifts somewhere else for a few seconds, somewhere darker than planning my wedding. I imagine she's thinking about couples who have been and gone and been again. Annette looks so effortlessly classy, and her make-up is absolutely perfect. Somehow, even though her eyes deceive the rest of her face, it's the flawless make-up that manages to keep her looking both professional and happy. Her eyes eventually snap back to me, and her smile finds its way to her face again. I imagine it is kind of depressing being the man behind the curtain, making the big day happen. But someone has to arrange for the swan shit to be cleaned up, I guess. Yes, *for an additional fee*, there was the option to hire swans for something that wasn't entirely clear.

'Speaking of happy couples, where is the groom? Has he left all the planning to you?' she asks, in a sort of friendly way, like she's just making conversation. I doubt she actually wants to know.

'Matthew has work,' I reply. 'He works such long hours, so I'm doing all of the preliminary work.'

'That's very sweet of you,' she says. 'I'll bet he knows he's got himself a good one.'

'I hope so,' I say with a smile.

'Do your families get along well?' Annette asks.

'For the most part,' I reply.

Annette nods knowingly.

'Because we here at The Chadwick understand families can be hard work – never mind when you try to merge two of them – and with all the champagne our happy couples usually purchase, there might well be certain individuals that are best suited, shall we say, out of each other's eyeline,' she explains. 'Our seating planners work with you to decide where everyone should be. We also have temporary pillars – in keeping with the decor of the room, of course, that we can place to prevent people from seeing each other.'

'Oh, that sounds fantastic,' I reply. 'Our uncles tend to butt heads about Brexit anytime we put them in the same room, so that sounds like just what we need.'

'Perfect,' she replies. 'Would you like to see the honeymoon suite?'

'Yes, please,' I reply. 'Is it included in the packages?'

'Only in the Platinum package, otherwise this does run an additional cost, but I'm sure you'll agree it's worth it. Please, do follow me,' she instructs, leading me out of the function room.

'So, are you keeping your name, or are you going to be Mrs Hemsworth?' Annette asks, making polite conversation while we're in the lift.

'I'd really like to be Mrs Hemsworth,' I reply.

'I am a firm believer in taking the man's name,' she says approvingly. 'Penelope Hemsworth – that sounds beautiful.'

It really does.

'Here we are, the honeymoon suite,' Annette announces as she opens the door.

Wow, the honeymoon suite is bigger than my flat. A large four-poster bed is the centrepiece of the room. At the foot of it, a freestanding bath is just crying out for me to climb in and relax. Not right now, obviously – I don't think Annette would be all that impressed if I did. The room is somehow traditional but modern. Classic but clean – everything looks brand new, even the antiques.

'This is just... Wow,' I say.

'We get that a lot,' Annette replies. 'At present it isn't set up for guests, but when it is, we fill the room with champagne, fresh fruit, chocolates, et cetera. And, of course, the finest products for the bath, with big, fresh, fluffy robes to cuddle up in.

Our happy couples never want to leave the room, but it's because of the facilities, not each other.'

I laugh, because I'm pretty sure she's joking, but her face suggests a real pride in her work that makes me think this could be true.

I walk over to the large windows to see what kind of view the room boasts.

'Excuse me,' Annette says, stepping in front of me.

The windows aren't windows at all, they're doors. Doors that open out onto a private terrace with vistas stretching across the grounds. This just keeps getting better and better.

I take a deep breath, sucking in the summer air, savouring the smell of the flowers and the heat of the stone wall that surrounds the terrace.

'So, do you think you can see yourself getting married here, future Mrs Hemsworth?' Annette asks hopefully.

'I can,' I reply. 'I really can.'

Everything here is just perfect – beyond perfect. It makes all the other venues I've visited look positively crap in comparison. It just has it all. The setting, the room, the menu – this room! God, this room. Now that I'm in it, I don't want to leave.

Yep, this really is the perfect place to get married. So it's a shame I'm not actually getting married.

'Perfect,' she replies. 'Well, allow me to give you a copy of our prices to peruse at your leisure. You'll find they're quite competitive.'

Eeesh. The only way these prices would be competitive is if they were put forward for a competition to find the most expensive wedding venue.

'That's great,' I say. 'I'll take this to Matthew, see what he thinks of it all. I'm sure he'll be as charmed as I am.'

'Let's hope so,' Annette replies. 'If not, I'm sure you can twist his arm. By the size of that rock on your finger, I think he might just do anything to make you happy.'

Ah, yes, my super fake engagement ring, given to me by my entirely fictional fiancé Matthew Hemsworth (but actually bought for myself from ASOS), and yes, I did name him after Matthew McConaughey and Chris Hemsworth because, come on, that man would certainly be marriage material.

I say goodbye to Annette, promising to call, even though I know I won't.

I do jobs like this all the time, I don't know why it's left me feeling so blue today. Ah, well, at least I've found the perfect venue, should I ever want to get married – and at least I know to start saving, like, yesterday, to ever stand a chance of tying the knot in a venue like this. But, to be honest, I've been single for so long now that finding a man feels just as likely as finding the fortune to pay for this place.

Don't give up the day job, Peach. At least I get to play at getting married, even if I don't actually get to do it.

2

Growing up in a town on the outskirts of York, I'd always dreamed of living in the centre. Then, when I landed my dream job and the commute started to get on my nerves, it made sense to leave the family home and find somewhere of my own.

Well, I say on my own – it's 2021 and I'm a millennial. We're the generation who can't afford deposits or to have babies. They say it's because we're frittering our wages on brunch and latte macchiatos – like forking out for eggs benedict multiple times a month is why none of us have any savings, and not because we have to pay rent. But don't get me started.

Luckily, I managed to find a flat-share, but not just any old flat: one located on York's most famous street – The Shambles. Like something fresh out of a movie, the long, narrow medieval lane is lined with overhanging timber-framed buildings, some of which date back as far as the fourteenth century. With its quirky shops and its resemblance to Diagon Alley, the street is a tourist hotspot. You get to the front door down a tiny snickel-way, which I love. It feels so hidden away. I could never afford a place like that on my own, but thankfully, when a friend of a friend was looking for someone to share a place with, I got in touch.

It was all going so well until recently, when my flatmate decided she was moving to London to live with her boyfriend. Great news for her. Terrible news for me.

Our overlord – sorry, I mean our landlord – was on my case, right away, asking if I had someone to take her place, or would I be paying the other half of the rent too? The latter was unfortunately off the table, but so was the former, it turned out, when I started trying to find someone to rent the other room. So our landlord put the flat back on the market, which meant it was only a matter of time before someone rented it from under me. Amazingly though, he hasn't had any takers yet, and with only days to spare I have managed to find someone – my amazing sister, Di – to move in with me. As soon as we sign the paperwork, the place is ours for another twelve months. Obviously I'm delighted because my only other option would have been to move back in with Mum and Dad again, and no one wants to move back home, do they?

I worried about my parents when I moved out originally. Di did too. Well, with both of their children moving out in the same week, you would think that would have had some sort of impact. I'd heard all about empty nest syndrome, and with Mum especially being the typical mother-hen type, I thought it would hit her the hardest.

I don't know what I was thinking. There's no empty nest – they couldn't get rid of the nest fast enough. The week Di and I moved out, my mum took over Di's room to make a sewing workshop, and my dad commandeered my room to give himself an office. I don't begrudge my parents taking back rooms in their own house, I just didn't expect them to do it the week we left, and to seem so over the moon about it. In a roundabout way, it's a good thing. I was worried they would be upset, and they weren't, so that's good, but they were genuinely happy to see us go so that they could start the next phase of their lives.

Still, at least they let me come back for dinner, but it doesn't come without its strings.

This desk, here in my childhood bedroom, is the only thing left that is mine.

I twirl in my old desk chair before pulling out the handle on the side so that I can bob backwards and forwards in it. Back when I was studying, when presented with a frustrating problem or when I was stressing about anything (I do love to stress) I would do this to try and relax – not unlike a rocking chair, but a sort of sad millennial version, preparing me for a lifetime of stressing in desk chairs. Funny, that I would do this to relax, because that first tip back of the chair always takes me be surprise, making me feel like the whole thing is going to fall backward, my life flashing before my eyes. But every time, I live to see another day.

It's not so much that I'm stressed today though, more that I'm just frustrated at having the same conversation, again and again, with my dad.

'I'm telling you, I got a text saying my PayPal account had been compromised and needed to verify my information to take control of my account again,' my dad insists.

David Cole – Big Dave to his mates – is sixty-eight years old and has only recently discovered the internet. I remember when I was thirteen or fourteen, getting my first dial-up modem and being blown away by the World Wide Web, going into chatrooms (which in hindsight seems like a terrible idea) and playing games, reading about anything and everything, messaging with my friends. Well, my dad is going through that phase now, but he's somehow more technologically inept than a child at the turn of the millennium, and on a World Wide Web that is far more tangled with... well, I don't need to tell you what the internet is like these days. It's all misinformation and porn – neither of which you want to see in the hands of a technophobe pushing seventy.

'Right, but do you use PayPal?' I ask him, already knowing the answer.

'No.'

'Do you have an account?' I continue.

'Well, no,' he replies. 'But—'

'It's a scam, Dad. Just like the text you got supposedly from HMRC, and the email from your Wakandan uncle who died and left you his fortune.'

I can never quite get it to sink in with him that these types of messages are usually spam, and to always just assume they are. Some of them are very convincing – others not so much. At least he checks with me, even if it is pretty much every time I come here for dinner.

'It would have been nice though, wouldn't it?' he says, staring thoughtfully into the distance, obviously thinking about what he would have done with his millions.

'If the uncle you didn't know you had from the entirely fictional country of Wakanda had died and left you millions? Sure, Dad, that would have been nice.'

I can't help but laugh.

'And I thought I'd get less cheek tonight, with your sister being on holiday,' he points out with a chuckle.

'She's been texting me from Greece, telling me to be extra cheeky while she's away,' I joke.

Di isn't just my little sister, she's my best friend too. She's only three years younger than me but, growing up, thanks to her being smart and my parents' finances changing for the better, we wound up going to different schools. This didn't drag us apart though, it just made us closer. She's currently away on holiday – well, at a destination wedding for one of her old school friends. Do destination weddings count as holidays? I suppose they do when you stay for a week. She must be having a good time because I've hardly heard from her.

'Dinner's ready,' my mum shouts from the bottom of the stairs.

'Lasagne tonight,' Dad says as he pulls himself to his feet.

'Uh, I can't wait,' I say. 'I'm going to stick my face in it.'

'Let me get mine out of the dish first,' he says with a smile.

I follow Dad's lead downstairs. As he walks down the stairs he holds on to the banister on one side, and steadies himself with his other hand on the wall.

I feel a heaviness in my heart. No one likes to think of their parents struggling as they get older.

'Do you need a hand, Dad?' I ask, wincing as I watch him carefully shuffle down the stairs, terrified he's going to fall.

Mum reappears at the bottom of the stairs.

'Oh, he's fine, he just had a few too many with lunch,' she says with a laugh and a bat of her hand.

I breathe a sigh of relief.

'I thought you couldn't walk!' I say.

'Well, he can't,' my mum replies. 'But it is only because he's a bit pissed. Come on, dinner.'

Retirement really suits my parents. It's nice. My mum, Julie, spends her days sewing and cooking and doing all the house-wifey stuff she wishes she'd spent her entire life doing. My dad spends his surfing the web and drinking, apparently.

'I'm not ready to look after you yet,' I say with a smile. I'm kidding, of course, but then again, I'm definitely not ready to look after them. I'm still not all that great at looking after myself.

'You could forgo having kids to look after us,' Mum says through a smile – I'm sure she's kidding.

'Di and I could take one of you each,' I suggest. 'Not that I'm sure which one I'd want. Actually, now that I can smell the lasagne, I'll take Mum.'

'Di is my favourite anyway,' Dad teases. 'She's bringing me a big bottle of ouzo. Are you sure you don't want me to pick her up from the airport?'

'It's OK, I have a job at Mote, that fancy hotel near the airport,' I reply.

We all take our seats at the table as Mum serves the lasagne and Dad pops open another beer. I can't resist grabbing a piece of ciabatta bread while I wait.

'Another wedding gig?' Mum asks. 'How did it go today? Would Matthew have liked it?'

I can't help but smile.

Everyone knows all about Matthew Hemsworth, my fake groom. Intimidatingly tall and impossibly handsome, Matthew is one of the big wigs at Owen's department stores – but don't look it up online, because he isn't really, obviously, because he's made-up. I did think that sounded like a good job though. It means he has money, so can afford fancy weddings, and it sounds like a dream, to be married to someone who can get me employee discount on Yves Saint Laurent, because unless I get stuff like that from work, I can't exactly afford it on the regular.

I know, I probably sound deluded, but my job requires me to be convincing, so it makes sense I should have a detailed cover story.

I'm a mystery shopper, which basically means I am paid to go to shops, restaurants, hotels, et cetera to pretend to be a customer. I'll usually have a brief, telling me what I need to do while I'm there. Sometimes it is my job to go through the motions with a hotel wedding coordinator, planning a fictional wedding with them, before I write my report, which ultimately makes its way through my employers and back to the hotel in question. It's such a fun job, and best of all, it allows me to enjoy the finer things in life, even though I can't afford them.

'It isn't a wedding one this time, just a regular hotel visit,' I explain. 'They have this super romantic suite that comes packed with food and drink. Totally luxurious. I can't wait.'

'It's a shame you don't have a man to share it with,' my mum half-teases as she places my plate down in front of me.

'Oh, isn't it just?' I reply sarcastically, glancing over at Dad who already has tomato running down the front of his shirt. He dabs at it with the piece of pre-emptive kitchen roll Mum must have left under his side plate.

'You get red sauce out by dabbing white sauce on it,' I tell him.

He points at me, as though I've just hit the nail on the head.

'Right!' he replies.

'Wrong,' Mum chuckles, taking the kitchen roll from him before he can dab it in his dinner. 'Just, take your shirt off.'

'What? No!' I reply. 'At the table?'

'I'm spending more and more time naked these days,' Dad says. 'Your mum too. Our therapist says we've spent so long raising kids that we're no longer acquainted with one another's naked bodies.'

'Therapist?' I say, trying not to sound too worried. 'Are you OK?'

'We're fine,' Mum insists reassuringly. 'It isn't couples counselling or anything like that.'

'It's a sex therapist,' Dad says confidently.

Sex is a perfectly normal and natural thing. No one should feel ashamed for having it. Except children talking to their parents about having it, and even more so parents talking to their children about having it.

'I should probably set off to pick up Di now so I'm not late,' I joke uncomfortably.

'I thought you were picking her up tomorrow?' Dad replies, clearly not getting the joke. But then he gets it and he laughs. 'Ohhh.'

They're lucky this lasagne is good or I'd be out of here. Mum's cooking is always so amazing, in a way I've never been able to emulate, even though she gave me a book of recipes the day I moved out. I think, short of them doing it on the table in front of me, I'd struggle to walk away from this table without clearing my plate.

'You must have missed her,' Mum points out. 'It's like the two of you are joined at the hip.'

'Yeah, I really have,' I reply. 'And seeing as I don't have a man, I thought she could visit Mote with me. We can have a girly night, eat all the chocolate, watch movies.'

'She'll love that,' my mum says. 'And it will be great practice for when the two of you live together.'

'Yes!' I say excitedly. 'It's timed so well, with my landlord not finding anyone to rent the place yet, and Di's rental agreement being up next week.'

'Yes, but no one wants to pay that rent to live there, not when there are so many fancy new apartments for much cheaper,' Dad offers up.

I suppose he has a point.

'I like the place – it has charm,' I reply. 'Plus, it really does feel like my home now.'

'Well, don't forget that this was your home first,' Mum says.

'I try not to, but it's hard when there's not a trace of me left,' I point out through an amused grin.

'It will be nice, the two of you living together again,' Mum says. 'And I'm sure you'll have a lovely time tomorrow. Do you both fancy coming over for dinner on Sunday?'

'That would be nice,' I reply. 'We can celebrate me and Di moving in together.'

'Or commiserate you both being homeless,' Dad says, 'if your landlord flogs it before you sign on the dotted line. The women in this family always fly far too close to the sun. Cheers!' Dad raises his beer before swigging the last from the bottle.

Di and I had previously talked about living together, but with her already renting a place, moving into my flat with me just wasn't on the cards. But things have lined up perfectly now. I need someone to move in with me, Di needs somewhere to live, and it really will be nice to live together again.

I'm so lucky to have a sister and best friend rolled into one, and there's no one I'd rather spend a night eating and drinking with, except the legendary Matthew Hemsworth, maybe, but he's almost too good to be true.

3

I've never actually visited Mote hotel before, despite it having been open for two years now and me living and working not too far away. I've driven past it a bunch of times and every time I do, I can't take my eyes off the place. It's always been my dream to have a job here.

You know how, when you need to stay in a hotel near the airport, you usually just check into a cheap and cheerful Hotel Premier Travel Inn Lodge kind of place? Well Mote was built by an eccentric billionaire who decided that the world was missing a sort of luxury take on a budget hotel. Somewhere you could live it up, rather than just crash for the night, and with a popular bar, restaurant and spa thrown into the mix. Having looked at the prices, this certainly isn't somewhere your average person would stay the night before a flight – unless, of course, they get to sneak in, like I do.

It's a massive, brilliant-white building, floodlit with the brightest black light, which gives it such a luxurious, modern finish. I can see it glowing, across two roads, from the airport window I'm peering out of. I stroll a little further, to look out of the window that faces the runway. It seems strange that I haven't heard from Di yet. She said she'd call me just before take-off.

I locate a departures-and-arrivals board, find Di's flight, but there's just a blank space next to it. That can't be good.

'Excuse me,' I say at one of the info desks. 'I'm supposed to be picking up my sister. She's flying home from Greece, but I haven't heard from her and I can't seem to work out when her flight is due in.'

'Oh, that must be one of the flights held up by the strikes,' she explains.

'Strikes?' I hear a male voice ask from behind me.

'Yes, staff strikes,' she replies. 'Unfortunately you'll just have to wait for further updates. I can't say what's happening – I don't really know myself.'

'I suppose there are worse places to be stuck than Greece,' the man behind me says brightly. 'Thanks.'

'Are you waiting for someone too?' I ask as I turn around.

I didn't know who to expect – I don't think I had any expectations at all, which is why I'm a little taken aback when I clap eyes on him.

He's tall – really tall, maybe six foot two, I actually have to shift my gaze upward to make eye contact with him. He reminds me of Zac Efron, just a little, but not an old school *High School Musical* Zac from the noughties. I'm talking the circa 2020, big, buff, manly version with the dark hair, the rugged beard and those piercing blue eyes shining through.

'Yeah, I was supposed to be picking up my mate,' he replies. 'He's lucky I love him – this quick favour isn't turning out to be all that quick.'

He laughs, and I melt. A good-looking man who does

favours and is not only polite but also comfortable enough to say he loves other men. I wonder what the catch is.

'How about you?' he asks.

My brain – a little confused by what I can only file under 'lust at first sight' – takes a breather. It's tuned out. It's just me and the voice in my head, staring at him, hoping he doesn't notice how weird I'm being for what feels like eternity, but in reality is probably only a second or two.

'Are you picking someone up too?' he prompts.

Perhaps I was staring for longer that I thought.

'Yes, sorry, my sister,' I say. I have such an impressive way with words.

'Last time I offer to do anyone a favour,' he says with a smile. 'I'm always too quick to do favours. Well, no more – unless you need something?'

Oh, and he makes naff little jokes too – I love naff little jokes, they're like 80 per cent of my vocab when my mute button hasn't been hit by someone handsome.

'Can you go for dinner with me?' I joke.

To ask a man out to dinner would be totally out of character for me – but to make a joke that doesn't really land, resulting in things feeling kind of awkward, is totally my style.

The man raises one eyebrow curiously. I should probably say more things now, to make that less odd.

'My sister was supposed to be having dinner with me at the hotel over the road, but now that I don't know when she's going to get here, I'll have to go by myself,' I explain as casually as I can. 'It was just a joke, don't worry about it.'

Smooooooth as silk. From an awkward joke to a babbling mess of an explanation. Oh, and in my attempt to sound casual, I've probably gone a little too far. Not just like I don't care but like I *really* don't care. Why can't I just say something normal?

'It's a shame you're joking,' he replies. 'Because I'm going to have to go back to propping up the café here, all on my own.'

Does he... does he actually want to have dinner with me? *Him*? With *me*? Obviously he's knocking on the doors of being a ten, and it's not that I think I'm some kind of monster, but I've given off pure weirdo vibes since the second I turned around. I don't know whether to retreat or double down.

'You are welcome to join me,' my mouth says, oblivious to the fact my brain was thinking it over. 'If we're both waiting for the same flight and you're at a loose end.'

'I'd love to,' he says. 'We can wander over now and keep an eye on our phones in case we get any calls.'

'Sounds great,' I say. I awkwardly shift my weight between my feet for a few seconds. 'OK, let's go then?'

I didn't intend for that to sound like a question.

'Yeah, let's do it,' he replies. He actually sounds excited, but in reality, I bet he's just hungry.

We make small talk as we make the short journey from the airport to the hotel across the road.

'So, where are you from?' he asks.

'I live in York,' I reply. 'Grew up just outside the city, went to uni there – I never wandered far. You?'

'Almost identical, but I'm a West Yorkshire version,' he explains. 'My family live in Kirkstall. I've got a place in Leeds city centre, in Bridgewater Place, if you know it?'

'The Dalek,' I say to show that I not only know the building, but I know its nickname.

'That's the one,' he replies. 'I rent a room from my mate. He's got a penthouse on the thirtieth floor. As apartments go, it's so out of my league. I could never afford it on an Oliver Strand salary.'

'You work at Oliver Strand?' I say. 'The department store?'

'Yeah,' he replies. 'In PR. But they don't pay you enough to shop there.'

He laughs, and I laugh with him, but he can't truly know how funny this is, because Oliver Strand is a big, fancy department store, like Harvey Nichols or John Lewis – or Owen's, which is where the man of my dreams, Matthew Hemsworth, works.

'Well, don't worry about paying for dinner tonight,' I tell him as we walk through the doors at Mote.

'Oh, I wasn't pleading poverty,' he insists. 'I just didn't want you to think I was a rich dick, living in a penthouse – *my friend* is the rich dick.'

He smiles. I love his smile. I also love that he's a little bit embarrassed to live in such a nice place. I totally relate to that. As much as I'm playing a part when I go on these fancy mystery visits and get to enjoy all the expensive products I wouldn't have otherwise, there's a little voice in the back of my head telling me that I'm a fraud – what's a working-class girl like me doing in a place like this? I feel lucky more than anything, but there's always a tiny niggling feeling of awkwardness. I'm glad he has it too.

'It's not that,' I say quickly, reassuring him with my smile. 'I'm not paying for it either.'

He stops in his tracks.

'This isn't something weird, is it?' he asks. 'Because there's no such thing as a free lunch – or dinner – especially in a place like this.'

'Relax,' I insist. 'I'm here for work. I can tell you all about it over dinner.'

He eyeballs me suspiciously. Looks like I'm not the only one thinking things are too good to be true.

'I promise,' I insist. 'I'll just nip into the ladies' and then we'll get a drink.'

'OK, I'm so intrigued now I'll risk it,' he says with a smile. 'But, before you disappear, what's your name?'

I laugh. I can't believe we've managed to get this far without swapping names.

'I'm Peach,' I say. 'Lovely to meet you.'

I put on a sort of faux-formal voice, keen to focus on the humour of the situation, rather than the awkwardness.

'It's nice to meet you too,' he replies. 'I'm Matt.'

I can't help but purse my lips as my eyebrows shoot up towards the ceiling – which is seriously high in this swanky hotel lobby, but I can't even get into the decor right now because, did you hear that? He said his name is *Matt*. Matt who works at a department store.

'I, er... I'll be right back,' I say, forcing a normal smile (which can't possibly look normal), hoping he hasn't clocked my odd reaction.

'OK, see you soon,' he calls after me, before playfully adding: 'Hopefully.'

Once I am safely inside the sanctuary of the ladies' toilets, I wash my hands and touch up my lipstick with the only one in my bag. When I left my room, I put on a deep-red shade, but the only one I have in my bag is hot pink. Luckily my lipstick has been fading from the inside out, so when I top it up with the pink, it gives it a sort of fashionable fade effect that you can guarantee I wouldn't be able to achieve if I set out to do it.

Urgh, I wish I'd tried harder, but I thought I was having dinner with my sister, not a man. I did make an effort, because how could I not at a place like this, but there's a difference between how you dress for your sister and how you dress for a date, even when you are dolled up. Thankfully I've just had my buttery blonde highlights topped up, and my hair is still enjoying the after-effects of being styled by a professional, even though I've washed it a couple of times since. I did actually wash it a matter of minutes after checking in because I wanted to try out the fancy French hair products in the bathroom, and the even fancier hairdryer that was set up at the dressing table. I didn't exactly go over the top with my make-up though (no one takes the time to contour their forehead for a sibling), and I'm wearing a pair of leather-look pants (thankfully it's a cool summer evening or I'd be needing help peeling them off) and a white silky off-the-shoulder top – appropriate for where we are, but it's probably not going to have Matt rushing to help me get out of them, is it?

I once read in a magazine that wearing trousers on a date gives off the message that you're not interested. I hate stuff like that, it's such bullshit. In the same magazine I also read that you're supposed to slap your moisturiser into your face to stop you from looking old. I knew sexism could be harmful, but wow. Hit yourself in the face, show men they have easy access? I'm going to stop reading the trashy magazines they have at the hairdresser's while I'm there. I might start a petition for books, instead of magazines. The amount of time I'm there, I'd certainly get through one.

I don't know why I'm blabbing on about dates, this isn't a date at all, is it? It might look like one, but it isn't. It's just two strangers who met at the airport taking pity on each other, that's all.

But that doesn't explain why I'm so nervous...

4

One of the amazing things about Mote (and there are many) is that the restaurant and bar area have a sort of Wimbledon-style roof, which means that on a gorgeous summer night like tonight, you are essentially sitting outside. It's not only great for enjoying the gorgeous evening sky, but you also get to see the planes taking off and landing – though not my sister's plane, obviously. Being next to a runway was bound to be noisy but, by making it part of the view, they've somehow managed to style it out and own it. It's a feature, not a nuisance. Amazing that, if you put a fancy spin on *anything*, people will lap it up.

To be honest, I'm not all that bothered with the way things have worked out. Well, Di gets to extend her holiday, even if it's only by half a day, and I get to have dinner with Matt.

We're currently sitting at the bar, waiting until our table is ready. Our drinks have just been placed down in front of us and they look spectacular. I'm having a Wow Woo, which is absolutely packed with glitter, making it look like a red-and-gold snow globe. I don't know what Matt's drink is exactly, it's called a Smoky Joe – I can tell that it's smoky though because some kind of actual smoke is billowing out of the tall glass.

'Can I at least get the drinks?' Matt asks in hushed tones, while the barman is off keying out drinks into the computer behind the bar.

'They're paid for too,' I whisper back. 'I'll explain in a second, I promise.'

'So' – the barman claps his hands together – 'would you like the drinks to be placed on your table tab, or would you like to pay for them now?'

'I'll pay now please,' I reply. 'And can I get a VAT receipt too?'

'Of course, you can,' he says, suddenly even brighter than he was before. 'I'll be right back.'

'I am frustratingly intrigued,' Matt groans as we wait for my receipt. 'Come on, let's go sit on the viewing terrace so you can tell me all about it.'

'Don't get too excited,' I insist as we walk over, weaving in and out of the tables. 'It's nothing interesting, I just have a job that has its perks.'

'Pretty decent perks,' he says, nodding at our surroundings.

'I feel like this may be overhyped now but, basically, my job is to go to places, try out the facilities and then write a report on it.'

'For a newspaper or a website?' he asks curiously.

'It's actually for the business,' I reply. 'So I get to eat in restaurants, stay in hotels, stuff like that, and then I write about the experience so that they can learn from it.'

'Wow, that's pretty sweet,' he says. 'So you just get to lap up all the freebies while you're doing your job?'

'Yep,' I reply, with a slight smile, not wanting to seem like I'm showing off, but it is pretty amazing.

I don't mention the wedding assignments because something about that is especially sad. When I'm staying in hotels, I'm not pretending to stay in them, I actually get a room, sleep in it, and enjoy the facilities. But, obviously, when I'm doing a wedding visit, I am straight up pretending to get married, and I don't even have a boyfriend, so there's something so delusional about it.

I definitely get the better jobs in the office because I'm good at role play and thinking of things to say to keep up the act. It's nice to be appreciated, but I do still feel like a bit of a loser, pretending to be loved-up. I suppose I should probably be a bit more upfront about this part of my job, because last time I was seeing someone (which feels like forever ago), he found a stack of brochures under my coffee table and I had to try and explain them away. The reality was that I just hadn't got around to recycling them, because I'm kind of lazy sometimes. To me, it was no different to blasting my hair with dry shampoo for the fifth day in a row or leaving empty bottles of bubble bath around the edge of the tub, but given the wedding-crazy rap women get, I don't think he believed me, and we didn't last long after that.

'Top tip,' I start. 'If you go to a bar, always ask for a VAT receipt. I have to for work. But the savvier employees know that the mystery diners and mystery visitors have to ask for VAT receipts, so they'll usually treat you better.'

'That's kind of depressing,' he replies. 'People will try harder if they think you're someone important and not just a regular customer.'

'I suppose we all do stuff like that sometimes,' I admit. 'Don't you work harder if you think someone is watching?'

'I guess you're right,' he replies. 'Like I'm on my best behaviour right now.'

Before I get a chance to ask him why, a waiter hurries over to us. He almost goes flying after clipping his foot on a chair leg, but he rights himself just as he puts the brakes on in front of us.

'Ms Cole, good evening,' he says as he catches his breath. 'Forgive my colleague who made the mistake of saying you had to wait for your table, it's ready for you now. If you'll allow me to carry your drinks, please follow me.'

'Oh, OK,' I say with a smile. 'Thank you.'

As we follow him closely, I look back at Matt who widens his eyes. He's impressed.

'My name is Tim, I'll be your waiter today,' he says as he hands us our menus. 'I'll give you a few moments to browse before I come back and take you order. Any questions or if you need any recommendations, just give me a wave, OK?'

'OK, thanks,' I reply.

Tim dashes off as quickly as he appeared.

'OK, what was that?' Matt asks. 'We just got rushed through the system, this place is packed.'

'It's the VAT receipt,' I say with a smile and a shrug. 'Another interesting fact: Tim isn't a waiter, he's the manager, see how he's dressed differently to the rest of the wait staff? Report forms always ask if you can see the manager, usually identifying them by what they're wearing. In a place like this, it's always a suit.'

'I feel like you've just changed my life,' Matt replies.

'Just make sure you only use these powers for good,' I insist through an amused chuckle. I didn't actually think this would impress him.

'Oh, Scout's honour,' he says through a cheeky smile.

I watch Matt's eyes darting from side to side as he takes in the menu. 'Do you know what you're having?' he asks me.

'I think... the camembert to start followed by...' It's hard to choose. 'I think I'll have the steak. Probably the rib-eye.'

'I can't believe they pay you to eat this stuff,' he says. 'I think I'll have the same.'

'I even get a wine budget,' I reply. 'Some with dinner – and my brief specifically requests I have a bottle delivered to my room too.'

'I've never been more jealous in my life,' he admits.

'Well, don't be too jealous. I was supposed to be staying here with my sister, having a girly evening, and now I'm going to be staying here alone and ordering a bottle of wine. I'm going to look so tragic. Especially because it's one of their romance rooms.'

I notice the look on his face. I'm not sure he knows what I mean by that, and given the fact he has one eyebrow raised, he must think it's something interesting.

'Think about it though, all the romantic junk you get, it's not all that different from the kind of stuff you'd have at a girly night. Wine, chocolates, spa stuff. And, don't worry, I appreciate you bailing me out by having dinner with me, but I won't make you come up to my room and drink wine.'

That was supposed to be a joke, but it just sounds weird as hell now that I've heard my own words out loud. I laugh, to let Matt know I was kidding. He laughs too. Crisis averted.

'I refuse to believe I am doing you a favour right now,' he says. He sips his drink before making what I can only describe as a thoroughly content face. 'So good.'

'Listen, I know he might be on to us, but if I do anything to intentionally blow my cover, then my report will be thrown out. So just don't let on that I just met you in the airport and invited you for dinner with me. That sounds made up,' I explain.

'Yeah, no worries,' Matt replies.

Sensing that we're ready to order, Tim reappears as if from nowhere.

'So, do we know what we're having?' he asks. 'And can I get you any more drinks?'

I hadn't actually noticed that I'd drained my cocktail glass until just now.

'Yes,' I say excitedly as I feel my stomach rumble, right on cue. I order a bottle of wine, careful not to go over my budget, and then my food, careful to ask for my steak without any coleslaw on the side because I absolutely hate it.

'And for the gentleman?' Tim prompts.

'I think I'll have the same,' Matt says.

'Exactly the same?' Tim replies.

'Yes, please,' Matt says.

Tim furrows his brow.

'With or without the slaw?' Tim double-checks.

'Without, please,' Matt says quickly. 'Hate the stuff.'

Tim looks almost upset, and like it's on the tip of his tongue to ask what rumour we may or may not have heard about the coleslaw here.

'You hate it too?' I say once we're alone again.

'It's basically cabbage in mayonnaise,' Matt says simply. 'No thank you.'

'I'm with you there,' I reply. 'Tell me some more things about you.'

I know it sounds like I've resorted to small talk, but I don't really know anything about Matt, so it's fine. I really want to know more about him because I am absolutely fascinated by him – I'm also waiting to find out what's wrong with him. No one is this perfect – well, perfect for me, at least – surely?

'Oh, I'm terrible at this stuff,' he says. 'When I go on dates and it's time to do the get-to-know-you stuff, that's when things go south.'

I feel my eyebrows shoot up. I quickly force them back down. I find it very hard to believe Matt could be bad on dates.

'You seem so confident,' I point out.

'It's not a confidence thing,' he replies. 'More just that... I'm not that interesting to a lot of people, I just don't have much to report. You know my job, you know where I live. I've got parents who love me, I watch a lot of TV, movies. I collect comic books, but that doesn't impress anyone. Do you ever feel like you might be a bit boring?' He laughs.

'My job is the most interesting thing about me,' I reply. 'Life is very undramatic. My parents never batted an eye when I left home, and they're both happy and healthy. I live in York in a nice flat. I also watch a lot of TV and movies – I've never read a comic, but I do love the movies they make from them. I collect keyrings, which has to be even nerdier than comics.'

Matt thinks for a moment.

'OK, yeah, keyrings are nerdier than comics,' he says seriously before that smile that just looks so natural on his face reappears. 'I'm kidding. That's pretty cool. So we're both boring, we both like superhero movies and we both hate coleslaw. This could be the start of a beautiful friendship.'

I laugh. Maybe it could.

Tim places our starters down in front of us.

'Enjoy,' he says with the smile of all smiles.

Wow, it really does look great. Baked camembert with warm, freshly baked bread to dip into it and a sweet berry sauce on the side.

'Oh wow,' Matt says. 'This looks amazing.'

'Mmm, it tastes amazing too,' I say, through my first bite, quickly remembering my manners and swallowing before I continue. 'I've never had a cheese I didn't like... apart from goat's cheese, but that doesn't count.'

'I *hate* goat's cheese,' Matt replies. 'I suppose I'm a little bit of a picky eater.'

'Me too,' I reply, almost excitedly.

This is amazing. We really do have so much in common. I swear, if this was a date, I'd be glad I kept the stack of wedding brochures under the coffee table because we're just finding things in common left, right and centre.

'Do you always order the same kinds of things wherever you go and struggle with trying new things in case you don't like them?' I ask.

'Yes!' he replies. 'Do you always ask for things to be taken off your food in restaurants?'

'Like the coleslaw?' I remind him. 'Yep, but then other times, there are things I absolutely love, that lots of people hate, like pineapple on pizza or pickles in burgers.'

'OK, this is just weird now,' Matt replies. 'It's like I'm talking to myself.'

'Really weird,' I reply with a smile.

I can't help but watch Matt as we eat. You can tell he really enjoys his food, but I love that he's just as fussy as I can be. I always feel like a big baby, still being picky as a grown adult, so it's nice to meet someone similar.

'How were your starters?' Tim asks.

'Oh, amazing,' I reply.

'Ten out of ten,' Matt adds.

'Wonderful,' Tim says. He gestures with his hand before another waiter appears and removes our plates. 'Your steaks will be with you shortly. Are you having a nice evening?'

'Really nice, thank you,' I reply. 'This is such a gorgeous hotel.'

'Are you staying with us tonight?' he asks.

'Yes,' I say. 'The rooms are just... wow. Everything here is fantastic.'

'Do you have a view?' he asks. 'The airport-facing rooms have a view that is simply stunning.'

'Oh, yeah, a really good one,' I reply. 'We're in the Together Suite, so we can see for miles from the terrace.'

'Oh, you're in one of our couples suites,' he says, all smiles. 'How wonderful. You make such a gorgeous pair.'

Tim is really grafting for his five-star review. It's impressive. I've slipped up though, saying 'we' because now he thinks that Matt and I are a couple, and Matt can't possibly be prepared for the amount of bullshitting that is involved with this job.

'We get that a lot,' Matt replies, suddenly snapping into character.

'I'll bet,' Tim says. 'How long have you been together?'

'Oh, how long is it now, babe?' Matt asks me.

'Gosh, it feels like no time at all,' I reply with a cheeky grin. I'm so impressed right now. 'Almost a year.'

'Ah, wonderful,' he says. 'How did the two of you meet?'

I know that Tim is sucking up to us, just a little, but he does seem genuinely interested.

'We met at Matt's work,' I reply.

'What do you do?' Tim asks.

'I work for a department store,' Matt tells him. 'I handle PR, and you wouldn't believe it to look at her, but this one kept causing trouble for me.'

'Oh, how so?' Tim asks curiously.

How so indeed?!

Did you ever play that game when you were younger where you would draw a head on a piece of paper, then fold it over, then someone else would draw the body, someone else the feet, and then you would open it up and see what you created? This is sort of like that. We're creating a story, bit by bit, and Matt has just passed it back to me.

'They kept sending me the wrong item, so I tweeted about it and it went viral, so Matt had to try and keep me sweet to stop me telling everyone they kept sending me two left shoes instead of a left and a right – they did it twice, can you believe that?'

'That's crazy,' Tim laughs. 'So he fixed it for you?'

'I insisted she came into the store and I personally handed her the correct shoes, and a gift card to say how sorry we were, and, as unprofessional as it was, the second I laid eyes on her, that was it. I wanted to get to know her. So I started chatting to her and then *she* invited *me* for dinner that very night.'

'A woman who knows what she wants,' Tim says, clearly warmed by our tale.

'Well, how could I resist?' I say. 'It was like a modern-day Cinderella.'

'You know what, I'm going to get you something,' Tim says. 'Something on the house, to celebrate the happy couple. I'll be back soon.'

'Wow, thank you,' I reply.

Tim disappears again, clearly on a high from such a heart-warming tale.

'So, people really do just fling free stuff at you,' Matt points out.

'Never mind that,' I say. 'Look at you, making up stories on the fly – that was amazing. That's exactly the sort of thing I have to do. And you were so good at it!'

'Well, PR is all about spin,' he says with a shrug. 'It was nothing.'

'Well, I'm impressed,' I tell him. 'And what an amazing

story. God, I should be so lucky to get swept off my feet like that.'

'Ah, so you're single too?' he says.

'Oh yeah,' I reply, somehow suggesting that I am more single than your average singleton, like my status is somehow set in stone and almost impossible to reverse.

'Well, this will be good practice for us,' Matt jokes. 'Perhaps playing at being on a date will help us get better at it – or at the very least, we can come up with better backstories for each other so we don't seem quite so dull to other people.'

Before I can say anything, Tim pops up again. This time he places a silver dish down on the table in front of it.

'For the happy couple,' he says as he removes the lid. 'Enjoy.'

Tim leaves us to enjoy our surprise. We both lean forward and peer down into the dish in front of us, before slowing looking up towards each other.

'Oh, God,' I say.

'You don't like oysters either?' Matt says.

'I've never even tried one – they look disgusting,' I reply. 'Have you?'

'I hate all seafood,' he replies. 'Well, fish fingers are OK, but that's it.'

'What do we do? We can't just tell him we're big babies who don't want them, can we? We'll look tragic.'

I know that I'm a grown woman who doesn't have to eat anything she doesn't want to... but people pay good money for things like this, and I would feel awful throwing them back in Tim's face. That said, if I eat them, I might still throw them back in his face, but with a little help from my gag reflex.

I pick one up and raise it to my face. I give it a cautious sniff; it smells like an ocean breeze, which sounds beautiful until you're applying it to something you're going to eat, then it just sounds disgusting.

'Yeah, I can't eat that,' I whisper to Matt through a forced smile, trying not to seem like I'm freaking out, even though I absolutely am.

'Not in a million years,' Matt replies. 'Just follow my lead.'

Matt picks up an oyster, raises it to his lips, but then instead of pouring it into his mouth, he stops short, causing it to just miss his mouth and fall into his lap.

'Into the napkin,' he whispers.

I look down at the napkin across my lap and then back up at Matt. This time my smile is genuine. That's brilliant.

I follow his lead, the two of us almost knocking back our oysters, but instead hiding them in our napkins.

Matt picks up the final one. We're almost home and dry when...

'How are they?' Tim asks.

'Oh, so good,' I reply. 'Thank you.'

Matt is frozen, the oyster held in front of his face as the cogs in his head turn. I can see it in his eyes. He's wondering what to do. Well, he looks as though he's about to eat it, so it would be strange if he changed his mind now, but his napkin trick isn't all that subtle when you're looking right at him.

He only gets a couple of seconds to think about what to do before he takes one for the team, knocking it back, swallowing it in one big gulp before returning the shell to the plate.

'I'll bet you're both feeling romantic now, huh?' Tim says with a smile as he takes our plate.

I just stare at Matt. I'm in shock. I can't believe he did that. I don't think he can quite believe it either. He looks ill.

'That's the last thing I was expecting you to do,' I tell him when we're alone again.

'Well, I didn't want to make us look like babies,' he replies.

'No one has ever taken an oyster for me before,' I say. 'How was it?'

'Like a giant chewy, slimy, snotty, rusty bogey,' he says, his face scrunched up in absolute disgust.

He practically chugs his wine to try and take the taste away, but it doesn't look like it's working.

'Thanks,' I reply.

'Don't worry about it,' he chuckles, like he's finally seeing the funny side of it. 'At least I'll have a story to tell next time I'm on a date.'

I know that Matt might think he's dull, and I know that this isn't a date, but even before he sank the oyster, I was already having so much fun with him. It's hard to imagine anyone not having a good time with him.

It's kind of a shame it's not a date really because, if it were, it would have probably been the best one I've ever been on.

5

Tonight has been so out of character for me I think I might have switched genres. Usually my life is little more than a gentle indie flick – tonight I feel like I'm in a romcom.

After a long and boozy dinner with Matt – and one hell of a baked Alaska for dessert – we semi-staggered our way to the hotel check-in desk so that Matt could book himself into the hotel for the night. Well, there's no way he can drive, and even if he could, Di and Matt's friend's flight could be landing at any point during the night, so it makes sense to stay close.

The woman behind the desk was impossibly snooty. Her nose practically pointed towards the ceiling the entire time she was talking to us. I don't know if it was because we were drunk or not 'posh' enough for this place, but the only time we saw any joy on her face was when she told us the hotel was fully booked.

'You could take her to the Travel Stop down the road,' she suggested to Matt as she gestured towards me with a nod.

What a confidence boost that was, having her look me up

and down and decide that the place most befitting for taking me was a budget hotel chain.

Needless to say, *Louise* is not going to look good in my report – yes, I made a note of her name in my phone, mostly because it's my job, but a little bit because I hate people who think they are better than others.

I don't normally think I'd be so bold, to do what I did, but not only is this an evening of firsts, but I really wanted to rub it in Louise's face.

'You can stay in my suite with me,' I insisted. 'Come on.'

I gave Louise a big smile before I took Matt by the hand and dragged him towards the lift. She did *not* look impressed.

'Was that for her benefit?' he asked me.

'We're both waiting for the same flight to get in, it's my fault you're too drunk to drive and my suite is made up of multiple rooms, so you can have the entire lounge to yourself,' I said. Eventually adding, 'And, well, yeah, a little bit for her benefit.'

'That's really kind of you, thank you,' he replied.

And so, here we are, in the most romantic suite in the general Yorkshire area, me and the man I just met. Surrounded by rose petals, heart-shaped junk, essential oils and more chocolate than even I can take down.

When we first got here, I charged a fifty-pound bottle to the room. Fifty pounds is my wine budget generally, not per bottle, but this bottle will be our last because I'm really starting to feel quite drunk. I'm going to start drinking water now to try to get the jump on my hangover.

The suite is pure luxury, with a separate living room and bedroom, a terrace that overlooks the airport and surrounding views, and a bathroom bigger than most Budget Inn rooms. It would be such an incredible space to share with someone you love but it's pretty great for sinking multiple glasses of wine with a stranger too.

I'm currently sitting on the sofa while Matt searches our room's minibar for bottled water.

'Oh my God, there's a vibrator in here,' he calls out from behind the fridge door.

'Please tell me that's just a cocktail I've never heard of?' I call back.

Matt sits back down on the sofa, plonking two bottles of mineral water and something called a Button Pusher Deluxe on the sofa between us.

'Do you think it has to be kept cold?' he asks curiously.

'No one likes room-temp mineral water,' I tell him.

He cracks up. He's so cute when he's drunk.

'Not the water, the vibrator,' he says. 'Do you usually keep them in the fringe?'

'Me? What are you asking me for?' I reply.

'Not *you* you, sorry,' he babbles. 'I just meant women.'

My serious face relaxes into a smile.

'I'm winding you up,' I tell him. 'I think they just put it in there because they charge you for it.'

Matt pops the silver cap off the tube-shaped container and tips it out into his hand.

'What?' he says, his disappointment apparent. 'It's tiny – I thought it was going to be way bigger.'

He discards the small, silver bullet vibrator, not that he had much use for it to begin with.

'That's a common theme for women,' I joke.

'You told Tim you couldn't resist me,' he playfully reminds me.

'Well, you told him the second you laid eyes on me, boom, that was it,' I reply flirtatiously.

I notice his face moving closer towards mine, so I meet him in the middle.

Matt glances down at my lips, then back up to my eyes.

'I never said "boom",' he whispers.

There's a serious look on his face that gives me goosebumps all over my body.

I don't often have moments with handsome men, so I'm no expert, but this really does feel like a moment. So I do what any women in my position would do – I feel around on the sofa, grab the vibrator, click it on and lift it up between our faces, which really are quite close now.

Well, I don't know what to do with a moment, so I may as well destroy it.

I place the vibrator on the end of Matt's nose. Yes, on the end of his nose. I don't think he knows what to say or do, so he just lets me. I really wish I hadn't done it, but now I need to own it.

'When my cousin Vanessa was younger, she was a rep for a lingerie and toys shop,' I tell him. 'She always told customers the best way to test these things was to hold them against the end of your nose, because it's the second most sensitive part of your body.'

I think this really has to be a new awkward low for me. Being too scared to kiss a man, so shoving a sex toy in his face instead, as though bringing a sex toy into the mix is the way to make this sexy moment less sexy. Then again, I did practically shove it up his nose.

'Your cousin sounds fun,' Matt replies, backing off a little.

'Oh, she's great,' I say. 'She lives in LA now, I really miss her.'

'What did she move to LA for?' he asks curiously. Now I think he's trying to dispel the sexual tension for me.

'A man,' I reply. 'She's divorced now – actually she's been divorced a couple of times – but she loves it there so much she decided to stay.'

'The things people do for love,' Matt says. 'LA isn't exactly a few hours down the A1, is it?'

'Yeah, although I think the fact he had a yacht and a seven-figure fortune did sweeten the deal,' I reply with a chuckle.

I don't doubt that Van loved Ian, but she would always be the first to tell you how much she loved his yacht. Well, her yacht now – I think she got it in the divorce.

'Could you imagine moving thousands of miles away for love?' he asks, relaxing next to me again now that I've holstered the vibrator.

'I can't imagine being in love,' I admit, before taking a big gulp of wine – bigger than I was intending. The expensive stuff sure does go down faster.

'Not been in love before then?' he asks, curious.

'Nope. I had a serious boyfriend for a few years, and I thought I loved him at the time, but we were together since we were in sixth form, and no one knows what they want back then, do they?'

'No. I don't think I've ever been in love either,' he says. 'But I'd move to LA just for the weather.'

'I wonder if they have good oysters there,' I wonder out loud playfully, hiding my cheeky grin behind my glass.

Matt stops mid sip. There's a horror in his eyes, like a soldier recalling an old war memory.

'I'll never do that again,' he says. 'Not for love or money or anything. That is my one oyster done, forever, so let's hope my life never depends on it.'

'Well, you'll always be my hero,' I insist, rubbing his bicep, and at first it's just a playful touch, but his arm is like a magnet that I can't seem to pull my hand away from. And just like that, the sexual tension is back, but with each sip of wine, the voice in my head telling me to shove sex toys in people's faces to stall becomes much quieter than the voice telling me to pounce on him.

I stop rubbing his arm and pat it for a few seconds, as if to say: 'There, there. Sorry I disturbed you.'

My gaze shifts from my hand to Matt's eyes. He's looking right at me. I mean really looking at me. It's the wine making me admit this, but all I can think about is doing kind of disgusting things to him. And the way he's looking at me, through my eyes, peering into my brain, I think he knows it too.

Matt slowly leans forward, only a matter of inches, then stops. I think he is thinking exactly what I'm thinking... but it's hard to think about thinking at all when you're this drunk. What point was I even just trying to make? Perhaps I need to stop thinking all together. Perhaps I need to just... lean forward a little... let Matt lean in a little closer... and... oh, screw it.

To say I throw myself at Matt would be correct in multiple ways. First of all because I'm handing myself on a plate to him, and second because I've launched myself at him with such a force I'm now on top of him, on the sofa.

The good news is that I'm not that rusty at figuring out if men are interested and Matt is just as into it as I am. He runs his hands down my body as we kiss, eventually resting them on my bum. He squeezes it for just a few seconds before, wow, in one swift motion we swap places. I haven't slept with many people (my cousin Van thinks I need to go on holiday with her to Malaga, pretend we're twenty-three and 'pad my sexual CV'), but of the people I have slept with, none of them have ever been so strong, and I don't recall any of them having any moves, apart from, you know, the usual rhythmic back and forth.

Matt whips off his shirt and he's straight back on top of me to kiss me more. As he pulls me up and leads me to the bedroom, alternating between removing pieces of my clothing and his own, he doesn't do anything for more than a few seconds before his lips are on mine again. Finally in the bedroom, in nothing but our underwear (you don't know how relieved I was my trousers came off without a fight), we finally pause for a few seconds, about a metre apart. It's that sort of calm-before-the-storm moment, where you can retreat to safety (the comfort of my uneventful day-to-day life) or just put your foot on the pedal and drive straight into the hurricane and see what happens...

I've never done anything like this – I bet everyone says that, but I haven't. My CV is all high-school sweethearts and lacklustre Matcher dates that only fizzle out (if they even get going), but when am I ever going to wind up in a situation like this again? I'm in a beautiful hotel suite that I haven't paid a penny for. I'm with an absolutely gorgeous, charming man (who actually seems like a really genuine person), who not only has the upper-body strength to fling me around like I'm weightless but can also make me laugh. And he wants me – he *really* wants me – possibly as much as I want him. And, perhaps most crucially, I've had just enough to drink that my natural confidence has been nudged out of the shell it sometimes hides away in.

I want Matt. I really, really do. I do usually make a guy wait a while before I'll sleep with him, to make sure he's actually interested in me. Then again, it's 2021, and I'm a modern feminist and... and I don't actually need an excuse, I don't have to explain myself to anyone, I can do whatever I want.

I reach out and take Matt by the hand, pulling him towards me so that our kissing can pick up where it left off.

He lays me back on the bed, and while I may not have ever done anything like this before, I just know that it feels right. And anyway, all that matters is this moment. We'll worry about the morning in the morning...

6

What the hell is that?!

I've had some hangovers in my time, but this one is really something else. My head feels fizzy, like my brain is being shaken up inside my head and it's going to burst any second. And then there's that deafening sound in my ears, like a jet engine, getting louder and louder and...

I carefully open my eyes, squinting as the bright summer-morning sun floods in through the open terrace door, and that's when I remember where I am. The good news is that I am not dying. That jet engine noise is real and not some kind of horrible tinnitus – it's from an actual plane. The bad news is that if I want to mute the sound a little, I am going to have to force myself to get out of this bed and walk over to the door to close it.

What seemed super charming and cute last night seems absolutely stupid and infuriating today. Who the hell builds a hotel next to an airport with a terrace overlooking the runway? I hate it. I hate it, I hate it, I hate it.

I've already kicked off my covers in my sleep, because it's so warm this morning, and I just feel so... yuck. You know on a hot summer night when your bed just gets so impossibly warm and you feel so sweaty and sticky and horrible? I feel like that. I can't wait to have a shower, just as soon as I work out how I can turn the volume down on that too, because I'll bet even the sound of running water is enough to make my headache worse.

I peel myself from the sheet underneath me and slowly but surely sit up, swinging my legs out of the bed, pausing for just a few seconds, before standing up. There's a voice in my head – well, it's more likely my blood pressure – telling me to lie back down before something makes me lie down, but I stagger over to the terrace doors to close them. I close the curtains too.

It's only as I'm making my way back through the now dim – and now even more roasting – room, that I realise something is missing. Well, two things. First of all, clothing of any description – I am completely naked – but that isn't the main thing. The main thing missing is Matt.

I quickly rectify the first problem by grabbing one of the hotel robes and wrapping it around my body, even though it's far too warm, but it was a lot easier to let Matt see me naked when I had half a bottle of fifty-quid wine in me.

Next problem: Matt. He wasn't in bed with me when I woke up, and he isn't in the bathroom because the door is open. Is he really that much of a gent that, after hours of rolling around between the sheets with me, he actually got out of bed and went to sleep on the sofa as promised? It does feel a little bit late for that. What's more likely is that I was sweating all over him – or doing what I'm told I often do when I've had too much to drink, which is flail around like a maniac when I'm asleep – and that's why he decided to sleep on the sofa instead.

I should nip in the bathroom first, shouldn't I? Brush the knots out of my hair, put on some make-up – take off last night's make-up first! That can't be looking too hot right now. Ideally, I should take a shower. I'm all sticky and gross, and not at all sexy, so he's not exactly going to be in a hurry to pounce on me again, is he? Because we met in such unusual circumstances, we've done things in the wrong order. Usually you have to impress people into sleeping with you, but given that Matt and I had only known each other a few hours (I can't stress enough that I *never* do anything like this), it's now that I need to put the effort in so that he doesn't feel like he's made a mistake.

It occurs to me, for a split second, that I may have made a mistake, but honestly, I don't think I have. Last night was just amazing. We had such a strong connection, we got on so well, and the sex... Oh my God. I've never felt this way about anyone before, or had so much in common or so much sexual chemistry. I might have been drunk, but I wasn't *that* drunk – I remember everything, and the more I think about it, the less I care what my hair looks like and the more I want to go and cuddle up on the sofa with him.

I spy my deodorant poking out of my overnight bag, so I grab it and give my armpits a quick blast before I tighten my dressing-gown belt again and head for the living room. I take a deep breath as the butterflies in my tummy (aggravated by my hangover) go nuts, but I smile, and I turn the corner and...

Oh. He's not here. That's odd. It's a big suite but, it's not *that* big, so if he's not in here or the bedroom or the bathroom, then he must have gone. Unless I locked him out on the terrace, which, now that I think about it, I could have easily done because I basically got up and closed it with my eyes closed. Here I am, banging on about making a good impression and I've locked him out on the terrace. He's not going to care how my hair smells compared to that, is he? Thank God I didn't stop to have a shower and do my hair. He would have been stuck out there for ages! And, there she is, the Peach I know, the one who always finds a way to mess up a good thing.

Huh? He's not there. He's nowhere. He's... I guess he's gone.

I wander back into the bedroom and plonk myself down on the bed. I'm so puzzled my brow is furrowing, and I'm so hungover that something as simple as the skin on my forehead moving is enough to make me feel worse. Well, I guess he's gone. I mean, obviously he's gone, but he's gone gone. Not-coming-back gone. He's woken up, snuck out and taken off. And he's done it a damn sight quieter than those planes out there because oh my God, they are loud, and oh my God, that has just reminded me that I have a sister I'm supposed to be picking up from the airport.

I grab my phone to see two missed calls, but thankfully they're only from half an hour ago.

I quickly call her back.

'Hey there,' she says brightly. 'What a night I've had.'

Uhh, same, but I'm not about to blurt it out right now.

'I'm so sorry, I've only just woken up,' I say quickly. 'Someone at the airport mentioned the strike – I figured your phone had died.'

'Of course it did,' she replies. 'Don't they always? But I'm home safe – well, on home turf, at least, I'm just in the airport, charging my phone. Can I buy you breakfast?'

'That would be great,' I say. 'I need to freshen up and get dressed, so why don't you meet me in the lobby of the hotel? They've got some pancakes on the menu that will make you forget all about your stressful night.'

'Ooh, sounds good,' she says. 'OK, sure, I'll head over and meet you downstairs.'

'OK, see you soon,' I reply.

I throw my phone down on the bed and spring into action,

whizzing around the suite, from the bedroom to the bathroom and back again, like a sad, stinky Tasmanian devil. I need to put on a lot of make-up, and a very brave face, and head down to meet Di.

It's going to take more than a big plate of pancakes to make me forget about my night though. But now it's unforgettable for all the wrong reasons.

7

'And how was your stay?' a very enthusiastic man who I'd guess was in his early fifties asks me. I can see from his name badge that his name is Walter. Just about. My eyes are so bleary.

'Oh, it was great,' I tell him. 'Amazing, thank you.'

The overly bright smile I force onto my face solidifies that I'm laying it on too thick. I need to dial it back a notch.

'Wonderful,' he replies. 'Your room charges will be charged to the card you booked your room with, so, all that's left is – anything from the minibar?'

'Hmm?' I reply.

'Peach, hello!' I hear my sister's giddy voice squeak from behind me.

I turn around to see her standing there, looking and sounding almost surprised to see me, given that we're supposed to be meeting here. Perhaps it's because I look so rough. Di, on the other hand, looks amazing, with her sun-kissed skin and her long light-brown hair. Even if you'd never met her before, you would still be able to tell she was just back from holiday because she has that unmistakable glow of someone who has just returned from somewhere nice.

'Oh my gosh, hello,' I reply as brightly as my hangover will allow. 'Look at how tanned you are!'

'Look at how hungover you are,' she replies with a cackle. 'Good night, was it?'

'Erm...'

'Anything from the minibar, miss?' Walter presses on.

'Yeah, maybe a couple of things,' I reply sheepishly. I remember exactly what was taken from the minibar. Two bottles of water, an overpriced tube of Pringles and *the bullet*.

'It's OK if you can't quite recall,' Walter says ever so helpfully. 'Housekeeping will have to replenish the items, so we can attach them to your final bill.'

'Oh, no, no, that's OK, I remember,' I quickly insist. The last thing I want is for my boss to look over my hotel bill and see that I took a vibrator out of the minibar.

'Come on, I'm starving,' Di whines from behind me.

'Yeah, OK,' I tell her, before practically leaning over the hotel desk. 'Two bottles of water, the Pringles and... *the bullet*.'

Walter, ever the professional, snaps into a mode I'm sure he often has to, where he adopts a more serious look and gives me a reassuring nod.

'Got it,' he says.

'Can I pay for those now?' I ask. 'On my card?'

'Of course,' he replies. 'One moment.'

I turn around to look at Di. She has the biggest, dumbest smile on her face.

'Peach!' she squeaks, her eyes practically glittering with amusement. 'You really did have a good night!'

'Oh, God, don't,' I insist. 'I can explain, I promise. Just, over breakfast, not here.'

'I don't think I want to hear about it while I'm eating,' she says with a laugh.

I quickly pay for the vibrator before trying to get away from the front desk as fast as humanly possible. Di is dragging her case behind her with one hand, so I link up with her on the other side.

'I don't think I could have lasted another five seconds of eye contact with that poor man,' I tell her as we head for the restaurant. 'That was so embarrassing.'

'And there's me thinking you'd be bored without me,' she laughs. 'I was stuck in an airport and you were sticking—'

'Table for two?' the hostess asks. She's all smiles, until she looks at me, and her customer-service grin falters for just a second. I must look bad.

'Yes, please,' I say quickly.

Once again, the roof is open on the restaurant. The hot summer sun is beaming down on us but, thankfully, we sit at a table with an umbrella for shade. It is really nice, with the slight breeze, the sunshine, all the beautiful green plants, the upbeat ambient music… but not today, not to me.

We order our food – cappuccinos and Nutella-and-cream pancakes, which hopefully I will be able to not only stomach eating but also successfully keep down – and the second we're alone, Di starts her interrogation.

'So, last night,' she prompts. 'What's this explanation you reckon you have?'

'Don't look at me like that,' I insist with a gentle laugh. 'I do have an explanation. I'll tell you the story now, but you have to promise to wait until the end before you say anything. No jumping the gun, OK?'

'OK, sure,' she says. 'Go on.'

'I met someone at the airport – a man.'

'Oh my God, Peach, that's amazing,' she interrupts excitedly.

'No. No, no, no,' I quickly add. 'See, this is why I told you to wait... So I met this guy, Matt.'

'Matt!' she replies. 'Matt like your fake fiancé.'

'Yep,' I reply. 'And the similarities don't start and stop there – he even had a similar job to my Matt. Well, he was waiting on a delayed flight too, so we got chatting, and I ended up inviting him to have dinner with me. We were both just stuck waiting, for the same flight too, so I was just being nice!'

I'm quick to reiterate that, before my sister playfully accuses me of trying to pick up men at the airport while I'm supposed to be there doing her a favour.

'So we had dinner, and we totally hit it off. We had so much fun.' I can't help but smile as I tell her about him. Well, just because the morning after is a disaster, doesn't mean the night before wasn't great. 'I told him all about my job, and he pretended to be my boyfriend so that the waiter didn't totally rumble my mystery visit. We chatted for ages, it got late, he'd had too much to drink to drive, and he still needed to stay close to the airport to pick up his friend, and then it turned out the hotel was fully booked so—'

'Peach!'

'I said he could sleep on the sofa in my suite,' I tell her truthfully. 'But then one thing led to another, and we had sex.'

'Wow,' she says, smiling widely. 'That does not sound like you at all!'

'It isn't like me,' I reply. 'I'm not a sex-on-the-first-date and minibar-bullets kind of girl at all. It was Matt who got the bullet out.'

'OK, I'm still your sister,' she playfully insists. 'I don't need the horny details.'

'Not to *use*,' I reply with a laugh. 'If anyone used it on the other, it was me.'

'Erm...'

'Oh, God, not like that,' I quickly insist. 'I practically shoved it up his nose.'

'Hey, I'm not here to kink shame anyone,' she jokes.

'This part you'll believe. I was being my awkward self, and I held it on the end of his nose, like Van used to do, because I was too scared to go through with kissing him, but I got over that.'

'It sounds like you had a great night,' she says. 'So why do you look so glum?'

I pause for a second, pursing my lips as I search for the words, because even though I can tell my sister anything, some things are hard to say. But that's the most wonderful thing about having a sister who is also your best friend, always having someone to tell anything and everything to. She's my agony aunt when I need advice. My priest when I need to confess. She's my lift from the airport, my Phone-a-Friend, the first person I'll hit up if I ever need a kidney. I can tell her this, easily, but I guess I just don't want it to be true.

'He'd vanished by the time I woke up,' I admit.

'Ah,' she replies. 'Well, there's nothing wrong with having a one-night stand, so you better not be beating yourself up about it.'

'Correction: there's nothing wrong with having a one-night stand when you know you're having one,' I reply. 'It would have been nice to have known that. I really thought we'd hit it off. I know that sounds naive – and you know I'm not naive – it just really did feel like so much more.'

'Well then, it's his loss,' she insists.

'I know,' I reply. 'I just don't know what's worse. If he woke up, took one look at me and realised what a massive mistake he had made, or if none of it meant anything to him. There I was, having the time of my life, thinking something special was happening, and he was probably just using me for the bed, and the roll around in it was just a bonus.'

'Oh, er, sorry – I have your food,' our awkward young waitress blurts. I guess she caught the end of that.

'Yes, thank you,' Di says. 'It looks great.'

Now that it's here in front of me, and looking incredible, my appetite comes crawling back. A stack of big, thick, fluffy American-style pancakes sandwiching together layers of Nutella, whipped cream and fresh strawberries. It looks so good I'll happily take my chances eating it.

'So, enough about me,' I insist. 'How was the wedding?'

'Oh, it was beautiful,' she replies. 'Everyone should get married abroad – it makes attending so much more pleasant.'

'You look great,' I tell her. 'So tanned and well rested.'

'You should see Lex – she's caught even more sun than I have,' she replies.

Alex – or Lex as she's known by her friends, but I am certainly not one of those – is Di's best friend from school. While I just went to plain old regular school, Di went to a really nice private school, and while I grew up and drifted apart from my school friends, Di is just as thick with Lex as she was when they were fifteen. Lex and I have never really got on, but we keep the peace for Di. It's not me, it's not me at all – it's all her. She can't help but look down her nose at me. Luckily, we hang out with Di at different times, so it's only really on special occasions I see her these days. I can live with that.

'Lovely,' I reply.

'Something interesting did happen though,' she starts sheepishly. 'I feel kind of bad telling you now but... I met someone too.'

'On holiday?' I reply.

'Yeah, well, at the wedding,' she says. 'He's a friend of the groom, so he's from round here.'

'Oh wow,' I blurt. 'Well, that's good?'

I can't quite put my finger on why, but for someone who just told me something positive, Di doesn't seem quite right. She isn't finding the words as easily as she would usually, she's fidgeting with her cup too and breaking eye contact, which is not like her at all. I imagine it's because she feels bad, because of the story I just told her, but I'd never begrudge my sister a little happiness just because my love life is going terribly.

'It's great,' she replies, finding a genuine smile. 'We met at the wedding, and then we spent pretty much every minute of the holiday after that together. He's amazing, Peach, he really is. Just the most gorgeous, most interesting man I've ever met. After He-Who-Shall-Not-Be-Named broke my heart, I never thought I'd fall for anyone again, but that wasn't real love, this is.'

He-Who-Shall-Not-Be-Named is Di's ex from a year or so ago, and not only did I promise never to talk about him again, I promised I wouldn't even think of him. The less said about him, the better.

'Anyway, on our last proper night there, he arranged this picnic on the beach for us. Everything was perfect. The lanterns, the violinist, the delicious food. I didn't think it could get better, but then he asked me to marry him... and I said yes.'

Di delivers this news so casually, the words falling from her lips with minimal effort. Unfortunately, the mouthful of pancake I shovelled in a second before she said it is nowhere near as graceful. I cough and splutter as it catches in my throat.

I quickly grab my water to wash it down. Well, I was already feeling queasy before the coughing fit. The last thing I need to do in this hotel is throw up in one of the nice plants.

'You said yes?' I say back to her. 'You're getting married? To a man you met on holiday? Who you've known for a week?'

'You said it yourself about Matt, when you hit it off with someone, you just do – when you know, you know,' she replies.

'Erm, yeah, and look how that turned out,' I point out.

'OK, but Charles loves me and I love him,' she insists.

'His name is *Charles*?' I reply in disbelief.

'Yes,' she replies. 'So?'

'Charles?' I say again. 'You'll be Charles and Di! And if that isn't a bad omen...'

'Oh, come on, P,' she replies with a roll of her eyes. 'So, we'll be Di and Charles instead. That isn't a reason not to do it.'

'Erm, no, the reasons not to do it are that you met him on holiday and you've only known him a week,' I say again. How can she possibly think this is a good idea?

'Well, we're doing it, and you're just going to have to force yourself to be happy for me,' Di replies. 'First of all, because I need you to be my chief bridesmaid, because you're my sister and my best friend. And I could have asked Lex, who was actually happy for me, but it has to be you.'

I soften ever so slightly.

'Also, we're pretty much tying the knot in a week or so, on a private island in the south of Italy,' she adds casually.

'What?!'

'Charles knows the person who owns the island,' she says excitedly. 'They said we can borrow their massive villa and get married on the beach – it's going to be incredible.'

'Believe it or not, I'm more shocked at the time frame than the location,' I reply.

'Mum and Dad need to meet him, so we thought we could

get together on Sunday – you too – and then go see his parents after. And then the plan is to jet off right away and spend a week there with our stag and hen parties, just us young ones, so we can all get to know each other, and then fly the family and friends out at the end of the week for the wedding! All expenses paid, don't worry.'

'Wow, you've really thought this all through,' I say sarcastically.

What makes this whole thing even more jarring is that Di is usually the sort of person to think things through. She plans things in great detail, always likes to know what she's doing, agonises over such simple decisions. A stunt like this is just so unlike her. If cousin Vanessa said something like this, honestly, I doubt I'd bat an eye. This couldn't be more out of character for Di though.

'Reckon you can get the week off work last minute?' Di asks. 'You said it yourself, your boss has been nagging you to use up all that holiday you have.'

'I guess,' I reply. 'Maybe. I'll have to ask.'

What is like Di, the baby of the family, is to expect the world to shape around her. I know that my parents will feel the same way as I do – that this is out of character for Di and that she's rushing into things, but she's never had much trouble getting her way with them. The baby of the family is treated as the baby pretty much forever.

'Please, please square it,' she says, 'or we'll have to move the whole thing. I can't not have you there – that would be weird.'

I mean, it would be no weirder than marrying someone you'd only known for a fortnight, but sure.

'Are you sure you know what you're doing?' I ask her.

'Of course I do,' she replies. 'Come on, you know me.'

'I do, that's why I'm asking,' I say.

'There is one downside,' she says, her face falling. 'It does mean I'm not going to be able to re-sign for the flat with you. I'm really sorry, but obviously I'll be moving in with Charles. Is that going to be a big problem for you?'

I was so blindsided by Di's announcement that I didn't stop to think about what it meant for me. Of course she won't be moving in with me now – and of course it's a big problem. I didn't think I could feel sicker, but her casual revelations feel like punches in the stomach. Still, she seems so happy, and she's my baby sister. Who am I to ruin this for her?

'Oh, don't worry about it,' I say. 'It'll be fine. I've been thinking about trying to find somewhere better. A bit bigger maybe.'

'Are you sure?' she says. 'I thought you loved it there?'

'Nah, I'm starting to get pretty bored with it,' I lie.

I do love it there. I really do. But what else can I say? I'll just have to figure it out.

'Well, I can't wait for you to meet Charles,' she says, her smile returning. 'Just promise me you won't think another thing about it until you've met him, OK? Just keep an open mind. I'm sure you'll love him just as much as I do.'

'OK,' I say because, again, what else can I say?

God, just when you think things can't get any worse. I thought my one-night stand was out of character but Di has topped that, hasn't she? It's one thing to sleep with someone you hardly know, but to marry them?!

I suppose I'll have to do what she says and meet this Charles and see what I make of him. I'll cross that bridge when I come to it. For now, I'll probably worry about where I'm going to live after a couple of weeks. Oh, and I need to write my report of Mote and send it today, so that will be fun. The place gets a glowing review, with the exception of Louise on reception last night, who was majorly rude, but as enthusiastic as my words will be, I'll know just how quickly my perfect night was over. When we were telling the manager the fake story about how we met, and I said it was like Cinderella, I guess I was right. The ball is over, the fairy godmother's magic has worn off, and now it's back to reality.

It is a shame though. I really thought I'd met Prince Charming this time.

8

It's nice to be back in my own bedroom. It's just a shame I'm probably going to have to move out. Well, I pretty much have today to come up with Plan B now that Di has decided she doesn't want to live with me, and I only have two options for staying: find someone else to move in, or pay the full rent myself. I could maybe, just maybe, afford to pay the rent for a month or two by myself while I found someone else to take on the other room, but it would be tight, so that's probably a non-starter. And what are the chances I'll find someone to move in with me? I don't know anyone looking for somewhere, and I don't fancy living with a total stranger.

I love my little room, my bed, the little fairy lights that hang above it. If there was anything I could do...

I've completed my mystery-visit reports, and I'm just browsing some website where people who are looking for flat-mates post and, just wow. It's not unlike a dating app; everyone has a profile, with a bio and photos, and just like on dating apps, some people try to be funny, some come across as psychopaths and basically no one looks like anyone I'd have stuff in common with.

I'm snapped from my thoughts by the ringing of my phone. It's Donna, my boss, and it's unusual for her to be calling on a weekend.

'Hi, Donna, was everything OK with my report?' I ask immediately, worried something might be amiss in there. I can't think why else she would be calling.

'No, everything isn't OK,' she replies. Shit, this sounds serious. There's never been a problem with my work before – I'm her favourite. 'I've seen your bill – the bill from your room.'

Fuck! How does she know about the vibrator? I thought I took care of that. I didn't expect it to find its way onto my room bill – I got a receipt and everything.

'Oh, I'm sorry,' I say. 'To be honest, I opened it by mistake and then just left it to one side, and I never intended it to wind up on the room bill.'

Whether it's a question of money or what Donna considers is or isn't acceptable in the privacy of a hotel room, hopefully that response has me covered.

'You wasted it?' she replies. She sounds shocked, but I guarantee I'm more shocked. Did she want me to get my money's worth or something?

'Well, I didn't want it,' I continue.

'That's a lot of money for something you didn't want...'

God, she sounds so angry.

'It was only £15,' I reply.

Donna says nothing for a few seconds.

'Peach, what do you think we're talking about?' she eventually asks.

'Erm, what do you think we're talking about?' I reply, because if she isn't talking about the vibrator, then things might not be as bad as I thought, so I absolutely shouldn't say it unless she does.

'The bottle of wine you ordered and charged to the room,' she says.

'Ohhh.' I have never been so relieved. 'It was fifty pounds, which was what the brief said, right?'

'Yes, the brief said fifty pounds,' she replies. 'But the bottle you bought cost *five thousand*!'

My small room gets even smaller as the walls close in on me. Did she just say five thousand pounds? For a bottle of wine?

'That can't be right,' I insist. 'I chose it – it was fifty pounds.'

I cast my mind back to last night, when we ordered the wine, and while it was technically Matt who called up and ordered it, it was me who chose it. The thing is, I'd already had so much to drink, and the one I wanted had a French name I couldn't pronounce, so I gave Matt the number from the menu. Did he hear the wrong number? Did I give him the wrong number? I don't suppose it matters, because we drank it. Holy shit, I drank a five-thousand-pound bottle of wine. I don't even remember what it tasted like, but it definitely didn't taste like a big chunk of a house deposit, that's for sure.

'It was five thousand pounds, Peach, of all the mistakes to make,' Donna replies. 'Obviously the company isn't going to cover it, so I suppose we're going to need to draw up some kind of payment plan where we take some money out of your wage every month, until it is paid for, OK?'

I sigh.

'OK, yeah, whatever you need to do,' I say, trying to sound as agreeable as possible, because now more than ever I need to keep my job, seeing as though I'm going to be giving a chunk of my wage back to them for the foreseeable. 'I am so, so sorry. I have no idea how it happened. I don't know what to say...'

So much for thinking I'll be able to rent this place on my own – I'm not going to be able to rent anywhere good, not while I'm paying off my wine debt. I just don't know how on earth it happened. I just wish I could strike last night off the record – what a massive mistake of an evening.

'Also, Ellie has very kindly offered to take on your workload next week,' Donna tells me. 'You've been working too much, and I think you're getting tired and making mistakes.'

Oh, that vicious little snake, I bet she has. Ellie doesn't work hard enough, mostly because she always has one eye on my jobs, and it looks like now she's finally got what she wants.

'So, what do I do?' I ask.

'I've just sent a brief to your inbox,' she replies. 'Things are a little quiet at the moment.'

I open it and skim through the details in a matter of seconds. Oh, shit, I really am being punished. She's got me spending the week travelling around all the Bargain Bonanza shops in Yorkshire, seeing how many packets of paracetamol they'll let me buy at once. Just when you think things can't get worse... I'm not usually one to give up on the task at hand, but this job is a real comedown from the high-profile gigs I'm used to.

'Actually, I could probably do with using up a week or so of holiday,' I say. 'If things are quiet, and with my holiday stacking up. Di is getting married in Italy.'

'That's great news,' she says, but she still sounds too mad at me to sound like she means it. 'Yes, by all means, take a couple of weeks while things are quiet.'

I think perhaps she just wants me out of her sight, but I'll take it because I really can't face going into the office and getting yelled at or, even worse, seeing Ellie's stupid, smug little face.

I hang up the phone and realise something else. My best, if not only, option on the home front is to move back in with my mum and dad. Just for a while, until I pay off some wine debt, save up some money and find someone I can share a flat with. No, I'm not excited about it, but at least I can move my things in and then jet off to Italy. Not that I can even get excited about my free holiday because it comes at the cost of watching my sister make potentially one of the biggest mistakes of her life.

I pull myself up and start packing up my things. Well, I'm already on borrowed time, and there's no time like the present to move back home. Plus, as tragic as this sounds, at least I won't have to pay for things like food if I'm there. That way I can overpay my wine debt, because I hate having this hanging over me – I feel like it's casting a shadow on my career.

I'll call Dad, make sure it's OK to stay with them for a while, and see if he'll help me transport my things there so I don't have to make two trips. Perhaps it will be nice, moving back in with Mum and Dad, getting to enjoy Mum's cooking every night and... well, I'm not sure what the perks of living with my dad are, I'll get back to you on that one. I'm sure I'll just end up being his secretary, managing all his bizarre spam for him in real time.

What I'm not going to do is focus on the fact that, while my sister is flying through the motions, I seem to be regressing. I'll pack up my things, tuck myself up in my parents' sofa bed and then, and only then, will I let out a few tears.

But really, the only thing to do is dust myself off, pick myself up, and try to get back on my feet properly. I absolutely can't afford to have a breakdown right now, because my sister needs me. I need to have my shit together when I meet this Charles fella so that I can figure him out. My own life might be going to hell, but I can't let Di do the same with hers.

Right on cue, I get a text from Di suggesting lunch tomorrow with Mum, Dad and Charles. As much as I think she's making a huge mistake, I am curious about him and interested to meet him. Well, come on, don't you usually have to drag men kicking and screaming into commitment? And there's Charles, proposing after one week. It sounds like this Charles might be too good to be true, and if anyone can figure out why, it's me, because when it comes to protecting my sister, there isn't much I wouldn't do. And anyway, it's not like I have much left to lose, is it?

I knew that my old bedroom was now my dad's office, and that I wasn't exactly going to be taking a trip down memory lane by sleeping in there, but I had latched on to the idea of some kind of positive nostalgia hit that I might get from sleeping in there again. Unfortunately for me, when I arrived home yesterday and started carrying in my things, I was instructed to take them to my mum's sewing room, not my old bedroom, because Dad, quote, 'isn't about to give up his office now.' I think he would have had me sleeping on the sofa every night before he would have surrendered his office to me, so I suppose I'm just lucky Mum loves me enough to give me my own room, with some privacy. Don't get me wrong, I don't mean to sound ungrateful – I know that they're doing me a favour – but it does sting, just a little, that my dad appears to be more concerned about his internet access than where his fuck-up daughter is sleeping at night.

I do feel like a bit of a fuck-up. The plan was never to move back in with Mum and Dad when I was thirty-one. And by the time the Student Loans Company and now my employer get at my pay cheque, there isn't going to be all that much left, definitely not enough to turn things around quickly. So I'll be sleeping in the sewing room for the foreseeable – and I'll probably be hiding in there more than I had planned to.

It turns out, in their retirement, and at the suggestion of their sex therapist, Mum and Dad have various, shall we say, 'customs' they observe day to day. My dad somehow thought he was sparing me by explaining the inner workings of Naked Wednesday to me so that I could find somewhere else to be moving forward, and when he started trying to explain what was special about Friday nights, I stopped him. I told him that once we were all back from the wedding, no explanation necessary, he just needed to tell me when he wanted me to make myself scarce. No details required. Please, God, spare me details. In a completely objective way, it's good that my parents are shaking things up now that it's just the two of them again. It makes sense and I'm happy that they are happy. But I'd just prefer not to have a front-row seat, and I can't help but remember how paper-thin the walls are in that house, because my dad could hear a dial-up modem trying to connect at 11 p.m. from basically anywhere in the house, and that terrifies me.

On the plus side, I did manage to get a decent night's sleep on the sofa bed, and after an epic lie-in, I am currently sitting at the breakfast table in my dressing gown, drinking tea and eating pastries.

'They were nicer when they were warm,' Mum tells me, clearly a dig at how late I've slept in.

'It's Sunday,' I point out.

'It's eleven fifty,' my dad replies. 'We'd been up, dressed, to church, and back for brekkie before you'd even kicked your covers off.'

'You did not go to church,' I reply in disbelief.

Dad just laughs.

Mum is currently spraying the kitchen cupboard doors with furniture polish before wiping them down with one of those bright yellow cloths. She's in that super full-on mumsy cleaning mode she always snaps into when she's expecting company.

'Wow, we really are all pulling out all the stops for Di's holiday romance,' I say through a mouthful of pain au chocolat.

I don't mean to sound so bitter – I'm just still in shock. Even more so because my parents don't seem to be bothered at all.

'Peach, we have to respect your sister's wishes,' Mum ticks me off.

'And I'm going to give him a good pat-down, don't worry,' Dad replies.

Mum and I both look at him for a second.

'Well, with my eyes, and my questions,' he replies. 'Make sure he's right for my baby girl.'

'You're scarier when you don't speak,' I point out. 'So maybe just stand there and look intimidating.'

Big Dave is six foot three and stocky, but he's also a gentle giant that isn't much of a threat to anything, apart from maybe whoever he does his online banking with. Still, when it comes to his daughters, he's always been the protective type. Take it from someone who dated their high-school sweetheart for years. As I got older, he was never quite able to shake the mentality that Chris (my ex) and I should be watched like a hawk. Imagine, being twenty-one years old and your boyfriend not being allowed upstairs to use the bathroom if you were in your bedroom getting changed.

Of course, it was all so easy for Di, with me having paved the way for her. It's the job of the oldest child to fight and break down barriers with their parents, and it's the role of the youngest to breeze through after them. My mum could be just as bad as my dad, despite being much shorter – so short she's standing on a stepladder to polish the cupboard doors – but what she lacked in height, she made up for in a series of different facial expressions that conveyed a world of emotions. I like to think I inherited Mum's dirty looks.

Bottom line: Di and that ex-boyfriend we don't mention had it so easy but, even so, I didn't expect Mum and Dad to be so chilled about her impending marriage.

'We're not pulling out all the stops, are we?' Mum says, not all that tactfully. 'Aren't you going to get dressed?'

'Obviously, I'll get dressed,' I reply, baffled my mum could even begin to entertain that I would meet my sister's fiancé for the first time in my scruffy dressing gown, with my knotty hair and pastry flakes raining down from my chest whenever I reach for my teacup.

We're interrupted by the sound of the front door opening and closing.

'Hello?' Mum calls out.

'Hey!' Di sings back. 'We're here.'

'Already?' I whisper to Mum.

'She did say lunch,' she whispers back.

'It's only just midday,' I reply, but to early risers like my parents, that won't mean much. 'Go distract them, I'll head upstairs.'

As my mum and dad head into the hallway, I plan my escape. I absolutely can't meet Charles looking like this – I look like I've escaped from somewhere – but I also can't get upstairs while they're in the hallway, because that's where the stairs are. If Mum and Dad can just get them into the living room, then I can dash through the hall, up the stairs, and I can make myself presentable. Urgh, why does this have to be even more stressful than it already was?

'Oh, Charles, it's so lovely to meet you,' Mum says. 'So tall! Isn't he tall, Dave?'

'Nearly as tall as me,' Dad says in that voice fathers reserve for talking to their daughters' boyfriends. 'Come here, lad.'

I imagine he's shaking his hand and not hugging him, but you never know. My mum, on the other hand, when presented with what she will probably decide is a younger version of my dad, will wrap herself around him like a pole.

'Where's Peach?' I hear Di ask.

'Oh, you know your sister,' Mum starts.

'She's in the kitchen,' Dad says obliviously.

'OK, Charles, time to meet my sister and my best friend, and the only person you need to worry about impressing,' she jokes.

Oh, God, please don't come in here. Please, please...

Di bounds through the kitchen door like a puppy after a tennis ball. Her smile drops when she sees me, but then she just starts laughing.

'Oh my God, you're not dressed,' she blurts.

'I thought I had more time,' I reply.

'We did say lunchtime,' she reminds me.

'Yeah, apparently I have a different idea to the rest of this family of what time lunch is,' I say, a little embarrassed.

'Well, it doesn't matter,' she insists. 'I'm too excited to wait. Peach, meet Charles.'

My sister yanks her fiancé through the kitchen doorway, and my jaw plummets.

He is tall with that kind of slender but muscular physique where his body is small but his shoulders and arms are broad. He's clean shaven with neatly swept-back blonde hair, and you can just tell he has money from his clothing, because if that polo player on his T-shirt were any bigger, the brand would probably be legally obliged to pay him for wearing it.

I just stare at him.

'Hi, Peach,' he says as he takes a step towards the table. 'I've heard a lot about you. It's great to finally meet you.'

It isn't the fact that he seems to be a catch that has me speechless – getting engaged after knowing someone for a week is unusual, so I knew he must be pretty special to have captured my sister's heart so easily – I'd guessed that much already.

The reason I'm sitting here, like an idiot, staring at him is because I know him, but for some reason Charles doesn't seem to recognise me. He should though – seeing as though Charles was the first person I slept with!

10

You know the whole Matt thing the other night, when I kept saying that I'd never done anything like that before? Yeah, well, that's not strictly true.

The second I clapped eyes on Di's fiancé, I recognised him. Charlie Blake. Charlie and I go way back, and they're certainly not fond memories.

The last time I saw him, we were both kids – I don't know if that makes it better or worse. Somehow, it's both. Charlie and I went to school together, and while Charlie was the most popular boy in our year, my social standing paled in comparison. Well, he was good-looking with rich parents, and I was kind of chubby and very quiet – a lethal combination when you're in secondary school.

It was like a fairy tale, every insecure teenage girl's dream come true, before it turned into a total nightmare. Towards the end of Year II Charlie wound up with a free house while his parents were away for the night. So he did what any sixteen-year-old would do: he decided to throw a house party. The best thing about house parties when you're that age is that because kids are so preoccupied with being popular, they don't worry about little things like inviting so many people their house gets destroyed, or inviting the uncool kids – anyone and everyone was invited. It was my first and last proper teenage house party.

I got all dressed up, after spending actual hours deciding which weirdly provocative Tammy Girl outfit to wear, and smeared myself in so much make-up I left blue eyeshadow and kohl eyeliner smears on my pillow for weeks afterwards. But it was all worth it when I got there and I finally felt like I fitted in. I was with the cool kids! To begin with, I let my hair down just a little. There was a table covered with a mixture of bottles of beer and those crappy Kapop alcopops that I don't think you can even buy any more. I had two – an orange one and a strawberry one – careful not to get too drunk because I was a good girl at heart. But being around the cool kids, being included, it gave me confidence, and as my confidence grew stronger, I got more and more into the party spirit. By the time party games were suggested, I was the first one to throw my hand in the air.

Charlie's house was massive, so someone suggested we play Sardines – you know the game, someone goes off to hide and then everyone sets about looking for them, joining them in their hiding place when they do eventually stumble upon them. Well, with only a small group of us playing, and with everyone being a lot drunker than I was, naturally I was the first person to find Charlie hiding in his parents' walk-in wardrobe. It turned out that everyone else got bored with looking, or easily distracted, so I was, in fact, the only person who found Charlie. But while we sat there, waiting for others to join us – we were still assuming they were actually searching, of course – we chatted, and we laughed, and we really hit it off. One thing led to another – and by 'another' I mean me losing my virginity to the most popular boy in school, in his parents' bed, at a house party. Granted it doesn't sound all that special, but that is peak teenage girl – as far as your peers are concerned you can't achieve any greater achievement than that. Well, no one gives a shit about the A* you're predicted to get in your French speaking GCSE exam, do they? *Non.*

I left that party with my head held high, excited for the next day at school when I thought I was not only going to be the new queen of Year 11, but I was naive enough to think that Charlie actually liked me. So I marched up to him with a confidence I shouldn't have had, and I spoke to him like I was on his social level. You know that scene in *Grease* where Sandy and Danny reunite for the first time and he treats her like shit in front of his friends? Well, imagine that, but it's every time they see each other for the rest of Year 11, while you're sitting your GCSEs!

In what I suppose was an act of self-preservation, Charlie, desperate for his friends not to find out he slept with one of the chubby, uncool girls, told everyone that I was pretending we had sex (making it a sort of self-fulfilling prophecy; I hadn't actually told anyone, so he was the reason people found out), and just to double-down, so that no one would suspect he had ever liked me at all, he bullied me for the rest of term. What an absolute bastard. I know teenage boys are horrible, but what Charlie did was really something else. I hadn't told anyone about it, and I wasn't keen to after Charlie's reaction, because I was so, so embarrassed. It took me ages to fess up to Vanessa but I could never bring myself to tell Di. Well, after what happened to me, I cautioned her about boys pretty much every day and I didn't want to undermine my position by telling her about my mistake. At some point not too long after, I started dating Chris, the ex I wound up staying with until we were twenty-four (who only started going to our school for sixth form, so he missed all the rumours about me and Charlie), so I pretty much just did my best to pretend Charlie didn't exist. He didn't stick around for much of sixth form anyway, so I just pushed him out of my mind.

And now he's here. In my house. Calling himself 'Charles'. Chatting with my parents – he's going to marry my sister. And the worst, worst thing of all is that he said 'Nice to finally meet you', which means he doesn't remember me. But how can he not remember me? I certainly remember him.

What am I supposed to do? I can't tell my parents. God no! I'm not sure I can tell Di either because, well, it was years ago. She seems so, so happy. It would completely ruin things for her if I told her the truth. Perhaps Charlie – I mean *Charles* – has changed since school? He was an arsehole back then, but that was fifteen years ago. I should keep my mouth shut for now, head back downstairs, now that I'm dressed, and 'meet' him properly. Perhaps he'll remember me, he might even apologise. Well, clearly we all make mistakes when we're teenagers, don't we? And as adults too, it turns out. I think my history with Charles is the reason I'm so annoyed at myself. After what happened with him, I swore I would never land myself in a situation like that again, that I would always take it slow, just to make sure things were actually going somewhere. And it was going so well until I fell for Matt. I fell for him in more ways than one, didn't I?

I look myself up and down in the full-length mirror in my parents' room. I've thrown on a long, strappy summer dress and a generous layer of make-up. I check my outfit, then my hair, then I scowl at myself because why do I care what I look like? It's as if he's still the most popular kid and I'm still worried about what he thinks of me. What if he hasn't changed? What if he's still an arsehole? It isn't escaping my attention that, back when we were at school, pretty much everyone believed him that I'd made the whole thing up – he could just say that again, he could even call around his old friends and have them back him up if it came down to it!

OK, I'm regressing to teenage me. I just need to get a hold of myself, head downstairs, and try to figure out what his deal is now.

Back downstairs, everyone is sitting in the dining room. Seemingly from nowhere, Mum has laid the table with the most delicious-looking afternoon tea – I'm talking professional-standard cakes and fancy-looking sandwiches. I sank two cold pastries less than an hour ago but I would have to be really, really full to walk past this table. That being said, the fact Charles is sitting at it could put me off anything.

'Peach!' Di says, jumping from her seat to rush over and hug me. I guess we're starting over now that I'm dressed. She seems so nervous, but in the best kind of way, like our approval is the missing piece of the puzzle.

'Sorry about before,' I say. 'If anyone was going to embarrass you, I would have sworn it would be Dad.'

'So would I, to be fair,' Dad chuckles.

'Please don't be embarrassed,' Charles insists. He stands up and walks over to us. 'You're going to be my sister – you shouldn't let me make you feel uncomfortable in your own home.'

Charles leans forward and hugs me, and I learn about whole new levels of uncomfortable. I'm only in his arms for a second, but it feels so bizarre. And I feel like everyone must somehow see what I'm thinking because I'm all stiff in his arms and can't pull away fast enough. Thankfully, no one notices – or they just think I'm so hopeless with men that I can't even execute a platonic hug with one.

'You're just in time,' Di says. 'Mum and Dad were just about to start grilling him.'

'I was not,' Mum insists. 'I was going to ply him with sandwiches and cakes first.'

'Well, that's the way to get anything you want out of me,' Charles replies as he heads back to his seat.

He is undeniably charming, but with the context I have, I kind of feel like he comes across as smarmy.

'Oh, my kind of man,' Mum says with a sigh. 'So, tell us about yourself, Charles. What do you do?'

'Charles works for his dad,' Di explains. 'His dad owns BB's Fish & Chips.'

'You work in a chippy?' my dad asks curiously.

'Oh, no,' Charles laughs. 'My dad owns the chain, but he's an entrepreneur. I'm his head of development, so I travel around, starting up various business ventures for him.'

'An entrepreneur, eh?' Dad replies. I can practically see the pound signs rolling around in his eyes. Not necessarily in a selfish way, but more because, as vetting goes, someone who is rich and charming is exactly the kind of person you want to see your daughter tie the knot with, right?

'Last year Charles lived in Canada for six months,' Di says excitedly. 'Just imagine where we'll end up!'

'Perks of the job,' Mum says with a smile. 'And there's me thinking Peach was the only person who had a sweet job like that.'

'Oh?' Charles turns to face me again, and the fact that I can't see so much as a glimmer of recognition in his eyes genuinely frightens me. How, how, *how* can he not remember me? 'What do you do, Peach?'

Seriously, how? Fair enough, he won't know me by 'Peach' – I actually think he took to calling me Penelope Bullshitstop by the time we'd sat our GCSEs – but I don't look that different, and Peach is obviously just a nickname.

'I'm a mystery shopper,' I reply.

'She gets to stay in swanky hotels, gets sent free stuff to try out, eat in nice restaurants – and all she has to do is write it up afterwards, isn't that cool?' Di tells him.

'That is pretty cool,' he replies. 'When I was in Canada, buying into a start-up, we worked closely with a seafood restaurant, and I pretty much had lobster rolls coming out of my... Well, let's just say I ate a lot.'

He's being all smiley and charming, and it's making me want to hit him over the head with the silver cake plate.

'And I got to hang out with Drake – he was a regular at one of the restaurants, so that was cool,' he adds oh-so casually, like it's no big deal.

'Well, I don't know who that is,' Mum says. 'But it sounds lovely.'

'Do you remember at Auntie Jane and Uncle Mike's anniversary party, when Dad got really drunk and the cousins taught him that dance move to that song?' I prompt her.

'Yes,' she replies through a snort. We all have fond memories of the night back in 2016 when my cousins Jamie and Lawrence taught my dad the 'Hotline Bling' dance after he'd had a few too many. 'Oh, well that's lovely. You met him?'

'He doesn't dance it like me,' Dad insists. 'I could break it out at your wedding.'

'Are you really having it in a week?' Mum asks. 'Is that possible?'

Reading between the lines, I think my mum is more interested in why the two of them are so keen to get married so soon.

'Charles has pulled all the strings we need to get married in

Italy – I think he might have even broken some laws...' Di says almost nervously.

'A little creative backdating is all, maybe we have to do something to make it official here when we get back – I'm working it all out,' he insists. 'What's the point in having money if it can't make the woman you love happy? The best wedding planners are going to meet us in Italy and organise our dream day, put it all together in time – it's going to be incredible. And whatever this gorgeous angel wants.'

I glance around the table and the big, dumb, happy smile on everyone's face but mine practically pushes me out of the room.

'I just need to pop to my room and make a work call, actually,' I lie.

'Your room?' Di laughs. 'I don't think you're allowed to call Dad's office that any more.'

'Didn't you know she'd moved back in?' Dad asks in disbelief.

'What?' she replies. 'I thought you'd just slept over?'

'It was only yesterday,' I tell her. 'And it's not for long.'

'This is my fault, isn't it?' she says. Her smile drops, but I feel like I'm the person who has killed the mood. 'Because I bailed on moving in with you.'

'It's not a big deal,' I insist. 'I told you, I'm on the lookout for somewhere better. Living here is just temporary.'

'There's no shame in moving back in with your parents,' Charles insists.

There's something about his tone, I don't know what, but I feel like he can't possibly mean that. At best, he's just trying to say the right thing. At worst, he's being sarcastic. He seems almost too good to be true, but Di is clearly smitten, and I can tell you now, he's passed the test with Mum and Dad.

'Yeah, anyway, I'd better go and make this call,' I insist.

'I could do with nipping to your bathroom, if that's OK?' I hear Charles say as I'm walking out of the room.

'Peach,' Mum calls after me, 'can you please show Charles to the guest bathroom upstairs?'

That's just *the* bathroom – and must I?

'Sure,' I reply.

'Back in a sec,' Charles says before kissing Di on the cheek.

'Aww, he even kisses you goodbye when he goes to the bathroom,' my mum coos.

I roll my eyes, but only mentally.

'This way,' I say, nodding towards the doorway for Charles to follow me.

He follows me up the stairs in silence.

'It's that door over there,' I tell him, but he doesn't move. For a few seconds he just stands in front of me, just inches away, staring at me. I notice the corners of his mouth turn up slightly.

This is it. His moment to say that he remembers me. I'd totally get it if he did, because he was as blindsided as I was downstairs earlier.

'This holiday is going to be a great opportunity for us to get to know each other,' he says. 'Di worships you, and now she worships me, so I'm sure we'll be great friends.'

'Oh, I'm sure,' I reply. 'I'd better...'

'Yes, go make your work call,' he says. 'We've got plenty of time to chat. I'm not going anywhere.'

11

When you have the world's best wedding planner and money is no object, what do you even need a chief bridesmaid for, other than show?

Di must have realised this, so I feel like she's making up jobs for me, which I suppose is kind of sweet, but totally unnecessary.

Still, she is my sister, and I love her, and if she wants my support, then she has it, and if she asks me to send the flight details to her snooty friend Alex – sorry, *Lex*, she hates being called Alex – as much as I don't want to, I will. And I don't want to for two reasons. One: because this wedding is a terrible idea and I don't want to enable it. And two: Lex and I really, really don't get along, and this is too much like going on holiday/living with her. I can just about handle Lex in small doses, if I hold my tongue and clench my fists, but any more than that is a nightmare.

Di left me with her iPad, which she told me to use for my wedding duties, but genuinely this is it. Just booking myself a flight and sending the details over to Lex so she can book hers

(Charles said he'll reimburse us, which is a relief, as far as my finances go). Thankfully, it's a budget airline Charles has recommended to us, so that we can all get the same last-minute flight at the same time. That's me, Lex and someone from Charles' side, which I am frankly terrified is going to be some other bully from my school days who is also going to pretend they have no idea who I am. Though I do like to think I'm better equipped to deal with bullies these days.

I find Lex in Di's contacts and drop her a message. I'll be polite, but it pains me to be friendly to her, because she will not be polite to me in return.

Hi, it's Peach. Great news that Di is getting married! She says this is the flight to book for the people who want to fly there together. She has also suggested a flight back the following week, but says you can fly back whenever is best for you. The groom is going to reimburse both tickets. Meet you at the airport in the morning?

There. That's polite enough, right? Of course, she'll treat me like some poor dating-app boy she's negging into liking her, probably leaving me hanging for 12 hours, before sending some kind of...

I hear the notification noise and eyeball the screen suspiciously. It's been about four minutes. Surely this isn't her?

Hi Peach! Oh wow! Sounds amazing, I can't believe it, thanks so much for inviting me! I can't wait! I'll get it booked right now! See you in the morning!

I mean, she's obviously being sarcastic. That's so like her.

I massage my temples and tell myself to rise above it, but I can't resist sending an equally sarcastic reply.

Can't wait!

I say I'm being sarcastic, but I actually am really looking forward to the holiday – and I need a break from my parents already.

Now that I'm done with my wedding duties – if you can even call them that, given that all I had to do was send a message – I can go back to packing my case.

Thankfully, I don't need to go out and buy all new things (not that I could even if I wanted to) because I really have amassed so much stuff from work – things like bikinis, beauty products, and I even got a pair of designer flipflops that I've mostly just worn around my bedroom. It will be nice for them to have somewhere to go.

Me too, obviously. I just wish it were under better circumstances.

12

There's just something about airports. I'm never quite sure how I feel about them.

I suppose, on face value, they're basically a big, fancy service station – just one you can catch planes from that also has a room for strip-searching people. I guess it's the people in them that make airports what they are, and as I glance from person to person, the mood changes.

There's the gang of lad-lad-lads, already boozed up, even though it's only 10 a.m., probably on their way to Magaluf. You almost can't help but smile, seeing them laughing their way through the airport, but upon closer inspection, I notice one of the men is wearing a T-shirt that has the words 'Last chance to bang me before I get married' printed in big letters, accompanied by a cartoon penis with a sad face, and a ball and chain attached to its neck. Well, that just went from light-hearted to depressing. The next time he passes through this airport, he'll probably have a crushing secret from his future wife and at least one sexually transmitted disease.

Then there's the family – mum, dad and three kids of

varying ages – all charging past me in a mad hurry. I'll bet that the mum was so looking forward to her relaxing break, but she couldn't look more stressed right now if she tried. That's one of the things I remember, when I think back to family holidays during my childhood: Dad practically dragging me through the airport as I clung on to my Gameboy for dear life.

There is one couple, sitting on the benches opposite me, practically eating each other's faces as their coffees go cold on the table in front of them. Now here are two people who look happy, like they don't have a care in the world. They're so into their kiss that they could miss their flight without noticing and, to be honest, I don't suppose they would care all that much. I'm reassured by how happy they seem in this otherwise mostly chaotic building until suddenly I feel a bit lonely. I'm the first one here from our little group, and even if Lex is the one I'm waiting on, it would be nice to have anyone to sit with right now.

'Oh, you fucking bitch,' a familiar voice practically yells in my direction.

I totally take back what I just said.

'And a good morning to you, Lex,' I reply. 'Maybe try that a bit louder next time. There are some kids on a plane down the far end of the runway who didn't quite hear you screeching swear words at 10 a.m.'

She sits down next to me – but not right next to me, keeping a good two spaces away, as if to remind me that we're not friends.

'You tried to ditch me from Di's wedding, didn't you?' she says. 'You don't want me here, so you tried to sabotage things – well, it didn't work, did it?'

I yawn. I couldn't really sleep last night and was up early

today, so I'm pretty shattered. I don't normally have energy for Lex anyway, but she seems even worse than usual today.

'I'm going to get a coffee,' I tell her, ignoring whatever all that was. 'I'll be right back.'

I pull myself to my feet and head in the direction of the nearest coffee shop.

I am so pleased that we're flying with an airline that doesn't have designated seating, so all I need to do is drag my feet a little, wind up at the back of the queue, and then hopefully there won't be any room for the two of us to sit together – neither of us want to anyway.

'Peach?' a man's voice calls out. 'Hey! Oh my God, it's been ages.'

'Oh, wow, hello,' I reply through a fake smile. 'It has. How are you?'

You remember Di's ex? The one who broke her heart? The one we don't speak of? Well, I'm currently speaking to him.

Alex is tall, with dirty-blonde hair and bright blue eyes. He does look a little different from how I remember him though, like he found a good gym and a designer clothes outlet, because he isn't the skinny, scruffy boy-ish type I remember him being.

'I'm doing great, thanks. How are you?'

He looks genuinely pleased to see me, which is nice, I suppose, given that he was with my sister for three years. But the fact that he dumped her and broke her heart with the 'It's not you, it's me' speech means I could probably get excommunicated by Di just for being in the same airport as him.

'All great here, thank you,' I reply.

Oh, for the love of God, please don't ask me where I'm going, because I don't want to be the person who tells him Di is getting married. You never know how people will react, do you?

He might not take it well, even if *he* did dump *her*. I've noticed he isn't wearing a wedding ring himself.

'I haven't flown in ages,' he tells me. 'I'm a bit nervous. Less so for being with someone I know because, the last time I had to fly for work, I was alone and we hit terrible turbulence – I tried to hold hands with the person next to me. He wasn't impressed.'

I smile but I'm a little taken aback. This is not how you do a quick hello at the airport. You don't tell stories and crack jokes. To be honest, if I'd seen him first, I would have pretended not to notice him and hid behind a magazine stand until he was gone.

'I'm sure you'll be fine,' I reassure him.

'Yeah, I know,' he replies. 'I'm just being a baby. How long is the flight?'

That's kind of an odd question. How am I supposed to know?

'Erm...'

'I think it said, on the ticket, maybe.' He riffles around in his man bag for a piece of paper. I manage to eyeball where he's headed: Naples. The same place as me. 'I was so surprised to be invited to the wedding, my feet have hardly touched the ground.'

A deep, uncomfortable rush of warmth starts rushing around my body. I think I might have made a mistake.

'Could you just wait for my coffee for me, please?' I ask him. 'I'll be back in two minutes.'

'Of course,' he replies.

I thank him and hurry back over to where I left Lex.

'When you said I tried to sabotage things, and stop you being here, what did you mean?' I ask her quickly.

'Obviously you didn't invite me – I had to get the flight

details from Di. Luckily there was still room for me. Nice try,' she says, still as salty as she was before.

I slump down in the seat next to her.

'I've fucked up,' I admit.

It's obvious now what I've done, and I can't believe how stupid I've been. I think perhaps, because I didn't deem my one and only bridesmaid task a real thing, I didn't pay all that much attention to what I was doing. I pretty much flew through the motions on autopilot, not thinking too hard about the task at hand, so I sent the message to 'Alex' in Di's contacts. It just didn't occur to me, to look for her under Lex, and obviously Alex is what He-Who-Shall-Not-Be-Named is called...

'Why am I not surprised,' Lex replies with a sigh.

'No, really, I have – I've really fucked up,' I tell her. 'I didn't not invite you on purpose – I sent the text to Alex by mistake.'

'Ex-boyfriend Alex?' she says. 'Well, that was dumb, but I suppose it gets you off the hook for now.'

'With you perhaps – but he's only turned up here with his suitcase, ready to come with us,' I confess.

'What the fuck? He turned up? To go to his ex's wedding?' she replies. 'That's so weird.'

'I know, but what do I do? Do I tell him it was a mistake? He's here and has got a ticket and a big excited look on his face. He's probably taken time off work too.'

'I think, the fact he's turned up at all, means one of two things,' Lex starts. Here we go. 'Either he's genuinely happy for Di, and she'll see him and get the closure she needs, or he's doing that dumb thing men do where they decide they want something the second they realise they can't have it. We need to work out which it is.'

'Do we?' I reply. 'Can't I just apologise and tell him to go?'

'But here's the thing – we can't stop him,' Lex points out. 'He has his own ticket, and if he's here to mess with Di's head, best we try and figure that out so we can work out what to do about it. Seriously, if he's here, it might be to cause trouble. We have to tread lightly.'

'So, what do you suggest?' I ask.

'Let me sit with him on the plane,' she replies. 'I'll interrogate him, find out what his intentions are. But to be honest, you know how shaken he left Di – it would be therapeutic for her to have him see her happy.'

'I'm just not sure...'

I can't help but wonder if Lex means what she's saying. A part of me is worried that she just wants me to look bad in front of Di, but she wouldn't do that at the risk of ruining Di's big day, would she?

'It's what we're doing, Peach, and there's nothing you can do about it,' she snaps. 'You've done enough. Let me fix this. This is why I should have been chief bridesmaid.'

I wish Di has asked her instead of me, to be honest.

'Here's your coffee,' Alex says helpfully as he approaches us. 'I didn't want it to go cold. Oh, hi, Lex.'

'Alex!' she replies with a faux cheeriness. 'Let's sit together on the plane, I'd love to catch up with you, it's been ages.'

'OK, yeah, sure,' he replies. He seems pleasantly surprised, but he shouldn't be. He should be wary. It's like he doesn't remember what she's like at all.

I can't quite figure them both out. Has Alex really just turned up to see Di get married because he thinks she invited him as some kind of friendly gesture, or is he here to cause trouble? And what about Lex? Does she really think this is the best thing to do, or is she just basking in my mistake and hoping it will make Di mad at me?

Either way, I'm not sure what I can do about it now – it isn't that long until take-off.

'Let's make a move,' Lex says. 'The closer we sit to our gate, the sooner we can board. We need to get on first to get a good seat.'

Now that I know she'll be sitting with Alex, grilling him for the entire flight, I relax a little. I can sit on my own, listen to some music or an audiobook, just the usual relaxing holiday stuff. I do need to treat this destination wedding like a holiday too, because it's the only one I'll be getting for the foreseeable.

As we wait to board the plane, Lex gets a head start on her detective work.

'So, are you seeing anyone?' she asks him.

'Not at the moment,' he replies.

This is where I leave. I don't need to be here for this. I'm just going to look out of the window (one of the ones as far away from these two as I can possibly get – not that I can go far, as we'll all be boarding soon) and drink my coffee. Let's see if I can slip into super relaxed holiday mode now. I certainly can't do that if I sit with Lex and Alex.

I only have about four seconds to start the process when I walk straight into a man around the same time he walks into me. The blame is pretty evenly split, but I'm the only one holding a coffee cup that gets squashed against my body, causing the plastic lid to pop off. Thankfully, I'd had quite a bit of it already so there isn't much to spill, but it splashes all over my white trainers.

'Sorry, I was miles away,' I blurt.

'Totally my fault,' he says at the same time.

You know, this would be quite the meet-cute, if we hadn't *met already*.

'You,' I blurt.

'Oh, hi,' he replies, without a hint of warmth.

It's Matt. Wham-bam-thank-you-ma'am Matt. Not that he didn't make the decision for me when he had sex with me and then snuck out, but I was hoping I would never have to see him again, and yet here we are, at the airport together – *again* – and it looks like waiting to board the same flight. Being in a confined space with Matt is certainly not going to make me feel relaxed.

Matt must feel like an absolute piece of shit – or he must *be* an absolute piece of shit – because he looks about as pleased to see me as I am to see him, which is not at all. It has actively ruined my day and, let's face it, given the whole 'I just accidentally invited my sister's ex to the wedding I don't think she should be having but I have to be a part of it' thing, it wasn't going all that well anyway.

My phone rings in my pocket – saved by the bell.

'Anyway, bye,' I say, which is very polite, given it's not a courtesy Matt usually extends, but I'm better than him, and it does cap off this truly awkward moment.

'Yeah, bye,' he replies with an equal level of cold indifference.

It's Di calling from Italy, so I mentally psych myself up for a second before I answer. I should sound happy and excited. Not like I just ran into her ex. Or another one of mine. And let's not forget about Charles – honestly, once you've slept with someone, if you don't ever plan to have anything to do with them, they should just disappear.

'Hey, sis,' I say brightly. 'You just caught me at the right time, we're about to board the plane.'

'Amazing,' she replies. 'I am so, so looking forward to it. This place is just so, so amazing, and it has staff, and a private pool – you're not going to be able to believe it.'

'It sounds fantastic,' I reply. I have to admit, I'm excited about staying in the villa.

'I won't keep you because I don't want to delay you, but Charles said for you to meet up with his best man, because he's on the same flight. He just showed me a photo of him, so I could tell you what he looks like. He's seriously hot, Peach,' she says, lowering her voice on the last part. 'He's tall, he has a beard – he's just your type. Do you see anyone like that around?'

Just the one person...

'Do you have the photo on your phone?' I ask her. 'Can you send it?'

'Yeah, OK, two seconds,' she replies. 'But trust me, if this guy is around, you'll already be looking at him.'

I have a horrible, sinking feeling that I already am, and sure enough, when the photo comes through, it's a photo of a couple of shirtless men on a beach – it's Charles, with his arm around Matt. Because of course it is.

'Oh boy,' I blurt.

'I told you that you'd fancy him,' she says, and I can practically hear her grin over the phone. 'You would, right?'

Now does not feel like the time to tell her I already have.

'I'd better go find him and get on the plane. See you soon, love you, bye,' I say quickly.

'OK, fly safe. Love you too, bye,' she replies.

I can't believe Matt is Charles's best friend. Though I suppose it's not as wild as it first seems. We did originally meet at the airport, waiting for two people from the same small flight, who both come from the same town. But even so, this is really truly horrible, and I can't believe I'm going to have to spend more time with him. He's going to be gutted too. I bet he thought he'd shaken me off, no worries, by taking off before I woke up. In a way, it might be nice to watch him squirm, but only for a minute or two. Pah, of course they're best friends – the only two men to ever ghost me. It must be a trait they have in common.

Matt, unsurprisingly, has retreated to one of the benches and is keeping his head down. I wander over to him hoping that, by the time I get there, the right words will come to me.

'I... er...'

'Peach, can we not do this please?' he says quietly. 'Can we just leave it?'

'Believe me, I would love nothing more than to leave it,' I reply, 'but we have a problem. Remember when we met at the airport and you were waiting for your friend and I was waiting for my sister. Your friend Charles...'

It's funny, watching realisation hit someone. Their expression goes on a real rollercoaster ride, as though you have literally hit them in face.

'Your sister is Di,' he says simply.

'Yep.'

'So you're...' he continues.

'Yep.'

'So we're...'

'Yep,' I say, for the third time.

'Well, we're just going to have to find a way to be civil with one another,' he ever so helpfully suggests, although him saying such a thing makes me want to be anything but civil.

'Just stay out of my way,' I warn him.

He looks a little taken aback.

'Gladly,' he replies. 'Probably best we keep... things to ourselves.'

'Oh, believe me, I have bigger problems than you being

here,' I tell him, turning on my coffee-soaked heel and walking away.

As I approach Lex and Alex, she hops to her feet and hurries over to me.

'Yeah, he's clearly still in love with her,' she tells me under her breath. 'We need to keep him where we can see him. Now, who's that guy you were talking to?'

'That's Matt, the best man,' I reply.

'Oh, yummy,' she says. 'I'm going to sit with him.'

'I thought you were sitting with Alex?'

'Screw Alex,' she whispers to me, before turning to him. 'Alex, Peach really wants to sit with you on the plane, to catch up, so I've told her she can, is that OK?'

'It's fine by me,' he says with a smile. 'We've all got at least a week to hang out.'

Oh, God, we really do. So much for thinking this was going to be a relaxing holiday.

13

Welcome to San Valentino, the most romantic place on Earth. That's what all the brochures, signs and staff say anyway. I doubt I'm going to find the place all that romantic though.

Technically, we're not quite there yet. We are just a short boat journey away, which wouldn't be so bad if we weren't sharing it with a bunch of loved-up couples.

San Valentino is a private island resort just off the coast of Naples. It's a luxury romantic getaway for couples, and couples *only*, meaning you usually only get to come here with someone you love, so this is probably my one shot.

I know what you're thinking, a holiday resort for couples doesn't sound like somewhere you can get married, but there is nothing you can't do if you have money and power. It turns out Charles is big buddies with the guy whose dad owns San Valentino, and only half of the island is a resort, the other half is private, where their villa is, and they've loaned it to Charles for the week while they're at one of their other homes. You've got to love that – the more people have, the more people give them.

To access the private side of the island – unless you take *the villa's helicopter* – you have to catch a boat to the resort, and then a second smaller boat that takes you to the private dock. How is any of this real?

The weather in Naples this afternoon is glorious. The summer sun is beaming down on us, but there's a beautiful breeze taking the edge off. We're currently waiting to board the boat, which I can see from here has seats in pairs, and for a couple of reasons I really, really don't want to sit next to Alex again.

First of all, he has absolutely talked my ear off about anything and everything, to the point where I actually started to question whether he was doing it to throw me off the scent of whatever his agenda is. Secondly, from where we were sitting, we could see Lex and Matt, and she was flirting with him like her life depended on it. Seriously, we're talking the whole playbook – laughing at his jokes, touching his arm, clearly making cheeky little comments. Yes, I know that's everything I did with him the day I met him, which kind of made me wish they would just hurry up, initiate themselves into the Mile High Club and get it over with, because then Matt would never speak to her again, which would expedite the whole excruciatingly awkward process of me having to watch the two of them getting together. Obviously I don't want him now, but watching him plough his way through the female members of the wedding party would just be so demoralising.

Given that their plane flirting was PG at best, if I could just push myself between them, maybe I could nip their flirt fest in the bud.

'You know, Alex, I think Lex would really like to sit next to you on the boat, and hear all about your... Final... er...'

'My Final Fantasy games?' he replies with a hopeful optimism that I can't help but admire. That was never going to be true, was it? The only games Lex plays are with your mind.

'Yeah, that,' I say. I listened to Alex talk about his love for the Final Fantasy franchise for a while on the plane and didn't take much away apart from the fact that you ride giant birds, which Lex will absolutely hate to hear about. But I can't let her get her claws into Matt. Honestly that would be the final piece of the puzzle in making this week so unbearable that I have to back out.

Except I can't back out of my sister's wedding, so I have to get between them – at least until we get to Di, because as soon as I tell her who Matt is, I'm sure the girl code between her and Lex will be forced to extend to me.

'I think she's too shy to ask you though,' I continue.

'Wow, really?' he says. 'OK, got it.'

He approaches Lex and Matt right as she's giving him yet another 'Oh, you're so funny' bicep squeeze.

'Hey, Lex, I was wondering, can I sit with you on the boat?' Alex asks her. 'There's so much I'd love to chat to you about.'

'Oh, erm...'

As Lex searches for some words to say no that don't make her look bad, Alex glances back at me and smiles, like he's doing the right thing. And, look, I know Alex might seem nice, he's perfectly polite, but he did absolutely stomp all over my sister's heart, so I don't feel bad about lying to him about something so silly.

Lex looks at Matt.

'Oh, by all means, sit together,' Matt insists. 'You're old friends – you must have a lot to catch up on. Don't worry, I'll sit with Peach.'

And there's my punishment. If Alex sits with Lex, and

everyone else is coupled up, that just leaves me and Matt. Oh joy.

A gorgeous Irish girl instructs us all to board the boat, and I have to admit, it's strange being around so many loved-up couples. It's like everyone only has eyes for their partners, to the point where the beautiful scenery may as well not even be here. I doubt many people will be looking out of the boat on this trip.

'After you,' Matt says, stepping back so I can get on before him.

I purposefully don't take the seats behind Lex and Alex and sit at the back of the boat, like a naughty kid on a school bus, so that I don't need to worry about them listening. Matt sits down next to me – keeping as much space between us as possible – but he doesn't say much. The tension between us is practically visible at this stage. A body-language expert would have a field day.

We set off, and the boat tour guide stands in front of a screen and basically gets everyone hyped for the island facilities. She says things in multiple languages, which makes sense, given how popular the resort is with people from all over the world – something else I learned from the brochure I'm so glad I kept hold of because it's making a great fan now that we're inside the boat.

'I don't suppose it's all that peculiar that we met at the airport and now we've crossed paths again,' Matt eventually says, breaking the silence between us. 'They were on the same flight home, which was probably mostly people from the wedding.'

'That's exactly what I thought,' I reply, without a flicker of anything. Well, it's not like it was fate, is it? More like bad luck.

'Charles must really love your sister,' he tells me. 'To be

doing this – Charles isn't the kind of guy to settle down. At least he wasn't.'

'This isn't like Di either. She doesn't trust people this easily,' I reply. 'As well she shouldn't.'

'Lex mentioned that Alex is Di's ex-boyfriend,' Matt says. 'What was the rationale behind inviting him?'

'I did it by accident – did Lex leave that detail out?'

'I'd rather not get involved in whatever it is you two have going on,' Matt insists.

Urgh, what has she told him?

'I bet,' I say with a snort. Of course he doesn't want to be involved in anything.

'Go on, what is that supposed to mean?' he asks with a sigh and a roll of his eyes.

'I think you know,' I reply. 'Anyway, it doesn't matter. We're only here for a week. We just need to support our people and then we can avoid each other for the rest of our lives.'

'That seemed to be the plan anyway,' he points out. 'But OK, sure, fine. *I* can be civil.'

He emphasises the word 'I' as though he's suggesting I can't be civil. Pah, he doesn't even know me.

I stare out of the window, looking at the water and the city beyond it. Gosh, the sea is such a gorgeous colour here. You don't get sea like this in Scarborough, which is probably our nearest seaside town back home. I love a trip to Scarbados as much as the next Yorkshire girl, but the sea is freezing, and super dark, like it's hiding something. Here it is light and bright and – oh, wow, is that Mount Vesuvius? Christ, it's massive. I knew it was big, but seeing things in photos and having an idea of what they look like is nothing compared to seeing them in real life, is it?

I turn back to Matt just in time to catch him staring at me. I feel uncomfortable in his gaze – probably because he's seen me naked. Once you see someone naked, that's it, right? You can recall the image – accidentally or on purpose – anytime. I narrow my eyes at him suspiciously for a second before turning back to look out of the window because while I was taking in the scenery, I stopped thinking about him, and about all the wedding bullshit, and it was great. It's going to be a difficult week, but I am in a beautiful part of the world with so many amazing things to see and do. I just need to focus on that. That and not, y'know, the variety of ex-lovers who are all basically ticking time bombs, waiting to go off, because surely it's going to be a case of *when*, not *if*, something bad happens...

14

'Holy shit, I feel like I'm on *Love Island*,' Lex blurts as we walk up the driveway towards the villa.

After a plane, a taxi, and two boat journeys, we are finally here, and here is glorious.

The sheer grandeur of the villa alone is enough to take your breath away, and that's before you take in everything around it. A large, curved floor-to-ceiling window looks out over a massive infinity swimming pool – complete with a jacuzzi on the side – that couldn't look more inviting right now. It's surrounded by the ultimate holiday party garden, with cream cushioned rattan sun loungers, a gazebo, various seating areas (pull-you-for-a-chat-type seating areas) and one hell of a barbeque. On the other side of the villa is some kind of ornamental garden that I can't wait to explore – or hide in, when everything gets too much.

The villa is huge, with a flat roof and massive terrace upstairs that must be at least twenty-five metres long, and there's my sister, standing right in the centre of it, like the lady of the manor.

'Oh my gosh, I can't believe you're here, you're all here, you're...'

She holds a hand above her eyes, shielding them from the sun.

I can just about make out her mutter, 'What the hell?' to herself. She takes a few steps back before hurrying downstairs.

'We should head in to meet her,' I say to Lex, giving her a nudge.

'Right, yeah – boys, help the boat people bring the cases in,' Lex says.

I cringe.

We hurry to the front door and head inside the massive lounge. It has a large open staircase on one side, and on that staircase is majorly confused-looking sister.

'Hello,' I practically sing at her.

'Was that Alex outside?' she asks, cutting to the chase.

'Sort of,' Lex replies.

'Was it a cardboard cut-out of Alex?' Di persists.

'No,' I say.

'So, it was Alex?' she says.

'It was,' I reply. 'And it's my fault. I sent the message about the flight to Alex instead of Lex. Even so, I can't believe he turned up, but he does just seem to be genuinely happy to be here.'

'But we also thought he might have an ulterior motive,' Lex adds – you've got to love her use of 'we'. 'So, we thought best keep him close, keep an eye on him, but also it would be good for you, to find closure.'

'Do you really think so?' Di ask as she pulls a face. 'I must be in love, because I don't even really care that he's here. How's that for closure? It is a bit weird though...'

'A success,' Lex declares, giving me a look that says: 'I was right.'

'What's a success?' Charles asks as he joins us.

'Honey, there you are,' Di says as Charles wraps an arm around her waist, in a serpent-like way that totally suits him. 'Peach and Lex are here.'

'Oh, Di, I forget how gorgeous he is,' Lex says. 'And he clearly knows how to treat a girl – look at this place!'

'Only the best for my babe,' Charles says.

'Honey, we have an extra guest,' Di tells him. 'I'll explain all about him later, but for now, can you just show the boys to their rooms?'

'Yeah, of course,' Charles replies, ever the dutiful fiancé. 'I do believe we are out of bedrooms, but Matt is going to have a twin, do you think your friend would mind sharing?'

'I honestly think he would love that,' I chime in. 'I think they both would. It seems like they really hit it off on the journey here.'

Right on cue, Matt and Alex walk through the door, like chalk and cheese. Matt effortlessly carries a couple of cases in his hands whereas Alex is pulling two by their handles, except they've both flipped over, twisting his arms around.

'Ow, ow, ow,' he says.

'Here, let me help you,' Charles insists at he rushes over. 'Don't worry, we'll be fully staffed later – no one is going to need to lift a finger.'

'Nice to meet you, pal,' Alex says, offering him a hand to shake. 'I'm Alex.'

'Great to meet you, Alex. I'm Charles, the groom.'

'All right, mate,' Matt says.

Charles turns from Alex to his best man. 'Are you OK? You look stressed,'

'It was one of those journeys,' Matt replies.

'How about we put a pin in the introductions right now – we show everyone to their rooms, and then we all get to know each other properly at dinner?' Charles suggests.

'Yes, come on, girls,' Di says. 'I'm so excited to show you your rooms.'

I have to admit, I am a little excited.

Lex and I follow Di upstairs.

'Lex, this is your room here on the left,' Di tells her. 'Have a peep, make yourself at home. Peach's is a little further – I'll see her there then I'll be back to make sure you're happy.'

'Nothing could make me happier than seeing you so happy and loved-up,' Lex insists as she pulls Di close for a hug.

'Aww, that's so lovely,' Di says.

God, I think I'm gonna throw up.

Lex disappears into her room and Di leads me further down the corridor. 'Right, this way,' she says. 'So, correct me if I'm wrong, but I thought, if I know my sister, given the choice between a small room of her own or a massive room with an en suite that you *may* need to share with Van, if she turns up – you know how flaky she is these days – that you would choose the latter.'

'You would be correct,' I reply. 'And if Van does turn up, I'd love to share a room with her. It'll be fun, like when we were kids and we used to have sleepovers.'

Van is the same age as me, so we did a lot of stuff together growing up. I loved our sleepovers – especially when we were teens and Di was old enough to join in too.

'I thought so,' Di says, proud of herself. 'It's a stunning room, seriously, you're not going to believe it.'

Di opens the door and we step inside. It really is a massive room, with access to the terrace, and it has not one but *two* king-size beds. I could share this room with everyone here (history aside) and not feel uncomfortable.

'Oh, wow, Di, it's amazing,' I say. 'Seriously just... incredible.'

'I knew you'd love it,' she replies.

The decor is all creams and light browns – shades you wouldn't normally go for, but ones that feel right at home in an Italian villa. Anything else wouldn't look as good or authentic. The beds look so comfortable and I'm itching to take in the view from the terrace, and the idea of my own bathroom is definitely something I need to check out – I hope it has a bath. But I don't feel like I can take another step until I've come clean to Di.

'Listen, I need to tell you something,' I say. I sit down on the bed and pat the space next to me.

'Uh-oh, this seems serious,' she says as she takes a seat.

'You don't need to worry,' I say quickly. 'But you remember I told you about Matt, the guy I met at the airport, the one I slept with.'

I whisper the last few words for some reason. I suppose it's because I'm a little bit embarrassed.

'Shit, you're not pregnant, are you?' she asks, jumping to her feet.

'Di, it was like four days ago,' I remind her.

'Oh, right, sorry. So... *ohhh*!'

And she's got it.

'Wow, he really is your type,' she says with a chuckle.

'Let's not forget that he snuck out the next morning – I'm not even sure if it counts as ghosting because I didn't even have any contact details for him.'

'Do you not have the Shag and Trace app?' she jokes.

My face must look as unimpressed as I feel.

'Oh, Peach, come on, he's clearly a massive arsehole, but I'm not marrying him, I'm marrying Charles, and Charles is not like that.'

'Right,' I say. 'Yes, I know.'

I say nothing.

'Please don't let it ruin your fun.' Di smiles. 'Did I mention you have an en suite?'

Di wanders over to another door, so I follow her through it to the bathroom.

'This bathroom makes up for quite a lot,' I admit. 'Wow.'

The bathroom is huge – bigger than the bedroom I'm sleeping in at Mum and Dad's – and it has everything. Not only does it boast a massive bath and a separate shower, there's also a bidet, and an actual chaise longue, just for chilling on.

'Perhaps I could just hide out in here,' I say, and I open a cupboard door and peer inside to see where the towels and other extra bathroom products are.

Di laughs. 'It's going to be fine,' she insists. 'It's such a big house – you can just avoid him.'

'I guess so,' I reply.

I open another cupboard door expecting to find more of the same, only to find myself peering into another bedroom. And who should be standing right there other than Matt?

'Oops – I guess it's a shared bathroom for the two rooms,' Di says. 'That's kind of neat.'

Oh, yeah, that's super neat – I am sharing a bathroom with the man I am trying to avoid, and not just any bathroom, one with two doors. That sounds like an accident waiting to happen.

15

I don't think you'll be surprised to hear that we are (almost) all currently sitting around the dining table, and things are awkward, so awkward, and Alex – a strong contender for most controversial person at the wedding – isn't even here yet. We're just waiting for him, and then we're having gnocchi, which I would be far more excited about if it weren't for the general mood at the table.

'So, just to clarify,' Charles starts. I can practically feel the look on his face burning my skin. 'You invited Di's ex-boyfriend to her wedding?'

'By accident,' I say, for the fifth time now.

'*Her ex-boyfriend*,' Charles says again.

'OK, but it doesn't matter,' Di says, jumping to my defence.

'He is your one that got away though,' Lex points out, ever so unhelpfully.

'So he's a key ex,' Charles continues, turning back to me. 'And *you* invited him.'

Ahh, I can go for a sixth time, why not?

'*By accident*,' I say again.

Charles eyeballs me suspiciously.

'He seems all right,' Matt says. Now it's my turn to look suspicious – is he defending me?

'There really is nothing to worry about,' Di insists. 'I don't even care that he's here. I'm so over him. I'm...'

The room falls silent as Alex walks in, which would tip any other person off that people were talking about them, but Alex is oblivious.

'Right then, what's on the menu?' Alex asks with a clap of his hands.

'Gnocchi,' Charles tells him.

'Ooh, I'll have what he's having,' Alex jokes to mixed reactions. It's funnier, the more you know.

'So, I've been thinking,' Di says, changing the subject, 'it's really important, to me and Charles, that our chief bridesmaid and best man get to know each other.'

I can't help but shoot her a look – I do make sure it's as subtle as possible though.

'What a thoughtful idea,' Lex says, but she sounds like she feels pushed out.

'I thought I'd arrange for the four of us to have breakfast tomorrow,' Di suggests. 'Out of the villa somewhere – maybe a picnic?'

'That sounds lovely,' I say, referring to spending time with my sister and enjoying a picnic *only*. I'll just have to pretend Matt isn't there.

'Yeah, sounds great,' Matt says. I can tell he's trying to mask his discomfort just as much as I am.

'I'm sure we can all get along just fine, if we all play nice,' Charles says, and I swear he mostly looks at me while he says it.

'I just honestly could not be happier for you guys, and I just know this wedding is going to be amazing,' Lex says. She grabs her wine glass. 'A toast. To Charles and Di, may you be together forever.'

This is classic Lex, dominating the conversation, being sickly sweet, making herself the centre of attention.

'To Charles and Di,' I echo along with everyone else, but I do really think we should stop referring to them as that. Well, their namesakes, Prince Charles and Lady Di don't exactly provide a shining example of a marriage, do they?

16

I feel almost guilty about the staff working here at the villa. This is a house, not a hotel – surely we don't need people running around after us? Of course it's nice having someone cook our food, someone clean up after us and so on, but I do feel bad about it.

It's late morning and our prearranged meeting time for brunch, but Di and Charles are nowhere to be seen. It's just me, Matt and a lovely man named Salvo who says he's going to be driving us to our picnic. He directs us to a golf buggy and tells us to sit on the back seat.

'Morning,' I say to Matt, in about as polite a tone as I can muster.

'Morning,' he replies.

Last night, after the uncomfortable house dinner, I went back to my room and decided that a nice, long soak was exactly what I needed to try to chill myself out. Except I'd only been in the damn bath for ten minutes when Matt started banging on the bathroom door, saying he needed to use the toilet. I stomped out of the bath and back into my room, and I was so

angry and stressed out – not just about my bath being interrupted, but about everything – that getting back in it seemed
like a waste of time, so instead I just went to bed, hoping things
wouldn't seem so bad in the morning. But I now kind of want to
kick him off this golf buggy while it's at full speed – sadly, its
full speed is about five miles per hour.

We go off-road, onto a dirt path, through some trees, until
Salvo eventually stops.

'Here we are,' he says. 'Your breakfast.'

'*This* is breakfast,' I say as my jaw drops – which I think is
down to a combination of how incredible breakfast looks and
that thing some animals do where they dislocate their jaw so
they can get more food in.

In a clearing in the woods, surrounded by trees tall enough
to shade us from the increasing heat, there is a breakfast picnic
all laid out. With only Salvo here with us, it's hard to imagine
how it all got here. I'm not talking a few pastries and a couple of
thermos flasks full of coffee, this is a five-star breakfast, but one
that seemingly materialised out of nowhere.

'Take a seat,' Salvo instructs us. 'I'll give the two of you some
privacy and then I'll be back to pick you up in an hour.'

'Thank you,' I reply, politely but cautiously. Is that right?

It must be because Salvo zips away in his cart, leaving the
two of us here, all alone.

'Erm...' I start, kind of awkwardly, hoping words will come
to me, but they don't.

'This is incredible,' Matt says. 'Like a scene from a movie.'

I hate to say it, but he's looking great today, in a pair of
green shorts and a black T-shirt. He somehow looks casual and
smart, which is what I was going for with the blue strappy
sundress I'm wearing.

We both take a seat on the cushions set out for us on the

picnic blanket. I notice there are only two cushions, but they're big ones, which must mean we're supposed to share. I'll definitely be sharing with Di. The food looks so good, I can't wait to tuck in, but there's no sign of Di and Charles yet. God, I'm starving.

'I'll give Di a call,' I say. 'See where they are.'

'Good thinking,' Matt says as he pinches a grape from the fruit platter. He has a glint in his eye, like a naughty boy, which again I really like, but I hate that I like it.

The phone rings for a while before Di eventually picks up.

'Morning, sis,' she says brightly. 'How are you?'

'I'm great – I'm at the breakfast picnic, where are you?'

'Oh, you won't believe it, but we took the chopper over to the mainland, for a meeting with the designers who will be sorting the outfits, and we totally lost track of time. But you two should enjoy the breakfast, please, make the most of it, and I'll see you later. Love you.'

'Love you too, bye,' I say.

Hmm.

'Everything OK?' Matt asks.

'They took the helicopter somewhere first thing for wedding-planning stuff and lost track of time,' I tell him. 'They said we should eat without them.'

'I am too hungry to care,' he says. 'This looks delicious.'

'Yeah, but something stinks,' I reply.

Matt looks down at the incredible food and then back up at me, puzzled.

'Not literally,' I say. 'With Di... she organised this whole thing and suddenly she's miles away? Is it even late enough in the day for her to be running late?'

'She has no reason to lie,' he points out as he grabs a

lobster-tail-shaped pastry that is absolutely bursting with a thick vanilla custard. 'It's not like she knows about us.'

I involuntarily correct him with whatever expression is on my face right now.

'You *told* her?' he says through a mouthful of pastry. He pauses just long enough to swallow. 'Why would you tell her?'

'Well, I'd already told her the morning after the night before,' I reply. 'And it wouldn't have taken her long to figure it out anyway. She knows me better than I know myself, and obviously she's my sister and my best friend, so I tell her everything. She's promised not to tell anyone.'

I can taste the guilt on my words, no matter how many chocolate strawberries I cram in there to try to cancel it out. I feel bad for not telling her all about Charles, but I'm still not sure whether or not it's the right thing to do.

'Like you haven't told Charlie,' I say.

'"Charlie"? That's a bit familiar,' he says with a laugh.

'Charles,' I correct myself.

'I haven't told him.'

'I thought men liked to brag to each other?' I say.

'Well, yeah, but it wasn't exactly something to brag about, was it?'

OUCH!

I grab my glass of champagne and throw it back before refilling it. Perhaps we should talk less and eat more.

There's a huge platter of fruit, lots of pastries – my favourite has to be the little rectangular cake sandwiches with the sweet filling. Any of those that don't get eaten will be going back to the villa with me, for sure.

When we were younger, Di and I would fantasise about what life would be like for us when we were grown-up. We'd imagine living on the same street, with husbands who were buddies and kids that played together. We would do everything together and it would be amazing. Sure, that might not be the most realistic outcome for our adult lives, but nothing even close to that is going to happen now, is it? It's always going to be weird between me and Charles, and if this is his best friend... That reminds me of something.

'You said you lived in Leeds with your friend,' I start. 'Is that Charles?'

'Yeah,' he replies.

'Huh, so I guess you'll be homeless soon?' I say.

'Something like that,' Matt replies. 'We're still figuring it out.'

'I was supposed to be moving in with Di,' I tell him. 'So that's not happening now.'

'So you're kind of homeless too,' he points out.

'I'm living with my parents again,' I confess.

'How's that going?'

'Oh, I'm stoked for Naked Wednesdays,' I say before throwing back another glass of champagne. I think for a moment. 'Yesterday you said Charles wasn't the kind of guy to settle down.'

'I did.'

'Did he have a lot of girlfriends?' I ask.

'He had zero girlfriends, if you catch my drift,' Matt replies.

'That bad?'

'I suggested we have a revolving door fitted on the flat,' he replies, raising his eyebrows.

I'll bet that was for his benefit too.

'Di was never the type to rush into things – especially since Alex dumped her. She was with him for years, she trusted him, and then, when two of their friends got engaged, he dumped her, because of course he did. It spooked him.'

'That's rough,' he says. 'Charles has never done that, but like I said, he's never really had a girlfriend, not one that wasn't for show – no one stuck around.'

'So, either this is the real thing for him or...'

'Or?'

'Or he's making a mistake,' I say. 'And so is she.'

'Did you invite her ex here on purpose?' Matt asks curiously.

I feel my eyebrows shoot up.

'Of course not,' I say. 'Perhaps this should be more of a silent breakfast. I don't like you, you don't like me, we don't need to play nice when no one is watching.'

'If that's what you want,' he says with a casual shrug.

Matt eats another piece of melon, sips his champagne, and then lies back on the blanket. He looks so relaxed it's annoying.

Just you wait until I get my hands on my sister. I'm almost certain this was a set-up, and I don't know what she's playing at, but she needs to stop. The dream is definitely over, we're not going to be playing happy families side by side any more, and she needs to get used to it. And so do I. Even if that means I'm not going to see my sister anywhere near as much as I used to.

17

The golf-buggy ride back to the house is nothing short of awkward. Awkward, silent and uncomfortably long.

As requested, Matt didn't speak to me for the rest of our picnic, and he hasn't uttered a word on the drive back to the villa. Salvo has dropped us off at the bottom of the villa driveway, so we're currently walking up it, about two metres apart, both with a face like thunder. I really, really don't like him – how can I after the way he treated me? And he clearly doesn't like me, not that I did anything wrong, which makes me dislike him even more.

I get to the front door first, so I head inside and straight for my room, where I can hopefully hide out in peace until Di gets back, and then I can strangle her for trying to set me up with Matt.

The last thing I expect to find is someone in my bedroom, lying on the bed in a barely there pink bikini, flicking their way through the book I bought myself to start reading on the plane but didn't because I had someone more important to keep an eye on.

'Oh my God!' I squeak.

'That's the kind of reaction we like to hear,' my cousin Van says excitedly, jumping to her feet so quickly it's only thanks to her quick reflexes that I don't see one of her boobs pop out. 'Whoops!'

'I don't think I've ever been more pleased to see you in my life,' I tell her.

'Keep it coming, keep it coming,' she demands, lapping up the attention.

When Van moved to LA, she left a lot behind. One of those things, apparently, is her North Yorkshire accent. She couldn't sound more LA now if she tried – I imagine because she tried really hard to lose it when she first moved there, and now it's just stuck.

She looks very LA too, with her toned body, her perfect teeth, her long blonde hair that looks too perfect to be real, but if she does have extensions they're too good to tell.

'You look amazing,' I tell her.

'You don't look so bad yourself,' she replies. 'You're looking a little bummed out though.'

'You look like you've been here for weeks,' I deflect. 'How's the book?'

'Who brings a ghost story on holiday?' she complains. 'I was just reading about a ghost pushing someone out of a window. That's not a beach read.'

'I hope that's on one of the earlier pages...'

'Nope, that's the end. There, I saved you a bunch of time, now you can have fun with me! Seriously, Peachie, a ghost story?! You should be reading a romance.'

'Yeah, well, I'm not feeling very romantic,' I say.

Van's smile shifts into something more serious.

'Who is he and where can I find him to chop off his balls?' she jokes – God, I hope she's joking.

I sigh.

'You always could read my mind,' I say with a smile.

'We have that twintuition thing,' she says, 'even though we're only cousins. Speaking of sisters, where is yours, and has she lost her mind?'

'She's probably in a helicopter, and yes,' I reply.

'Ugh, I love helicopters,' Van says. 'Especially helicopter sex. That's a rush.'

'That can't be real,' I reply. 'You can't be having sex in the sky when I can't even master it on the ground.'

'Been a while?' she asks.

'It's not even been a week,' I say with a chuckle. 'But I've fucked up, big time, in a few ways, spanning fifteen years.'

Van runs back over to her case, searches around inside it and pulls out a bottle of champagne.

'I bought this for Di but I can replace it,' she says. 'It sounds like we need it more.'

'Oh, you don't have to—'

She pops the cork.

'Let's go sit on the terrace,' she says. 'We'll share this while you tell me all about it.'

'I had a couple of glasses with breakfast but... sure, why not?'

I whip off my sundress to reveal my bikini. I might not look as perfect as Vanessa, but I gave up feeling insecure next to her years ago because, honestly, what's the point?

Right outside our bedroom door there's a table and chairs, so we take a seat. It's quite hot now, and the champagne is far from chilled, but it's nice to sit and swig at a bottle with my cousin, like when we were naughty teens, except we weren't drinking Dom Pérignon back then.

'This is a really gorgeous place to get married, I'll give her that,' Van says as she takes in the view. 'My favourite wedding of mine was on a beach.'

'Your favourite wedding?' I laugh as I hand her the bottle.

'What? Yes,' she says with a smile. 'My first wedding was my favourite. You never forget your first.'

Her second wedding was probably my favourite, if I'm allowed to have a favourite, because they served pizza.

'That's kind of what I need to talk to you about,' I tell her. 'I'm just not sure which bit to tell you about first.'

'I can clearly see you're in pain, but I've never been more excited,' she replies honestly as she passes the bottle back. 'Spill.'

I take one big swig before I let it all out.

'How's this for a teaser,' I start. 'There are three men in this villa, all of whom I or my sister have slept with – and one we've both slept with.'

'Oh, God, stop it, you're making this up,' she says excitedly. 'Seriously?'

'Don't make that face, it isn't sexy – it's just sad and gross and depressing,' I insist. 'Do you remember when I was at school and I lost my virginity to that dickhead in my year who told everyone I was making it up?'

'Yes...'

'That was Charles,' I say.

'No!'

'Yep. And when I was waiting at the airport for Di last week, I met a man who was also waiting for someone on the same flight. Once again, sixteen-year-old Peach made a comeback, and I fell for him pretty instantly, slept with him, thinking we were both on the same page, only for him to piss off the next day. That was Matt, Charles's best friend-slash-best man. He's staying in the next room.'

'Holy shit!' she blurts.

I take another swig and pass her the bottle.

'And to top it all off, I accidentally invited Di's ex Alex instead of Lex, so he's here too, and sharing a room with Matt.'

Van chokes on her drink.

'I am your cousin and I love you and I *will* help you... but this is fantastic,' she says. 'I'm so glad I came.'

'You're welcome,' I reply. 'Just give me a good seat at your third wedding.'

'Working on it,' she replies.

The patio door that goes into Matt's room opens, and he steps out in nothing but his shorts.

'Oh, hello,' he says. He does a double take when he sees Van. They all do. 'You're new.'

Vanessa doesn't say a word. Instead she asks me, '*Is that him?*' in sign language.

'*Yes,*' I sign back.

Matt cocks his head curiously.

'This is my cousin Vanessa,' I tell her. 'Her dad – my uncle Mike – is deaf, so we all learned it.'

'Oh wow, that's cool,' he replies. 'It's nice to meet you, Vanessa, I've heard a lot about you.'

With her right hand, Van makes a sort of sideways thumbs-up gesture and wiggles it up and down.

'What does that mean?' Matt asks curiously.

'It means nice to meet you,' I tell him.

Van smiles widely at him.

It doesn't at all. It means 'piss off'.

My parents taught me how to sign when I was really young,

because Uncle Mike was born deaf, and naturally they wanted me to be able to communicate with him. I was so young I don't really remember learning, but it's something Van and I would use to talk to each other all the time, if only to keep well practised, but sometimes to have secret conversations. I wish it was something that was more widely taught. It's nice to be able to communicate in that way with people who otherwise wouldn't be able to understand. I feel really fortunate to have that skill.

'I'll have to remember that one,' he says with a smile.

I notice him clock the champagne bottle.

'We're just celebrating Van's arrival,' I tell him.

'Do you want some?' Van asks.

'Ordinarily I would, but I'm meeting Charles in five minutes – someone is here to measure me for my suit, apparently. I was just cooling down, before I go dress up.'

'Well, good luck with that,' I tell him.

I'm only being civil with him because we have an audience, even if Van knows everything now.

'OK, well, I'd better dash,' Matt says.

'Sounds about right,' Van replies. 'See you later.'

'Yeah, see you both later,' he says as he sweeps his hair back, flashing a bulging bicep at us as he does so.

'He might be a wanker, but he's seriously fucking hot,' Van says once we're alone. 'I'm not surprised you shagged him in an airport.'

'It wasn't quite like that,' I say through a laugh. 'It was in a hotel. But yeah, sure, he's hot, all right. Shame he's a wanker, really.'

'And as for his wanker friend,' she continues. 'I take it you haven't told Di?'

'I haven't,' I reply.

'For what it's worth, I think that's the right thing to do,' she says. 'If I was on the hook for everything I did when I was sixteen, no one would give me a chance – perhaps he's changed? He must have – it was fifteen years ago.'

'Exactly,' I reply. 'Although he is pretending he doesn't remember me.'

'Ah.'

'So that doesn't bode well. And then there's the fact that if he hasn't changed, he could do what he did back then, and say I made it up. And obviously I don't want to destroy Di's relationship for no reason, or for a weak reason,' I add. 'I'd feel awful if I ruined this for her – she's so happy.'

'You're doing the right thing,' Van assures me. 'Let me scope him out, try and figure out what his deal is – I can spot a douche a mile away.'

'That's why we love you,' I tell her.

'That in mind, I wouldn't have had Matt down as a proper douche. Sure, he's hot, but he has a kind face. It was the second thing I thought about his face.'

'What was the first?' I ask.

'How much I'd love to s—'

'Never mind,' I interrupt her. 'I get the picture.'

'You've had the picture,' she reminds me. 'But don't worry, he'll regret messing with you by the time I'm done with him.'

'What are you going to do?' I ask curiously.

'I'm not sure yet,' she replies. 'But you know me, it doesn't take me long to come up with a plan.'

'I really am so glad you're here, you know,' I tell her. 'I really miss you.'

'I miss you too,' she says, handing me the bottle. 'Have a little more of this and then show me around?'

'If I have any more of that, I won't be able to show you around,' I say with a chuckle.

She shrugs.

'I'll bring it for the road, just in case.'

I suddenly feel lighter, just for Van being here, because now it feels like someone is here who has my back, who knows everything, who loves me and never judges me. Any man would be lucky to be Van's third husband, but they'd need to be very brave too – she's going to make poor Matt's holiday a living hell.

18

After a long walk exploring the area around the villa, a tipsy Van and I managed to slink back inside and up to our room without anyone seeing us, so that we could smarten up (and hopefully sober up) for dinner this evening.

Now, we're dressed in our best and heading for the dining room. So far, apart from Matt, only Di, who popped up to our room to say hi, has seen Van, so she's yet to be introduced to Charles.

We're the last two to arrive at the dining table. All eyes are on Van the second we walk into the room.

'Vanessa,' Alex says brightly. 'Long time no see.'

'Yeah, I didn't fancy staying in touch, unsurprisingly,' she tells him, but there's a kind of light-heartedness to her voice that doesn't create a bad vibe, it makes Alex feel like it's something he can laugh off.

'Hello, Vanessa,' Lex says.

'Hi,' she replies with an unenthusiastic wave.

That's another fantastic thing about Van – she doesn't like Lex either! I couldn't ask for a better ally right now.

'Come meet Charles,' Di insists, grabbing her by the hand and leading her around the table.

'Hello, Vanessa,' he says, kissing her on both cheeks. 'It's so good to finally meet you.'

'You too,' she replies. 'I feel like I've known you for ages.'

For the briefest of moments – so brief I'll bet no one else even notices it – Charles glances at me.

'Pizza tonight,' Di tells me with a nudge. 'They've got a wood-fired oven outside, so they're just going to keep making different ones and putting them down in front of us! We're going to sit outside to eat now we've got our drinks.'

'Sounds great,' I reply. I do love pizza – who doesn't – and when in Italy...

'Let's head out,' Charles says. 'We can carry on getting to know everyone outside.'

The table next to the pool is all laid out, ready for dinner, and it looks like something out of a brochure for somewhere I could never afford to stay – so here, I guess.

The sun is setting and the light is changing. The pool is lit up, the garden boasts a variety of lights, and the villa is practically glowing. It's just such a stunning, inviting space. If you look beyond the infinity pool, you can even see the sea in the distance because we're so high up. This place really is a dream. I have to keep reminding myself to pull myself out of the drama and take in everything around me. Perhaps now Van is here, I'll find it easier to enjoy myself.

'Why is there an extra seat at the table?' I ask as I take my seat, noticing an additional set of cutlery.

'My cousin Ben has just arrived,' Charles replies.

'And that's everyone here, until the wedding, of course,' Di says. 'It's all getting a bit real now.'

She sounds nervous but still mostly excited.

'Oh, it's all real, hun,' Van says.

'Did you get everything done that you needed to do this morning?' I ask curiously, hoping to catch her out.

'Yes, thank you. I keep thinking it's too good to be true,' she says, changing the subject before I have time to ask any more questions. 'Like I'm looking at Charles, thinking, "What is wrong with you?"'

She says this in a sort of jokey way that maybe has just a little bit of truth in it.

'I'm the lucky one,' Charles tells her. 'I never thought I'd find this with anyone.'

'That's so sweet,' Lex says with a sigh.

'Sickeningly so,' Van jokes.

'Ah, Ben,' Charles announces. 'Here he is.'

We all look at the patio door to see Ben walk in, and oh my God. Tall, slim, super fit, a sparkling smile, chiselled good looks, brown puppy-dog eyes – he has the look of a younger Jon Hamm and I am here for it. Cousin Ben is hot!

'Hello,' Ben says. 'Sorry I'm late.'

He has such a deep voice, and his accent is so different to Charles's. Charles is unmistakably North Yorkshire but with subtle tweaks from all the different places he's travelled to. Ben can't have grown up where we did. I'm not great at placing accents but I'd say he sounds like he's from Oxfordshire or somewhere similar. He speaks the Queen's English, that's for sure.

'Let me introduce you to everyone,' Charles says. 'We'll work our way around the table. First up, this is Lex, she's a friend of Di's.'

'Hi,' she says in a voice much higher and softer than her usual tone. She gives him a flirtatious little wave.

'Then we have Alex,' Charles continues. 'Who is an, er, old

friend of the bride. Then we have Vanessa – cousin Vanessa, who I've just met myself.'

Vanessa looks at Ben, turns so that Di and I can see her, and signs something at us.

'Oh, that just means she feels hot,' I tell the table.

It doesn't, it means that she thinks Ben is hot.

'Her translator is Di's sister, Peach,' Charles goes on.

'Peach,' Ben repeats back. 'Now there's a name you don't hear every day. Are you as sweet as your name?'

'I, er...' I smile and scoff. Way to be cool, Peach. 'I don't know about that.'

Charles looks a little put out by Ben's friendly, almost flirty comment, so he quickly moves on.

'Matt, you know.'

'Hi,' Matt says bluntly.

Ben just gives him a nod.

That's interesting. Perhaps Matt and Ben don't get along.

'And this beautiful woman by my side is Di – my soon-to-be wife,' Charles says.

'It is truly wonderful to meet you,' Ben says as he makes his way around the table to hug her. 'Anyone who can make an honest man out of my cousin is a hero in my eyes. And he's right, of course, you are beautiful.'

Di almost melts in his arms.

'Everyone, sit down, sit down,' Charles insists. 'Let's get to know our new guests. Vanessa, you start.'

'Talking about myself, my favourite thing,' she jokes. 'I'm Vanessa, twenty-eight, single, currently living in LA.'

She isn't twenty-eight at all, she's thirty-one, the same as me. It seems almost silly, to lie about just three years, but I think Van might be playing the long game with that one. I get the feeling she's going to be twenty-eight for a long time – for as long as people will believe her or medical advancements will allow.

'What do you do?' Charles asks her.

'At the moment, not a lot,' she replies. 'Not for work, anyway.'

Everyone looks at her for more info, but she is unwilling to supply it. I know the truth. Van doesn't work because she's been through two very lucrative divorces – not that she planned it that way. It's just a coincidence that both of her husbands have been loaded, and an unfortunate coincidence that both of them cheated on her. Since her last divorce, she's decided she doesn't want anything serious for a while, and she's become a bit of a man-eater, and it really suits her. She's so sexy and confident and clearly having the time of her life. And then there's me, plucking up the confidence to sleep with someone on the first date – deluding myself into thinking it was a date at all – only to be ditched and left feeling all wounded about it. I wish I didn't care.

'Tell us about yourself, Ben,' Di says eagerly.

'Well, I'm Ben,' he starts. 'I am a professional polo player—'

'Is that a real job?' Alex pipes up.

'It certainly is,' Ben replies proudly. 'It's a lot of fun. I'm sort of like my team's battering ram.'

'I bet you are,' Van says as she sucks her drink through her straw. 'So do you wear the leather boots and the jodhpurs?'

'And the helmet and the goggles,' Matt adds.

'Yes to all of that,' he says with a smile. 'Don't knock the safety gear. Even with it, I've been hurt a few times. I've broken my ankle falling off the horse, I've taken a few mallets to the face, I've been hit in the face with balls...'

I quickly but subtly place my hand on Van's arm, as if to say

'Don't you dare say what I think you're going to say,' and thankfully she keeps it to herself.

'He's met Prince Harry,' Charles tells us.

Ben bats his hand, as though it's no big deal.

'He's a good lad,' he says, casual as you like, considering he's talking about actual royalty.

'So, Matt, you work in a shop,' Ben recalls, significantly underplaying Matt's actual role. Matt doesn't correct him, but he has a look on his face like he's tried to before. 'Alex, what do you do?'

'I'm a software developer,' he says.

'Oh yeah, how's that?' Ben asks.

'Pretty good actually,' Alex replies. 'I sold an app I'd developed recently, so I made quite a bit of money from that, figured I'd earned some time off – this holiday couldn't have come at a better time.'

'Anything we might have heard of?' Van asks curiously.

'It was a photo sharing app called SnappySend' he tells us.

'Oh my God, I love SnappySend,' Van tells him. 'I like that you can send whatever you want and then the photos just disappear.'

'Wait, I read about this fairly recently,' Charles says. 'It sold for *seven* figures.'

We all turn to face Alex.

'Like I said: great time to take a holiday,' he replies with a cheeky smile.

Wow, am I the only pauper at the table? That's depressing.

'What do you do, Di?' Ben asks her.

'I'm a solicitor, so nothing very exciting, I'm afraid,' Di replies. 'Peach has an interesting job though.'

'Oh really?' he says, turning to me.

'I don't know how interesting it is, but I enjoy it,' I start. 'I'm a mystery shopper, so I get paid to go to shops, restaurants and hotels, to basically shop, eat and sleep.'

'Surely you have the best job of all of us,' he points out. 'That's the dream.'

'Did you hear Charles say the thing about seven figures?' I joke. 'I do really enjoy it though.'

'I stay in a lot of hotels,' Ben says. 'So many I'm probably an expert too – so if you ever need an assistant...'

He's kidding, but, oh my God, I wish!

'I haven't had much luck with assistants,' I confess. 'The last time I did a hotel visit with someone else, we had too much to drink, we got a bit muddled ordering a bottle of wine, and bought one that was five thousand pounds, instead of the fifty-quid one we were intending to get.'

I tell this story like it's one of many zany capers I've had during my career. I suppose it is (although this has to be my biggest fail to date), but this time it's personal – I want Matt to know that actions have consequences – but I don't let my face slip.

'Five thousand pounds?!' Matt screeches.

'Oh yeah,' I reply.

'Did they make you pay for it?' he asks.

'Of course they did,' I reply. 'My friend and I drank it, so...'

I glance at Matt, briefly, and he looks mortified.

'It's a shame you don't want an assistant,' Ben says. 'You sound like you're a lot of fun in a hotel room. Five thousand pounds for wine? My kind of girl.'

One of the waiting staff comes out to see if we want any side dishes. Van takes this moment to sign a message to me.

He's flirting with you,' she says.

No way,' I reply.

Di walks around the table and crouches down between us.

'You're having to pay five thousand pounds for a bottle of wine?' she says.

'It's fine – well, as fine as it can be – they're taking it out of my wage a bit each month,' I say quietly.

'Do you want me to ask Charles for the money to pay it off for you?' Di suggests.

'Oh, God, no,' I say a little too quickly. 'Sorry, it's just I got myself into this mess, I'll get myself out.'

'Well, the offer stays on the table,' she says before she heads back to her seat.

'I could give you the money,' Van says. 'Or lend you it, if it makes you happier.'

'It's my own stupid fault,' I say. 'But thank you.'

'Yeah, but it's not just your fault, is it? It takes two to tango,' she whispers back.

I look over at Matt, who is chatting with Charles, but it's like he can't focus. He keeps looking over at me, only for seconds at a time, but I suppose the wine money is on his mind now. He looks like he feels terrible – well, good. My heart bleeds for him.

I mop my brow with the back of my hand. The summer heat just does not let up. I switch between loving it (almost all the time) and hating it (like now, when I'm all dressed up and feel like a sweaty mess).

'I'm just going to get another drink,' I tell Van. 'Back in a sec.'

I wander into the dining room, where there is a sort of DIY bar. I'm not a mixologist, but I search through the fridges and cupboards until I find some passionfruit juice and some vodka, which I mix together in a glass. I grab the champagne from the ice bucket and pour a little into my drink, making a poor man's Porn Star Martini – or a rich man's Porn Star

Martini, I suppose, given that I've used champagne instead of prosecco.

I take a sip and – mmm – it tastes so good. I tip my head to one side and hold the icy-cold glass on my neck for a second. It even feels good.

'Hey you,' I hear Ben's deep voice from behind me.

'Oh, hi,' I reply. 'I was just getting a drink. And cooling down a little.'

'Try this,' he says mysteriously.

Ben steps behind the bar and grabs a beer and a tea towel before removing the champagne from the ice bucket. He dips the tea towel in the ice water, and he walks behind me, standing so close I can smell his aftershave. My whole body shakes for a second when he first places the icy cloth on the back on my neck, but my body soon acclimatises and it feels great. Oh, he's got game. I'm impressed.

'How's that?' he asks.

'Ugh, amazing,' I reply.

I feel icy water trickling down my back. Ben quickly swipes it away with a dry tea towel.

'What does the beer do?' I ask.

'Oh, that's just for me,' he says with a laugh. 'And so I had an excuse to talk to you again. You seem like the most interesting person here.'

'Ah, well, that's where—'

We're interrupted by someone clearing their throat.

'Matt, buddy,' Ben says. 'Can I get you a drink?'

'I just came to talk to Peach, actually,' he replies.

The last thing I want to do is talk to *him* – especially when I'm talking to Ben! If he doesn't want me, the least he can do is leave me alone.

'The pizzas will be ready soon,' I tell Matt. 'We'll talk later.'

Ben smiles at me – it's as though he likes that I don't like Matt, which makes me think they must have some kind of history. Ha! Join the club.

'It won't take long,' Matt says. 'It's important.'

'I'm sure it's nothing to brag about,' I reply as I walk past him, echoing the words he used to describe sleeping with me earlier.

'I think you're barking up the wrong tree, buddy,' Ben tells him with a friendly pat on the back.

OK, I know, this is seriously petty, but let me have this one. Matt really hurt me. I felt so rejected, and so cheated, and kind of used. I thought there was something between us that would span twenty-four hours, at least, and for him to take off like he did just proves that, whatever I saw in him, he didn't see in me, and that hurts. So just let me have this, this small shift in power where suddenly he is interested in talking to me (I know it's probably just to offer me some money for the wine, and genuinely, he can piss off, if that's the only thing he feels bad about), and I get to be the one who blanks him. And, look, I know a sexy southerner who plays professional polo and pronounces his consonants is probably out of my league, but if that gets under Matt's skin, then I'm all for that too.

Now that I have more people here who I can get along with, things don't seem quite so bad. I have Van to talk to, Ben to distract me – and I'm actually interested to hear more about Alex. I had no idea he has such an interesting job.

I just need to keep looking forward, take things a day at a time and get this week over with. Oh and, you know, make sure my sister isn't making the biggest mistake of her life in the meantime.

19

It's lunchtime, and I have been summoned to the restaurant where the wedding reception will take place. Well, I say 'restaurant', but the term hardly does it justice.

I'm at Grotta Biancofiore, a super exclusive restaurant on San Valentino, best known for its location. I've never seen anything like it – there is this cave in the side of the cliff with a five-star restaurant inside it. It looks so bizarre from the outside looking in, and now that I'm inside, it seems even odder. It's kind of dark, with the bright sunlight from outside unable to get in, but it's so nice and cool.

At the heart of the cave, there is a big hole in the floor with a fence around it that looks down at the water below, in the – I don't know – downstairs cave, which is where my boat docked. I arrived here from the villa just a few seconds before Matt pulled up in a different boat, which had come from the resort. We're the only two people here, apart from the staff. We're supposed to be meeting Di and Charles here to help them pick their wedding food, but once again, they're nowhere to be seen.

'I'll call her,' I say to Matt as we're shown to the table.

Once again, the phone rings until the absolute last minute, and Di answers.

'Hey, sis,' she says.

'Hey – I'm at the restaurant, Matt is here too, where are you guys?'

'You're not going to believe it,' she says in a tone of voice that, yep, she's right, I don't believe it. 'But Charles surprised me with a trip to the mainland again – this time to taste cakes. We're in Alberobello. You'd love it here. The man at the bakery told me Alberobello means "beautiful tree" but, oddly, the place is famous for its buildings. They're called trulli, or something like that – I bought you a little one from a gift shop.'

She's waffling, which only makes me more suspicious.

'Di...'

'Anyway, we're here now, and running late with the cake tasting, and there's this two-hour walking tour that I fancy, so we may we well do that while we're here.'

'Right, so for your food tasting?'

'Can you two do it for us?' she says. 'You know me. You know what I'd pick.'

'Do I have a choice?' I say with a laugh.

'Thanks, sis, you're a babe,' she says. 'Love you.'

'Yeah, yeah, you too,' I reply. I look up at Matt. 'Yeah, they're not coming.'

'Again?' he replies.

'Again,' I confirm.

Not turning up once was a little shady, but twice, two days in a row, that's got to be on purpose. Is this Di trying to play matchmaker? Does she think if she keeps pushing the two of us together, in these ultra-romantic scenarios, we'll just throw ourselves at each other? Of course, the alternative is that it's Charles orchestrating this, but I'm just not sure why. To keep me away from my sister? To distract me? That sounds like something he'd do if he remembered me and was worried I was going to say something...

'We have prepared a selection of sample dishes for you to try,' our waiter tells us. 'I will be back with the first ones in just a moment. But first...'

He leans forward and lights the candle on our table before disappearing into the kitchen.

'Another day, another romantic meal, just the two of us,' Matt points out.

'It's like *Groundhog Day*-te,' I point out. 'The two of us repeating the same awful date again and again and again.'

'I can't wait to put that on my dating CV,' he replies.

'Just don't ask me for a reference – you won't like what I say,' I add.

I can't help but notice that joking with him like this feels like we're wandering back into the territory we were in at Mote that night... but we can't actually get that back now, can we? We ruined it by having sex.

'Would it help if I offered you some money for that bottle of wine?' he asks. 'Or all of it. Whatever you're paying per month, I'll pay it. I feel so guilty about it – how did it happen?'

'I have no idea,' I reply. 'We were drunk. We did a bunch of stupid stuff. It's fine, just forget about it. Please.'

'I'll leave it for now, but I don't think I can live with myself if I don't give you something,' he says.

'Seriously, you've done enough,' I say.

Our waiter looks a little puzzled as he places two small plates of pasta in front of us. I think he was expecting a couple in love.

Sitting here with Matt, in such an amazing setting, is like one of life's cruel jokes. We're in a super romantic restaurant, in a cave, at a resort for lovers, all alone apart from our own personal waiter. It's so lovely and cool in here, with such a stunning view and the sound of the water hitting the rocks below. And it's all totally wasted on us.

'This is orecchiette with sausage and fennel,' he tells us. '*Buon appetito.*'

'That sounds really good,' I say, digging in the second our waiter disappears. 'Ugh, it tastes good too.'

'Oh wow,' Matt says. 'This is really good. Do we really have to pick for them?'

'They've just flown probably hundreds of miles to taste cakes,' I tell him. 'There's no way they're letting us pick anything. This is a set-up.'

'Are we being *Parent Trap*-ped?' he asks with a completely straight face.

I raise an eyebrow.

'Didn't think I'd know what that meant?' he asks with a smile. 'I grew up with two sisters... and... neither of them watched it. I watched it. I wanted to watch it. I've just realised I don't need to pretend to be cool in front of you any more. I can do what I want.'

Matt puts down his fork, picks up one of the little ear-shaped pasta pieces with his fingers and pops it in his mouth. He looks at his saucy fingers and pulls an amused face.

'Too far, right?' he says with a laugh.

'Maybe,' I reply, with a smile I can't help or hide. 'I get it, I get it. You don't care what I think.'

'You know what I mean,' he says. 'We can relax now.'

'Chance would be a fine thing,' I say with a sigh.

'Is everything OK?' he asks as he wipes his hands on his napkin. He goes back to using his fork to eat. 'You're pretty grumpy for someone staying in a five-star villa, who is about to watch one of the people she loves the most get married...'

'If I say something, do you promise not to repeat it?' I start cautiously.

'Of course,' he says. 'What's up?'

'I am not in favour of this wedding *at all*.'

Matt's jaw drops as his fork drops to his plate. The clattering sound is almost as loud as his gasp.

'*What*?!' he says in a way that is immediately and obviously sarcastic.

'OK, it's not *that* obvious,' I insist.

'You're clearly not having the best time,' he says.

'Well, that's largely to do with your presence, if we're being honest,' I say.

'Fair play,' he replies, suddenly going back into his shell a little. 'Look, honestly, I'm not all that happy about the wedding either.'

'No?'

'Of course not,' he replies. 'It's natural though, right? We feel like we're losing our best friends, our homes, our plans. We feel like we're getting left behind.'

'Well, yeah, there is that,' I admit. 'But it's more than that. I'm just not sure Charles is the right kind of guy for Di...'

Matt thinks for a moment.

'OK, yeah, he's not the type to settle down,' he says. 'He's tried a couple of times and failed after... well, a matter of days. But who are we to say anything?'

'So you think it's a stupid idea too?' I say.

'Is that what you want to hear? Yes, OK, sure, I think it's a bad idea. But other than a little light "Are sure you know what you're doing?"s and "As long as you're happy"s, there's nothing we can do.'

'Hmm,' I reply.

'All finished?' our waiter asks.

'Mmm, yes,' I reply. 'That was amazing.'

'I will be back immediately with your next dish,' he replies.

'Can't wait,' Matt tells him. 'Thank you.'

'So you think we should just keep our mouths shut?' I continue.

'That's all we can do,' he replies. 'And if it does all go tits up, we'll be there for them and it will all be fine.'

'Well, first of all, I'm going to try and find ways to subtly highlight what a terrible idea this is – and you should too. Secondly, you're pretty blasé about this kind of stuff, aren't you?' I point out. 'Just get married and if it doesn't work, never mind. Just sleep with—'

'Food's here,' he interrupts me.

'Your next dish,' the waiter says. 'Calamari. *Buon appetite.*'

'Oh, God,' I whisper through my smile when we're alone again. 'Tried it, hated it.'

'Yeah, squid is a no-go for me too,' he says. 'And I told you, never again – I'm not eating any more grim sea shit for you.'

'We could set it free,' I suggest, fully aware we wouldn't be it doing any favours, given that it's battered. 'Just chuck it over that fence, back into the sea – you're a fit guy, I'm sure you could throw them from here.'

'Not without being seen,' he says. 'And typically people don't throw things in the sea.'

'I know, I know, I just don't know what we're supposed to do with it,' I say quickly.

'Have we ruled out just saying neither of us likes it?' Matt asks.

I stare at him and tip my head.

'Right, OK, honesty is the worst policy. Should have known that one,' he replies with a smile. 'So...'

I grab my napkin and place it on the table.

'Quick, dump them on here,' I say.

Matt follows my lead. I bundle them up in the napkin before stuffing it into my handbag.

'Do not let me forget they are in there,' I laugh.

'Oh my, clean plates already,' the waiter says. 'You must have loved it, no?'

'No' is correct.

'Mmm, yes,' I say.

'There are some left, if you would like some more?'

'No, no,' I say quickly. 'We don't want to get too full to taste the other dishes.'

'*Si*, OK, no problem,' he replies. 'Your next dish will be just a few moments.'

'*Grazie*,' I reply with a lump in my throat. I really hope the next thing isn't gross.

'I know you might not think this wedding is a good idea, but Charles is a good person,' Matt tells me. 'I wouldn't be best friends with him if he weren't.'

I nod thoughtfully, but it's hard to imagine the Charles I grew up around, who now has the job of basically buying up small businesses and absorbing them into his dad's empire, could be all that different. Do people really change that much?

Matt is right about one thing – and, yes, I do hate to admit that – but there's nothing I can say to Di to try and put her off going through with it. She'd only resent me for it.

I do need to have a word with her about these dates though because if it is her setting me up with Matt, she needs to stop. The *Groundhog Day*-te scenario is a little tired now – I don't have the patience for it.

I do feel a little less uncomfortable now that Matt and I have had a civil conversation, and it seems like we're both down for ignoring the elephant in the room, which suits me fine. It's nice to know I'm not the only person feeling scared about losing my best friend too. I've been so focused on Charles being all wrong for Di that I haven't been thinking about what it's actually going to mean for me, when my best friend isn't around any more. That sucks, no matter who the man is.

20

Walking up the villa driveway with Matt today, things aren't quite as awkward as yesterday, which is progress, I suppose. I'm still annoyed at him, and I still think he's a giant dick, but I'm tired of being so angry about it. It's done now.

As we approach the front of the villa, we hear noise coming from outside, where the pool is, so we walk around the building to check it out.

Sure enough, Ben and Alex are in the pool, whacking a beach ball back and forth, while Lex watches on from the comfort of a sun lounger.

'Hey there,' I call out.

'Well, hello there,' Ben says back in his silky smooth, sexy deep voice.

'You look like you're having fun,' I point out.

'Where have you two been?' Lex asks nosily, looking at us over the top of her sunglasses.

'We've been to a food tasting, for the wedding,' I tell her.

'And you didn't bring me anything back?' Alex jokes.

I pause for thought.

'Actually, I have a handbag full of calamari,' I tell him.

'What, seriously?' he replies. 'Can I have it?'

'Erm, yeah,' I reply. 'It's kind of cold and kind of gross.'

'No worries,' he says as he wades towards the pool steps.

Oh, wow, he's really coming for it. Amazing really, the man is a multimillionaire staying in a villa that pretty much has a chef around the clock, and he's going to eat out of my handbag. I have a lot of time for that.

'Jump in and play with me,' Ben calls out.

I look at Matt, then at Ben.

'What, me?' I say.

'Yes, you,' he says with a smile. 'I can see your bikini straps under your dress from here. Get it off and jump in. The dress, that is.'

Lex has a face like thunder, which makes me think she must be into Ben. To be honest, that makes jumping in the water with Ben more tempting, but I can't.

'I can't jump in,' I tell him. 'I can't swim.'

'What?' he replies.

'You can't swim?' Lex echoes. 'Seriously?'

'Yeah, seriously,' I reply.

'Wow, that's interesting,' Ben says. 'You're, what? Twenty-six, twenty-seven? And you don't know how to swim?'

'Flattery will get you *anywhere*,' I joke, but he doesn't seem like he's kidding. 'I just never learned,' I explain. 'And I'm not embarrassed by it.'

I'm not. There's no shame in being a thirty-one-year-old who can't swim. It's not even like I tried and failed, I just never got round to it. I've been strictly a shallow-end girl my entire life.

'It is a bit pathetic,' Lex points out.

I shrug.

'Well, I feel obliged to teach you,' Ben says. 'Now that I know, should anything happen to you, I would feel responsible. Do you want me to have to live with that?'

'Ah, but what are the chances I'm going to need to know how to swim in an emergency?' I say.

'We are on an island,' he points out. 'Surrounded by sea, covered in pools and lakes – the baths are pretty deep in the villa. Come on!'

'OK, OK, fine,' I reply as I tug at my dress straps, slipping them off my shoulders, allowing my dress to hit the floor.

'Matt, Matt, why don't you sit next to me?' I hear Lex say behind me. 'This sun lounger is made for two.'

'Erm, OK,' Matt replies.

I kick off my shoes and hurry around to the pool steps. I carefully step into the water, which is freezing! Ben offers me a hand to help me in.

'Ooh, it's a saltwater pool,' I say. 'It's lovely. Freezing though!'

'We'll soon warm you up,' Ben tells me. 'Right, first things first. What I want you to do is hold on to the side of the pool with your hands and just let your body float up onto the water. We'll practise moving just your legs.'

'OK,' I say, suddenly a little nervous.

'Hahaha! Matt, you are so funny,' I overhear Lex say loudly – probably for my/Ben's benefit.

Last night Di told me that she had let slip to Lex about my recent history with Matt, and I wouldn't put it past Lex to be flirting with Matt to try and make me jealous, just to distract me from Ben so that she can have him all to herself. Like I'm going to fall for that. Lex is the one who is *so funny*, if she thinks that is going to work.

I grip the edge of the pool with my hands and try to float,

but it's one of those things that is hard to do when you don't know how, and no one can quite explain it to you.

'Just let your body rise to the top of the water,' Ben says.

'I'm trying,' I tell him as I lift my feet, but I just feel my body being pulled under the water every time.

'OK, Plan B,' Ben says. 'Do you mind if I...?'

He holds his hands up in front of me.

'Oh, sure, go ahead,' I reply. Now I'm even more nervous.

Ben places his hands out in front of me, under the water.

'Rest your body on my hands,' he suggests. 'Don't worry, I won't let you drop.'

'OK,' I say. I take a deep breath and slowly lean forwards, placing my body in Ben's hands. One of them lands just below my bikini top, the other just above my bikini bottoms. It's so strange, feeling so weightless – it's even weirder having a gorgeous man's hands on my body.

'Hey, look, you're floating,' he tells me. 'Now, just try moving your legs, to keep yourself up there.'

'I don't feel very graceful,' I tell him.

'You're doing great,' he replies. 'Do you want me to take my hands off you?'

'Leave the hands on for a bit,' I hear Van's voice call out. She sounds far away, like maybe she's on the terrace. 'If you can get your hands on a girl like that, never let her go.'

There's a tone to her voice, like this information is for the attention of everyone, and I can't help but smile.

'Sorry,' I whisper to Ben.

'It's OK,' he laughs. 'Sounds like solid advice.'

'Hahaha! Matt! Stop!' I hear Lex again.

'I'm glad you're here,' Ben whispers. 'That Lex girl keeps aggressively flirting with me. I've tried dropping subtle hints, but she's just not having it.'

'She is never going to pick those hints up,' I whisper back. 'If you kissed me right now, she'd just think you were playing hard to get.'

'Is it worth a try?' he asks.

Ben says this with such a sexy, cheeky grin. It's hard to resist giving the kissing thing a go.

'That calamari was great, Peach,' I hear Alex say, interrupting us at the worst possible moment. 'Did you pick it for the wedding?'

'No!' Matt and I reply, perfectly in sync.

'Right, let's get you on your back,' Ben says. 'Same kind of thing, only you won't be holding on, it will be just my hands under you, sound good?'

'Sounds great,' I reply.

And it really does. Suddenly I can feel all my stress melting away, and it's all thanks to this saltwater pool, and Ben.

Who knew swimming lessons were so fun?

21

It turns out, if you walk down the driveway and turn left, there is a hidden pathway that leads to a secret beach.

After dinner, we all agreed it might be nice to head down there for a bonfire, so we gathered blankets and bottles of wine, and made our way down the winding, grassy pathway until we hit the genuinely perfect sands of the beach. We were like children, all racing to see who could reach the sand first. On the beach, there's a fancy metal firepit surrounded by benches covered with big, cosy-looking cushions – the perfect spot for chilling out after dark. It stands out from all the natural beauty that dwarfs it, but at the same time it looks like someone put a great deal of time and attention (and money) into making it blend in.

Di, the perfect hostess, poured us all a drink while we each chose our spot for the evening.

We're all settled now. Matt is sitting opposite me, which means I can see his face peeking over the top of the flames, which seems appropriate. Charles and Di are sitting next to him. Van was quick to claim a two-seater bench for herself, so she could lie across it, cuddled up under her blanket, with her giant glass of red wine cradled in her hands with all the love and care you'd give your first born. That left just two two-seater benches, and me, Lex, Ben and Alex to decide who sat where, and oh-ho, the look on Lex's face when Ben sat down and patted the seat next to him, for me to sit there.

'The two Alexes together,' Alex announced happily as they sat down together – which only made Lex look angrier.

We've been sitting here a little while now and it's glorious. This side of the island faces out to sea, so there is nothing to see but water that fades into the dark night sky, and given that there's nothing else around us, it's like nothing exists outside the glow of the firepit. It does feel a bit like that when you're on holiday, doesn't it? Like real life doesn't exist. You forget about your job, your family, where you live, what you do for fun. You create this whole new life for a short period of time, and it's hard to imagine much else mattering while you're in the holiday bubble.

'Are you cold?' Ben asks me softly.

'A little,' I reply, but I'm not, it's a nice evening and I'm feeling just right.

Ben scoots a little closer and wraps an arm around me, pulling me in to his body. He gives my arm a rub, but only for a few seconds before settling his hand on me.

I feel even better now.

It's a beautiful, calm, clear night. Perfect for sitting around and taking in the scenery, just having a drink, relaxing...

'We should play a game,' Lex says with a clap of her hands.

I can't help but roll my eyes. Thankfully she doesn't notice.

'Games,' Van groans. 'Urgh.'

I love that she says what she thinks. Then again, she doesn't have to live in the same continent as Lex.

'Erm, technically, your cousin isn't getting a bridal shower,' Lex reminds her. 'And we don't really have time to squeeze one in, so we'll call this Di's bridal shower. Lucky boys, you're invited too.'

Ben lightly pinches my arm, which I reckon is supposed to fill in for a sarcastic remark or an outright refusal to take part, but I guess he's scared of angering Lex too.

'I've never been to a bridal shower,' Van says. 'I didn't even have one, not for either wedding.'

'Either wedding?' Ben asks.

'Van is a double divorcee,' I tell him.

'People usually find it pretty hot,' she points out. 'Never figured out why.'

'We're not talking about failed marriages at a bridal shower,' Lex quickly snaps.

'Check my bank balance and then tell me they were failures,' Van mumbles under her breath.

'We're going to play a couples game, but just for the happy couple, because that feels appropriate,' Lex starts. 'How about a game of Mr & Mrs?'

Is she stupid? Doesn't she get that having a couple who have only known each other for two weeks play a game like Mr & Mrs, which tests how well couples know each other, is a terrible idea? They can't possibly know each other well enough to play this...

Oh. *Ohhh*... Maybe this isn't a terrible idea after all.

'I think it's a great idea,' I say. 'Lots of fun.'

My enthusiasm makes Di smile, which does make me feel a little bit bad, but I'm simply going to do what I told Matt I was going to do, and just highlight how little they actually know about each other.

'It is?' Lex says in disbelief. 'Of course it is. I figure the two of you can use the notes apps on your phones. We'll take it in turns to ask you the usual Mr & Mrs-style questions, and you both use the pen tool to write the answer on your phone, then hold it up so we can all see if you're right.'

'OK, sounds fun,' Di says. 'Let's do it.'

'I'm asking the first question,' Van calls out loudly from under her blanket. 'Who is best in bed?'

'Vanessa!' Lex shrieks. 'You can't ask that!'

'Are we playing it PG or anything goes?' Alex asks. 'Because one sounds much more fun.'

'We're all adults,' Charles says confidently. 'Anything goes, let's do it.'

'Oh, God. OK, fine,' Lex says. 'If it appeals to the plebs... OK, write your answer, then turn your phones around in one... two... three!'

Charles has said *Di*. Di has said *Charles*. Obviously that's the only way to safely play that one.

'I've got one, I've got one,' Lex says far too excitedly, given how boring this game is for everyone apart from the couple playing. 'What was the other person wearing the day you met?'

'Wasn't that only a week ago?' Ben points out with a laugh.

'So?' Lex replies.

'So, I'd be worried if they didn't remember,' he says.

'Just, shut up,' Lex insists. 'Answer guys. One... two... three!'

Charles's phone says *blue dress*. Di's says *slate-grey suit*.

'Is that right?' Lex asks.

'It is!' Di replies.

'Yay, another point,' Lex cheers. This is so lame. 'Who's next?'

'I've got one,' I say. 'What's the other person's favourite pizza topping?'

Charles looks quietly confident. Di looks like she's giving it some thought.

'One... two... three!' Lex says, and my God, it gets more annoying each time.

Charles has written *pepperoni*. Di has written *ham and mushroom*.

'So, are they the right answers?' Lex asks, knowing full well at least one isn't.

'Well, mine is wrong,' Di says.

'Mine too,' Charles adds. 'What's your favourite pizza topping?'

'God, don't make her say it,' Alex says through a wince.

'What?' Charles ask him.

'The answer is gross,' Alex says. 'The mucky mare, she likes a Hawaiian, but she swaps the ham for anchovies.'

'That can't be your be your favourite pizza topping,' Charles says with such an intense seriousness, I wouldn't be surprised if he called the wedding off – I know I would if I met someone who thought that was a good pizza topping. Di only gets away with it because she's a blood relative.

'Erm, yeah, it is actually,' she confesses.

'I absolutely love anchovies on pizzas,' Charles says as a smile blossoms on his face. 'I put them on Hawaiians, but I leave the ham on too. That's my answer.'

'What are the chances?' Lex says excitedly.

'What *are* the chances?' I wonder out loud.

'I've got a question,' Matt says.

I look over at him, only for him to give me a subtle little wink. I think he gets what I'm trying to do, and he's going to join in.

'Favourite thing in your bedroom,' Matt says, scooting to the edge of his seat as he awaits the answer. As he leans forward on his arms, I catch myself staring at his shoulders. I remember, that night at the hotel, when we were in bed together, I couldn't keep my hands off his strong shoulders. Urgh, I need to snap out of it.

'Ooh, interesting question,' Lex says. 'Three... two... one!'

Charles has written *dressing table*. Di has written *PS4*.

They look at each other's phones. Their faces fall, confirming wrong answers.

'Not really a gamer,' Charles tells her.

'PS4s are outdated now,' Alex chimes in. 'And I've never known Di have a dressing table, so unless she's got one since... erm...'

Alex, who has had a few too many, lets his sentence drift off into the night, but Charles wants answers.

'So, I suppose you know the answer to this one too, do you?' he asks Alex through gritted teeth.

I glance over at Matt, who wiggles his eyebrows at me.

I knew that highlighting just how little the two of them knew about each other was going to be a useful tool in showing them they were rushing into things, but Alex knowing the answers that Charles doesn't is just an added bonus.

'She'll probably say her electric blanket,' Alex says sheepishly.

Matt's face falls.

'Electric blanket?' Charles says.

'I like a toasty bed,' Di says. 'But, look, if you don't, I'm not so attached to it that I would choose it over you.'

She laughs awkwardly.

'I like a toasty bed,' Charles insists. 'I love my electric blanket!'

'You really do?' Di asks with stars in her eyes.

'He really does,' Matt mutters under his breath.

Just like when I asked my question, he really thought he had them there.

We go around the circle asking questions, but no matter how many times we highlight how little Di and Charles know about each other, it almost always turns out to be something they agree on or both like. So anything they didn't know before, they do now, and the only thing we've highlighted is how much they have in common.

I exhale deeply. Maybe they are perfect for each other. Maybe there is a way to just know if someone is the right person for you – something inexplicable – when you first meet them. Di and Charles (I refuse to say it the other way around) knew they wanted to get married before they knew about all this weird and wonderful (mostly weird) stuff they had in common – does that mean you can actually meet someone one day and know by the end of the week that they're the right person for you?

I'm sitting here with Ben, with his arm still wrapped around me, and he's obviously gorgeous and talented and passionate about what he does, and he seems like a really nice guy, but if someone told me I had to decide right now if I wanted to marry him or never speak to him again, I'd have to go with the latter, because I couldn't possibly know. And, take Matt (seriously, take him!), after just a few hours I felt like I was falling head over for heels for him – turns out I was just falling for his charm. He was gone by morning. So I ask again: how can you know? How can anyone know so quickly?

It's a big decision, and one that I need to make sure Di takes seriously, but Charles is seeming more and more perfect for her so... I don't know. But just because they both think *Hamlet 2* is the best musical (I'm not even sure it counts as a musical, never mind the best one), doesn't mean they'll be happy together for the rest of their lives, does it?

I don't know the ingredients for a happy marriage (Naked Wednesdays and individual hobby rooms, if my parents are anything to go by), but I do know that my sister deserves the best husband. And while Charles might seem like the best on paper, he just seems too good to be true. I just need to figure it out, and quickly, like over-the-next-few-days quickly. Oh boy...

22

It's official, I'm getting old.

Look, I know thirty-one isn't old – I'm not that person, whining about how I'm an OAP on my birthday when I'm clearly far from retiring (and don't I know it). What I mean is that this is clearly the beginning of the beginning of the end... if that makes sense? I'm not that old, I could be older, but I could be younger too. I remember a time when I didn't even get hangovers. Now I get them from simply staying up late watching TV shows with wine in them. Those few glasses I had last night have left me with a thumping head and eyes that refuse to acknowledge the daylight. I can only open them one at a time, briefly, before I have to rest them. And then there's the fact that my hip clicked like a mother just now when I pulled myself out of bed to go to the loo. I'm too old to stay up late drinking on hard seats. It's official. The beginning of the beginning of the end.

I put my premature midlife crisis to one side to head to the bathroom. That's another thing that makes me think I'm getting old, I used to be able to sleep in for hours and hours. Now my body wakes me up to pee.

I slowly make my way to the bathroom, careful not to take a trip in my sleepy, eyes-half-open state, and plonk myself down on the loo. I lean forward and place my head in my hands for a few seconds. I'm definitely getting back in bed after this, and getting a few more hours of shut-eye before the day ahead, because considering holidays are for relaxing, I feel like this one is commanding a lot of energy.

Someone coughs to clear their throat.

I slowly lift my head and peel open my eyes, and right there in front of me, lying back in a bath full of bubbles, is Matt.

'Morning,' he says casually the second we make eye contact.

'Oh, fuck,' I blurt, jumping to my feet, pulling my vest top down as I pull my knickers up, and I know that he's seen it all before, but 'it' never involved me peeing. People are in relationships for months before they dare pee in front of each other – if they can ever do it at all – and here I am, going for it like a hungover racehorse. I am mortified.

'Sorry, sorry,' I say quickly as I rush back towards the bedroom.

'My fault,' he calls after me through a laugh. 'It's the stupid double—'

I imagine he's going to say 'doors', and yes, they are incredibly stupid. But not as stupid as me. Why didn't I just look around the bathroom before I sat down? It's big, but it's not that big. If I hadn't been so bleary-eyed and hungover...

As though it weren't hard enough coexisting here with Matt, given that we slept together less than a week ago, now I've had this little booster shot, it's going to be even worse.

I just want to get back in bed, but there's no way I'm going to sleep now because I'll be replaying that look on Matt's face for the foreseeable future. Urgh.

* * *

Maxime, the lovely Frenchman who works shifts in the kitchen here, will make you anything you want for breakfast. You just have to ask.

I thought the pancakes at Mote were good, but suddenly they seem amateur. Maxime has made me crêpes, drizzled with Nutella and sprinkled with crushed-up pistachio nuts, but I could honestly eat them plain, because the crêpes themselves are the best I've ever had. The Nutella and the nuts just makes them next-level amazing. I swear, I'm going to eat this every morning until I go home.

It's relatively early, given how late we all were to bed last night, so I'm the only person sitting at the table by the pool. I can feel it starting to get warm out already, and it somehow sounds like summer while also sounding like nothing at all, which is so relaxing. It's a lovely place to eat crêpes and drink coffee, and my hangover really appreciates the silence.

'Good morning,' Matt announces.

He places an omelette down on the table and takes a seat opposite me.

'Morning,' I reply sheepishly.

'You're up early,' he says.

'You know I am,' I reply.

I somehow take comfort from the fact I'm wearing sunglasses, like they give me something to hide behind, even if it is just my eyes.

'I thought you were headed back to bed – you looked tired,'

he says. He pauses for a second. 'Sorry, I'm just trying to make you feel less embarrassed. Is it working?'

'No,' I reply. 'But thank you. I think we just need a better system with the doors, to make sure we lock them both.'

'Honestly, that bathroom is the least of my worries,' he says as he tucks into his omelette. 'I'm sharing a room with Alex, and I think he thinks he's well endowed, so he likes to be naked pretty much every second he's in there.'

I almost choke on my crêpe.

'And is he?' I ask curiously.

'Oh yeah,' Matt replies. 'Intimidatingly so. I wear two pairs of boxers around him. One to cover mine, and another over my face so I don't see his.'

I laugh. I wish I didn't like him as a person as much as I do. I keep feeling little sparks when I see hints of the Matt I spent that evening at Mote with, but given what happened the next day, it just feels like a sad waste of energy.

'I'm sorry you've wound up sharing a room with him,' I say. 'It was such a dumb mistake, the way I invited him. Almost too dumb. I'm starting to wonder if my subconscious did it.'

'Nah, you just did a ditzy thing,' Matt replies. 'We all make mistakes or don't quite do the right thing sometimes, even if our intentions are good...'

I wonder if he's talking about our night together, but was that a dumb error, or something he didn't handle right?

'To invite someone's ex to a wedding, just to screw with them, would be manipulative and mean, and you're neither of those things,' he says. 'Don't worry about it.'

'I worry Charles thinks I invited Alex on purpose,' I say. 'To try and drive a wedge between them.'

'Just because you don't think they've known each other long

enough?' he replies. 'I don't think Charles would worry about something so minor.'

I mean, it's not just that. If Charles is worried about anything it will be our history (which I'm sure he must be pretending not to remember). Surely he must realise that anyone would want to protect their little sister from a man who behaves like he did?

'There are some things you should know about Charles – and they have pros and cons. First, there's no problem he won't throw money at,' Matt explains. 'And second, he can go pretty nuclear when he wants to. So the fact he's being so level-headed about this wedding makes me lean towards thinking maybe they are doing the right thing.'

'Hmm,' I say through a mouthful of food – some breakfasts are too good to be paused for conversation. 'Maybe I'll back off a little with the highlighting then.'

If Matt thinks Charles is seeming really grounded and mature, then maybe he has changed. Perhaps he really is nothing like the horrible, manipulative teenager I knew, who would do anything in the name of self-preservation.

'I'm just as worried they're making a mistake as you are,' Matt says, leaning across the table to squeeze my hand. There's one of those little sparks again. 'But I'd be a lot more worried if "Bad Charles" reared his ugly head.'

'Ooh, look at you two eating breakfast together, holding hands,' Di sings as she sits down at the table with us.

I quickly whip my hand away.

'You're up early,' I point out. I don't actually know what time it is, but so far Matt is the only other person I've seen up so far.

'Yeah, well, Charles was up early – he said he had a surprise guest to go and meet off the boat, so I was too excited to go back to sleep,' she says before grabbing my coffee and taking a sip.

Her face scrunches up.

'Urgh, that's cold,' she points out.

'Oh, I am so sorry *my* coffee is too cold for you, Lady Diana,' I tease.

'Don't take that tone with me, Lady Penelope,' she replies.

Matt smiles.

'Did your parents do that on purpose?' he asks.

'God, I hope not,' I reply.

'Our parents are called David and Julie,' Di explains. 'They always said they wanted us to have names that were a little different.'

'So they had me, and called me "Penelope", then realised that was a horrendously mean name to force a kid to learn to spell in Reception or whenever it is you have to do that, so Di got off a little easier,' I add.

'I think they're both beautiful names,' he says. 'And I get it. Matthew is a pretty basic name.'

'Oh, wow, you are called Matthew, aren't you?' Di says with a big grin, aiming in my direction.

'Erm, yes,' he says with a confused laugh.

'Peach knows a Matthew, don't you?' she teases.

'I do,' I reply. 'Through work.'

'Is he cool too?' Matt jokes.

'He's basically perfect,' Di tells him. 'So perfect you'd think he was made up.'

'Oh, look, Charles is back,' I say, happy to change the subject. 'He's got someone with him... a man.'

Walking alongside Charles is a man in a cap and a pair of mirrored aviator sunglasses, dragging a suitcase along behind him. After the bombshell arrivals of Van and Ben, I'm not sure who could top either of them.

As they get closer, the man starts to seem familiar. It's the shape of his chin, the dimples... They're cloaked by a stubbly beard I don't recognise, but those lips, that slight smile...

As they arrive at the table, he whips off his hat, to reveal his messy, dirty-blonde hair, and that's when things start clicking into place for me. By the time he's removed his sunglasses, it only confirms what I already suspected. It's someone I know. Someone I know really well.

'Hello, ladies,' he says.

'Wha— what is he doing here?' Di asks Charles, absolutely horrified.

'Oh, do you two know each other?' Charles ask her with an innocence that I have every reason to believe is put on.

'He's my ex-boyfriend,' I say, with a poker-straight face and nothing but indifference in my voice. The reason being, Charles knows Chris is my ex-boyfriend, because we all went to school together.

'*Is he?*' Charles says. 'What a small world. Chris and I went to sixth form together.'

'Mate, Peach went to sixth form with us too,' Chris reminds him. 'Don't you remember her?'

Charles looks me in the eye and feigns concentration. As he examines my face for signs of familiarity, I feel like his eyes are doing something different. Conveying a message to me that says, 'If you're going to invite your sister's ex to this wedding, I'm going to invite yours.'

'I don't,' Charles says. 'That's funny.'

'Wait, so the three of you went to school together?' Di says in disbelief.

She looks like she can't quite believe it – I'm having trouble myself, and I know it's true.

'Apparently so,' I reply.

'I did leave sixth form pretty sharpish,' Charles reasons.

'You were there long enough to establish a lifelong friendship with Chris, at least,' I point out, knowing full well the two of them were not friends.

'I was a bit surprised to be invited to the wedding,' Chris says. 'But I wasn't about to turn down a free holiday. So who is the lucky bride?'

'That's her over there,' Charles says, pointing out Di, who has a face like thunder.

'Huh,' Chris says, kind of amused. 'So you're marrying my ex's sister? It really is a small world.'

'Crazy, right?' Charles muses. 'Anyway, let's find you somewhere to sleep. Come with me.'

'I'm sure I'll catch up with you two later,' Chris tells us – and it almost sounds like a threat.

Di waits until they're inside before she speaks.

'Oh my God, Peach, I'm so sorry. I don't know what he was thinking,' she says. She really does look upset about it. Tears are forming in her eyes. 'In fact, he clearly *wasn't* thinking. I told him, a couple of nights ago, about the ex who cheated on you, so there's obviously no way he would have invited Chris if he'd known it was him.'

Di's brow furrows as she processes all of the information. 'Do you really not recognise him from school?' she asks.

'We must have been on different sides of the timetable,' I reply with a shrug.

'Huh,' she says. 'Look, let me go talk to Charles. Perhaps he can ask Chris to leave.'

'Look, don't worry about it,' I insist. 'I stopped thinking about Chris a long time ago. It doesn't bother me that he's here.'

'I'm still going to have a word,' she says, jumping to her feet, marching off after them.

And then it's just me and Matt again, but it's as though a

tornado has passed through an otherwise peaceful breakfast, and now it's gone again but it's left a trail of destruction in its wake.

'So, just so you know, when I talked about "Bad Charles" and his nuclear behaviour that he seemed to have put behind him when he fell in love – this would be a classic example of that,' Matt informs me.

'It does seem too coincidental to be an accident, doesn't it?' I point out.

'Yep,' Matt replies.

And he doesn't know the half of it.

23

'Do not let that wanker – either of them – ruin this holiday for you,' Van insists as she semi-aggressively brushes my hair.

'I'm not going to let him ruin it, I just don't plan on leaving this room unless I have to,' I say. 'That's all.'

'Look, Charles is just screwing with you because he probably thinks you invited Alex here to throw a spanner into the works, and last night you were obviously asking questions you didn't think he'd know the answer to.'

'I was just playing the game,' I insist.

'Well, you were definitely playing on expert level,' she replies. 'He's just trying to mess with you. Don't let him. Don't get mad, get even.'

'What, invite one of *his* exes?' I reply. 'I'm definitely not going to do that.'

'No, of course not, that would completely ruin the wedding – he would probably have you set adrift in the sea if you pulled a stunt like that. No, no, nothing so extreme. You just need to fuck his big, buff cousin.'

'Thank you, Vanessa, that is fantastic advice,' I say sarcastically.

'What? I'm serious,' she insists. 'I would, if he wasn't so clearly into you.'

'He's not "into me", he's just being nice,' I say. 'And even if he was, I may only have slept with five people in my *entire life*, but if I were to make that six with Ben, then two thirds of those people would be *under this roof*, and suddenly the club wouldn't seem quite so exclusive, would it?'

'I'd slept with five people before I could drive,' she tells me.

'No you didn't,' I reply with a scoff.

'Well, by the time I could legally drive an HGV then,' she says. 'I'm exaggerating, to show you that you're being precious about a number that doesn't matter. Zero, five, fifty, five hundred. Whatever.'

'No judgement on five hundred, if that's where you're at, but the thought of having to be around that many men, even for a few minutes – if you're lucky – sounds like a nightmare, because all the men I've had to interact with recently, I kind of hate.'

Now I'm exaggerating.

'Alex seems all right,' she says before biting her lip thoughtfully.

'Alex seems rich,' I say with a laugh. 'I guess he seems better though. He seems more easy-going now. But he did break your cousin's heart.'

'Well, that's starting to seem like not a very exclusive club either, so start having revenge sex with Ben. Show Matt that he's old news. Chris that he's older news. Show Charles that he can't get under your skin. And show me photos afterwards, please,' she jokes. At least I hope she's joking.

'Come downstairs with me,' she says with a pout, now that's she's finished my hair. 'We're going to have drinks and eat – I've eaten my body weight in *taralli* today, and I could go for more. Plus, Lex says we're going to play games again.'

'You hate games,' I point out.

'Exactly, so I need you there to help me get through them,' she replies. 'Now, come on. I'll even do your make-up. Oh my God, you could borrow one of my outfits! Nothing says that you don't care like a new look.'

'To save us some time, is saying no an option?' I ask with a smile. But to be honest, it sounds like fun.

'Nope,' she replies. 'Now come on.'

Van drags me by the hand over to the dressing table, where she plonks me down and immediately begins messing with my face.

'I'm going to give you a cut-crease so flawless one of those pathetic boys downstairs is going to ask you to marry him, but also so good you're going to say no.'

'I don't think eyeshadow is what makes men commit,' I point out. 'But I also wouldn't know, so knock yourself out.'

The amount of make-up Van travels with is enviable, so what she has back home must be immense. She doesn't just have the good stuff though, she knows how to use it and in a way you'd probably only know if you'd been taught, so I know she's going to do an excellent job with my face.

My body, on the other hand...

After getting a face full of make-up, which I highly approve of, Van starts taking me through the contents of her suitcase. It's not so much I don't approve of her clothes, but her clothes can't possibly approve of me.

'OK, maybe I should just wear my own clothes,' I suggest.

'Don't chicken out now,' she replies.

'It's not that I'm scared, it's that your clothes aren't going to look on me like they do on you,' I point out.

Van holds up one of those swimming costumes with all the cut-outs.

'Oh, God, I can't even look at that,' I insist, as I imagine all lumps and bumps spilling out of the various holes.

Van laughs as she throws it onto the bed.

'Ah, here we are,' she eventually says. 'I'm thinking this one for tonight, and I have another one in mind for the bachelorette party.'

'Are we doing that?' I ask.

'Yes, but I have good news.' Van climbs up onto the bed and stands proudly in the middle of it with her arms out. 'I get to throw it!'

'Well, now I'm even more worried,' I joke.

'I did have to promise I'd throw a sort of joint thing,' she says with a bat of her hand. 'But no matter. It will still be crazy!'

'I'm so glad she didn't ask me to do it,' I admit.

'I figured you would say that, which is partly the reason I offered. But it was mostly because I thought it would be fun! Certainly more fun than if anyone else did it.'

'Well, that's true,' I admit. 'Go on then, what have you got for me?'

Van hands me a short, strapless dress. It's black and looks like it would be clingy around the chest, with a loose, floaty skirt.

'I can't pull that off,' I tell her.

'Yeah, but Ben can!' she replies.

'Nah, I think his legs are too big,' I joke.

'Oh, God, those legs,' she says, looking off into the distance. 'They must be durable, to spend all that time on a horse.'

'I'm not going to think too much about that one,' I laugh. 'Go on, give me the dress.'

'That's my girl,' she says as she grabs a tiny denim skirt and puts it on over her bikini. 'Ready!'

I hurry out of my clothes and into the dress before looking myself up and down in the mirror.

'Wow, it doesn't look that bad,' I say, turning from side to side.

'Of course,' she says. 'Because I know clothes and I buy good ones, and all the women in our family are babes.'

'It's like it highlights the things I want to highlight but it hides the things I want to hide,' I marvel.

'Now let's go downstairs and find someone to rip it off,' she insists as she grabs me by the hand again.

* * *

We arrive in the large living room, where two corner sofas face each other to form a square with a coffee table in the centre. The table is covered with snacks and bottles of beer and wine.

'Oh, there you are,' Lex says. She clicks her tongue. 'We were about to start without you.'

'How would we have coped?' Van asks me sarcastically.

'Oh wow, Peach, look at you,' Di says. 'You look amazing!'

I instinctively – and annoyingly – look for Matt's reaction. He quickly looks away.

Isn't it strange how a makeover makes you feel both so confident and so uncomfortable? Simultaneously wanting people to notice how great you look, but not knowing how to graciously take the compliment when they do. I do feel good about myself, but still so nervous, and Van's clothes do feel a bit like a wardrobe malfunction waiting to happen.

'Can you believe she just found that dress in the bottom of her case?' Van says. 'It would have been a shame for that bad boy to not see the light of day. Or the dark of night.'

'Anyway, what are we playing?' I ask, changing the subject because I'm so not comfortable with all eyes being on me.

'The groom has chosen a game,' Lex says. 'He's just about to tell us what it is.'

'I thought we could play something a little more physical than sitting around asking questions,' Charles starts.

'Wehey!' Van calls out.

'Hey, save that sort of game for tomorrow night,' Alex replies. 'Stag, stag, stag!'

All the females at the table exchange groans and eye-rolls.

'So, the game I want to play – and you all have to say yes, because I'm the groom, and I'm paying for this place.' Charles pauses for laughs. He gets a few. 'I want to play Sardines!'

'What's Sardines?' Lex asks.

'Oh, we used to play Sardines all the time when we were kids,' Ben chimes in. 'It's sort of a tradition in our family.'

'Basically, it's like Hide-and-Seek,' Charles explains. 'Except only one person hides – everyone else has to find them, and when they do, they have to hide with them. The aim of the game is to not be last! And I think the person to hide should be...'

Charles stands up and twirls around with his finger pointing forwards. Eventually he stops, and he's pointing at me.

'Peach,' he says. 'You can hide first – if you're sure you get the game?'

He says this so casually, and I'm sure his words seem empty to everyone else, but I can read between the lines.

'Yep, I get it,' I reply with a smile.

He knows very well I get it – there's no chance this is just a coincidence. I know now, for a fact, that Charles does remember me, and what happened, and that's fine by me. Now that I know it's a game, I am happy to compete. It's on. It's *so* on.

24

Here I am, back where it all began, in a large wardrobe in the master bedroom.

With Charles letting me know that he remembers me in such a subtle way, I wanted to prove to him that he can't psych me out, and that I know he knows, so I hid where he hid, all those years ago.

I feel strangely nervous, hiding in here all alone, surrounded by someone else's clothes. For the most part, the house shows no trace of the people who own it, and staying in a guest room, all the furniture was empty, but in here I have my first glimpse of what the owners are like, and they're rich. Stinking rich. Not rich like Charles or Van or Alex. Richer. I'm in their holiday home, and there is a Birkin bag just chilling on the shelf in this wardrobe, sitting there like my River Island ones do at home, except this one is probably the equivalent of a healthy deposit on a house.

I can only just about see it in the little bit of light filtering in through the slats in the door, but it's definitely a Hermès Birkin. Everyone who knows anything about handbags recognises a

Birkin – I've never touched one before, and I probably never will, and this one is just sitting there, practically begging me to try it on.

I bite my lip thoughtfully as I wonder what to do. It's just a handbag, it's not a dress, I'd only be hooking it on my arm, only for a few seconds... I'm sure no one will mind.

I slip my arm through the handles and let it just rest on my forearm. Wow, it's kind of heavy, but so comfortable, and it just feels so... wow. Some of these bags are worth hundreds of thousands of pounds, which is admittedly a lot of money for a handbag (or for most things, actually), but they do feel like they're worth more than your average bag.

I'm so into strutting around in the limited wardrobe space with the bag that I don't notice the first person discover my hiding place until they're whipping the door open.

'Do you two want to be alone?' Matt asks, nodding down towards the bag.

'I was just trying it on,' I insist as I put it back on the shelf. 'Now, quick, come in and close the door before anyone sees you.'

'Wow, you're really into this game,' he replies quietly as he does as he is told.

'It's not that,' I whisper back. I take a breath. 'We need to talk. Look, I know Charles is your best friend, but he's officially insane. You just want what's best for him, right?'

'Of course,' Matt replies. 'What has he done?'

'I can tell you, but you've got to promise not to say anything because I do not want this getting out. Di would be devastated.'

'OK, I promise,' he replies. 'Now what's up?'

I hear the bedroom door open. Then footsteps getting closer.

'Meet me in our bathroom after everyone has gone to bed?' I suggest. 'We can talk then.'

'OK, sure,' he replies.

Seconds later, the wardrobe doors open again. It's Ben.

'Aw, it's a shame he got to you first,' he says. 'I'm my family's Sardines master.'

'Surprising, really, given how big you are,' I point out.

Matt shoots me a look.

'Well, best get hiding before someone else walks in,' Ben says, stepping inside the wardrobe, pulling the doors closed behind him.

Once the three of us are inside, Ben squeezes past me so that he's on my left, Matt is on my right, and this is very awkward.

'You really do look amazing tonight,' Ben tells me in a whisper.

'Thanks,' I reply.

For some reason, I look at Matt, and I do so just in time to catch the end of his eye roll.

'The joint stag and hen party is going to be bizarre tomorrow, right?' I say to change the topic of conversation. 'I've never been to a joint one before.'

'I'm not sure how common they are,' Ben replies. 'It's usually an excuse for a last night of debauchery for the happy couple, but I'm not sure how smoothly that will go, if they're both there together. It might be quite tame.'

'If my cousin Van is planning it, it's going to be far from tame,' I tell him. 'I had a big birthday last year, and Van lives in LA, so she couldn't come. She sent a stripper in her place. They called him Magic Spike. He was a Viking themed stripper, because of course they exist. He had a terrifying weapon – in more ways than one.'

'Well, that beats sending flowers,' he replies with a slight laugh. 'Perhaps it will be fun. Although, I may have got my wires crossed, but did I hear someone say Charles's friend Chris is your ex-boyfriend?'

'Yeah,' I reply sheepishly. 'It's a small world.'

The world is small, but in this villa it seems even smaller. Di, Van and I are related. Charles and Ben are related. Charles and Matt are friends. Di and Lex are friends who went to school together. I went to school with Charles and Chris. Di is marrying Charles. Alex is her ex. And finally, I have been romantically involved (for lack of a better term) with Charles, Chris and Matt (to give you them in chronological order). But when you really stop and think about it, it doesn't seem all that fantastical.

It's somehow so messy and yet the pathways that lead to everyone being here are so clear. We definitely can't afford to have anyone else turn up though, so when our families start arriving for the wedding, let's hope no one brings any extra guests.

'Is it awkward, having him turn up here out of the blue?' Ben asks.

'Oh, I've had far more awkward encounters over the past week,' I say casually, without explanation. 'Chris being here doesn't bother me at all. We're such old news, it's a miracle I recognise him.'

'Di mentioned the circumstances around your break-up earlier,' Matt starts cautiously.

'He cheated on me,' I tell Ben, bringing him up to speed. 'Honestly, I'm over it, I can talk about it without feeling upset. We got together when were in sixth form – so, like, seventeen– and we stayed together until we were twenty-four.'

'That's a long time,' Ben says.

'Yeah, I guess it is,' I reply. 'Somehow, when you're younger, and you grow up with someone, it almost feels like no time has passed at all. Anyway, over the last couple of years we were together, Chris had what today you would call a "glow-up". He started going to the gym, got in great shape, then cut off his long hair, and stopped dressing like the drummer from an indie band. I guess the new attention was too much to turn down.'

Even in this dimly lit cupboard, I can see the pitying look on both of their faces.

'Honestly, I don't care now. It was a long time ago, I'm over it – I feel nothing for him, I'm not upset,' I insist, although I worry that the harder I try to protest, the more upset I'll wind up looking.

Sure, it's rubbish to be cheated on, especially by someone you've been with for so long, but that wasn't the part that hurt me the most. The thing that wounded me so, so deeply was the fact that, after Chris gave himself a makeover, he somehow felt like he'd levelled up, that he could do better. So he went out and found 'better'. That was the bit that stung – that I suddenly wasn't good enough. Yes, I know I clearly have terrible taste in men, and that I can't seem to spot a rotter until it's too late, but I'm working on it. My trust issues served me quite well until Matt managed to break down my defences, otherwise I was on a good run.

All of a sudden, the wardrobe doors open to reveal Van with a big smile on her face and an open bottle of wine in each hand.

'Ay!' she somehow successfully shouts quietly. 'I thought I heard noises coming from in here.'

She looks at Ben, then at me, then at Matt, then back to me.

'What's going on in here?' she asks with a wiggle of her eyebrows.

'Quick, get in,' I insist.

'I brought wine,' she whispers excitedly, sounding like she's a had a fair bit already while she was searching the house. 'I thought it might make hiding more fun.'

She offers the bottles around.

'Sorry for interrupting,' she says in an even quieter whisper, that seems like it's only intended for my ears. 'And for disturbing your Ben–Matt sandwich.'

I hear the boys snigger.

'It's OK,' I insist. 'Just keep quiet, we're supposed to be hiding.'

'Ooh, sorry,' she says like a teenager who is ticked off about being told off.

'Look, someone's coming,' Ben whispers.

We all pipe down.

At just the right angle, it is possible to peer through the slats of the wardrobe and see into the bedroom. I watch as Di walks into the room. She sits on the bed and puts her head in her hands. Eventually she lies back and exhales deeply.

'Di,' I call out, just loud enough for her to hear.

'You're not supposed to help,' Ben reminds me.

'I know, but we're in her bedroom, and she will rightly expect a degree of privacy in here that is cancelled out by the four people in her wardrobe,' I explain. 'Di!'

I open the door. This time she hears me.

'Oh, you're in there,' she says, squinting to get a better look. I could swear she was blinking away tears.

'Quick, get in,' I say.

Di does as she's told and hurries into the wardrobe with us.

'Red or white?' Van asks her, holding up both bottles.

'Oh, neither, thanks,' she says. 'My reflux is majorly flaring up at the moment.'

I'm not all that surprised. When Di sat her uni exams, she wound up with such bad acid reflux from the stress that she ended up with a stomach ulcer. Weddings are stressful generally, but ones planned in a week, to someone you've only known a fortnight, with a cast of characters like we've got here must be extra stressful.

'Are you OK?' I ask her.

'I'll tell you later,' she says softly.

'Helloooo,' a man's voice calls out.

I peer through the slats.

'It's Alex,' I whisper.

'Come out, come out, wherever you are?' he practically sings.

I don't know why but he has an almost creepy vibe, like we're teens in a slasher flick and he's the maniac hunting us all down one by one to murder us. Well, if anyone at this villa was going to be a maniac, my money would be on Alex.

'Still not found them?' Lex asks as she peers her head into the room.

'Not yet. It's just a matter of time though,' he says menacingly, as though it's intended for us, on the off chance we can hear.

Yep. Definitely a potential serial killer.

'We could look together,' Lex suggests. 'Gives us a chance to catch up.'

'OK, sure,' he says. 'I have a feeling we're getting warmer.'

'So, how's single life?' she asks him, skimming her hand across a chest of drawers.

Is she... is she flirting with him?

I glance at Di who is watching them like a hawk.

'I might be single, but I think I'm in love,' Alex says. 'So it has its ups and downs.'

'Oh,' Lex replies. She sounds a little put out. 'How do you go from single to suddenly being in love?'

I don't think she believes him.

'It's like, when you haven't seen someone in a really long time, and then you see them again, and it's like...'

I have to stop this before he says something that isn't up for interpretation.

I cough loudly. A very theatrical throat-clearing sound that not only tips them off to where we are but also that we can hear them.

'Wow, a wardrobe, seriously, Peach?' Lex rants as she storms over. 'I thought you would have hidden somewhere a bit more original.'

Wow, she doesn't need to take it out on me just because the rich bachelor she's trying to get her claws into isn't interested in her. I'm not bothered about that, it's kind of funny really, but he was definitely about to say that he's still in love with Di, and that's a problem. Or is it? Alex not only has the money to compete with Charles (not that Di cares about money, but it does make them more evenly matched in terms of game playing) but he has history on his side too. It's not that I think Di should get back with Alex – he did break her heart after all – but just the existence of the option should hopefully be enough to make her stop and think about what she's doing with Charles.

The wardrobe doors close, we shuffle around to try and fit in a little better (we're really starting to feel like sardines now), and a matter of seconds later Charles and Chris stroll in.

'It's not that weird,' Charles says.

'Mate, it's really weird,' Chris replies. 'She was definitely my girlfriend for a chunk of Year 12 while you were still there. You really don't recognise her at all?'

By the time Chris joined our sixth form, Charles had stopped terrorising me so intensely, and most of the kids who found it funny didn't stay on to do A Levels, so Chris never saw that side of him.

'It was nearly fifteen years ago,' Charles insists. 'And Peach is a pretty plain-looking girl – no offence.'

'None taken,' Chris replies.

I think I'll definitely take some though.

'She's looking really good now though, right?' Chris says. 'Not plain at all.'

God, this is so excruciatingly awkward. I almost wish it were darker in here, so I couldn't see the others cringing for me.

'Not really my type,' Charles says as he peers inside the en suite. 'But you should go for it, if that's what you're into – I don't judge.'

I am going to assume that Charles is only protesting so firmly that he doesn't fancy me because he's trying to hide the fact that he did, once upon a time, as opposed to him just finding me both plain and repulsive these days.

'You might have to fight my cousin for her,' Charles says. 'He seems to have fallen for her fake cool-girl gimmick too. I don't fancy your chances against him.'

'Trust me, mate, now that I'm here, I'm going to get what I want.'

'Wanker,' I say under my breath, except it's not that under my breath, Charles and Chris definitely hear me. Both of their necks snap in the direction of the wardrobe as they eyeball it suspiciously.

'Hello?' Charles says. 'Anyone in there?'

'Good work, Peach,' Lex snaps at me in a whisper.

'Did you hear what they were saying about me?' I reply.

'You are pretty plain,' she points out. 'OW!'

Chris opens the wardrobe doors, flooding the small space with light, revealing the seven of us squashed together. Lex is hopping on one foot.

'Sorry, I didn't mean to give the game away, someone stood on my foot,' Lex says angrily.

'It is pretty squashed in here, accidents happen,' Van says, somehow instantly tipping me off to the fact that she stood on Lex's foot, and definitely on purpose.

'Well, come on, quick, squash in,' Ben insists.

Charles is first, pushing his way between me and Van, so that he can be next to Di.

'Hey, babe,' he says.

'Hey,' she says bluntly. I can see, just from the stiff, straight appearance of her eyebrows, that she's a bit pissed off at him.

Chris wedges himself in front of me. As the doors are closed behind him, he presses his body against mine. I feel so uncomfortable.

'Hey,' he whispers. 'We should probably have a chat.'

'Buddy, we should switch places,' Matt says, squeezing out of the spot where he's standing before practically dragging Chris into it. 'You're the shortest bloke here – you'll fit under the railings better.'

Now it's Matt who is in front of me, and strangely enough having my body touching his doesn't repulse me like Chris's did. I kind of like being so close to Matt, which I hate, because I wish I could turn the attraction off.

He smiles at me, as if to say, 'There. I got him out of your personal space *and* I called him short.'

'Thank you,' I silently mouth at him.

'You're welcome,' he mouths back.

'Wait a second,' Di says. 'Aren't we all here?'

'Oh, yeah, we are,' Charles says with a laugh. 'I suppose we can all get out.'

'So, what, how do you know who wins and who loses?' Chris asks.

'I suppose it's who found her first and who found her last?' Lex suggests as we all filter out of the wardrobe.

Matt gives Chris a meaningful pat on the back.

'Well, I found Peach first, and you were the last one in the cupboard,' Matt tells him. 'So I guess I'm the winner and you're the loser.'

I may not have felt upset when I saw Chris (just annoyed at Charles and with the overwhelming urge to keep away from them both), but now I feel happy to see him because now, after what Matt just said, Chris has a face like thunder, and knowing he's decided he wants me back, well, now it will be all the sweeter when I continue to want nothing to do with him.

Yep, Charles is going to have to try much harder than this if he wants to psych me out. Especially now that I have a plan.

25

'So, how do you know Charles invited Chris just to mess with you?' Matt asks curiously. 'What confirmed your suspicions?'

Matt and I are having a secret meeting in our shared bathroom. He's sitting on the edge of his bath, soaking his feet in cool water because it's such a warm night. I'm lying back on the chaise longue, eating one of those delicious chocolate cake bars with the milky filling they always put out at breakfast.

'It's going to sound crazy, but something happened when we were at school, when we played Sardines together at a party,' I explain, leaving out obvious details. 'So, on the same day he invited Chris here as a "surprise" guest and did that whole bit about not remembering me from school, he decided we should play Sardines and then he picked *me* to start.'

Matt thinks for a moment.

'There was something kind of wild in his eyes, when he was starting the game,' he says. 'I thought he was just drunk or really excited to play. But if you say the two of you have history with that game...'

'Trust me, we definitely do,' I reply. 'He's screwing with me.'

'Because?'

'Because he thinks I'm screwing with him,' I reply. 'I knew what he was like at school – he was a dickhead. He probably thinks I invited Alex here on purpose.'

'But you didn't,' Matt replies. 'I saw how freaked out you were on the day we came here.'

'But Charles doesn't believe that,' I say. 'And, honestly, what kind of man would treat his future wife's sister this way?'

'When I thought he was in love – well, I've never seen him like this with a girl before – I figured it had mellowed him, that he'd finally found the person he wanted to spend the rest of his life with, and that I could support,' Matt explains. 'But seeing the way he is with you, seeing the games, the manipulating, the lying – I think you're right. I think they both need to stop and think carefully about what they're doing, and if it's the right thing for them.'

'Well, we can't tell them,' I reply. 'If we tell them they shouldn't be together, they'll only want each other more.'

'Fair,' Matt replies.

'Also, the last thing I want is to create drama and upset and ruin their big day. If the wedding doesn't go ahead, it can't be on me or you. It has to be because they've decided it's the right thing to do. Or not do. Charles might be a dick, but I'm not, and if they're both sure about what they are doing, and genuinely in love, I will put a smile on my face and be the perfect sister at their wedding, and I'll do the same for the rest of my life.'

'That's fair enough,' Matt says. 'So, what do you suggest?'

'We need to keep highlighting the fact they hardly know each other – every chance we get,' I say. 'It was super obvious when we were in the wardrobe that Alex is still into Di, so if I remind her how amazing it feels to have someone who knows you inside out, and how horrendous it feels to have someone hurt you, then maybe she'll think more carefully about what she's doing.'

'Maybe I could talk to Charles about you without actually saying anything,' Matt suggests. 'If I can get him into a conversation about you, make it clear that I was at the airport with you and saw how freaked out you were about Alex being there, then he might lay off and be more himself. Think you're no longer a threat. Or I could just ask him what the hell he's playing at.'

'The first one,' I insist. 'We just need to give them the best tools to do the right thing. I'd never forgive myself if I let my sister make a huge mistake.'

I'd also never forgive myself if she really has fallen in love with the perfect man for her, in just a week, and I'm the person who ruins it by dragging up the past.

'Well, OK,' Matt says. 'Chuck me one of those cakes, please.'

I reach into the packet, grab a cake and throw it to Matt. It's oddly nice to be hanging out with him like this, scheming together. Nice until I remember our history, that is.

'So will this be our fifth date?' Matt asks with a smile.

'Fifth?' I reply.

'The hotel, the two you think your sister set us up on, breakfast and now,' he says. 'I don't count our brief time in the wardrobe together, but let me know if you do.'

I laugh.

'I don't think any of them were dates,' I say with a smile and a roll of my eyes.

'What about Ben?' he asks.

'What about Ben?' I reply.

'Rumour has it there's something going on between the two of you,' he replies, looking at his cake rather than me.

'Nothing is going on between me and Ben,' I insist.

'Well, that's good,' Matt replies.

'It is?'

'Yeah.' He pauses for a second. 'You think Charles is a dick-head – he's nothing compared to Ben.'

'Ben seems all right,' I say. 'He definitely seems like the best one here. The others aren't great, are they?'

'Well, no, given what you've told me about Charles, and the fact Alex and Chris both seem to have hurt someone in your family,' he replies. 'But, just remember not all men are like the ones in this villa, OK?'

'Oh, OK,' I say in a goofy voice.

'Trust me,' he says.

I don't really know what to say to that.

'I'd better get to bed,' he eventually says. 'Vanessa has really hyped up her stag and hen party game. We're going to need all the sleep we can get.'

'That is a good point,' I say. 'The biggest mistake a person can make during one of Van's parties is to fall asleep.'

'I feel like there's a story behind that comment,' he says. 'But maybe you can tell me after I survive it.'

'Sure,' I reply.

Matt makes a move for his bedroom door, but he stops when he gets alongside me, and places a hand on my shoulder.

'It's going to be OK,' he tells me. 'Whatever happens.'

'Thanks,' I reply with a smile. 'Sweet dreams.'

'You too,' he tells me with a gentle squeeze of my shoulder. Then he heads off to bed.

I suppose it makes sense in a way that Matt is the kind of guy who will sleep with a girl and then take off, because he really is so gorgeous, so funny, so thoughtful and so sweet. A catch like Matt could have any girl he wanted – what man wouldn't take advantage of that? Then again, his fantastic personality is also the reason this doesn't check out. He could have any girl he wanted, but he seems too nice to take advantage of it. He *seems* great. A little nerdy, sure, but I just think that makes him all the more attractive. Perhaps it's the fact that he has all of these amazing qualities, but in such a normal way, that makes him seem all the more perfect for me.

Well, he might not be interested in anything romantic with me, but at least he's willing to help me out with Di and Charles.

If this is the right thing for Di, then I will be behind her all the way. I'll be at every Christmas and birthday, I'll travel to see her wherever she is, and should I be lucky enough to find someone to marry and have kids with, I will make sure our families have great relationships with one another. But I'm only willing to do that if it's the right thing for her.

Thinking back to when we were in the wardrobe playing Sardines and her acid reflux was playing up because she's so stressed, is Di having second thoughts? Perhaps she's starting to think this is a terrible idea and wants to back out, but doesn't know how. I'll talk to her tomorrow, see how she's feeling, and promise her that no matter what, I'll be there for her. That's all I can do really – especially without the resources or the little black book to start flying in Charles's exes anyway. Then again, I suppose the worst ex for him to have here is already here. Me.

26

It turns out that our private beach seems just as isolated in the daytime as it does at night.

Miles and miles of sea in front of us. A wall of trees cloaking the hill behind us. If you had fallen overboard on a boat and washed up here, you would resign yourself to trying to stab fish with a stick and look for Wilson immediately because this place looks deserted. It sounds deserted too, except for all the noise coming from our party, of course.

Today we are enjoying a relaxing day on the beach, ahead of the joint stag and hen party Van is throwing this evening. The only thing I can take comfort in is that this island is largely a romantic resort, so she's not going to have access to all the tawdry stag and hen party junk people often have at these things. Then again, if Van can't access all the usual penis-shaped items, L-plates, inflatable sheep, et cetera, then she might have to use her imagination for alternatives, and that could potentially be even scarier.

'Remember when we went to Bali?' Charles muses. I'm not sure who to yet.

'Oh, Bali was epic,' Ben replies.

'Obviously this holiday is going to take its place,' Charles insists dutifully. 'But Bali was the best. Only thing missing was you, Matt.'

'Cheers, bud,' Matt replies from behind his sunglasses.

Matt and Charles are sunbathing on towels. Ben is in front of them, in his trunks, doing press-ups in between bursts of conversation.

'Oh, that's right, you weren't there, were you, Matt?' Ben says sympathetically. 'You couldn't afford it.'

That's kind of an odd thing to say.

'I couldn't take the time off work,' Matt says, still lying back, his face not giving away a glimmer of emotion.

'Yeah, you couldn't afford the time off work,' Ben says. 'Same difference.'

Ben must catch me staring at them, listening to their conversation.

'Peach, you would love Bali,' Ben says. 'You'll have to come with us next time.'

'Oh, I definitely can't afford it,' I say with a laugh. 'In any sense.'

For a second I wonder why I said that. I mean, obviously it's true, but I didn't have to be honest, did I? It was like a reflex, one that I had no control over, to make Matt feel better.

'Di, will you tell your sister to pounce on Big Ben?' Van says in hushed tones.

While the boys are sunbathing, Lex is having a bath, Chris hasn't shown his face yet today and Alex has just headed in for a shower after taking a dip in the sea. Then there's me, Di and Van sitting under a gazebo because Di doesn't want to risk having sunburn in her wedding photos. Luckily we're far enough away from the boys that if we talk quietly, they can't hear us.

'Do you like him?' Di asks me.

'He's gorgeous,' I say immediately. 'And he seems nice – although he's kind of mean to Matt.'

'Well, do you like Matt?' Di asks instead.

'Urgh, I do. Well, I did,' I clarify. 'Ben and I don't really have anything in common. Matt and I have loads in common, but he's already made his feelings pretty clear. I don't want anyone who doesn't want me.'

'Or anyone who *didn't* want you, I hope,' Van adds. 'We all heard what Chris was saying about you – gross as it was.'

'I did have a word with Charles about what he said, saying you were plain,' Di says. 'He told me he was just worried about what it would sound like if he was too complimentary about his bride's sister.'

'Ah,' I say. 'OK.'

Van dismisses that with a shrug.

'Just don't fall for Chris's bullshit,' Van says. 'Especially tonight, when I get you stupid drunk. You need to be more like your sister and handle having your ex here like a boss.'

'Actually, having my ex here is not going all that well for me,' Di says with a sigh.

'Oh?' Van says. 'What's up?'

'To say it's not going well is kind of an understatement, actually,' she continues. She's trying to keep a brave face, but I can see it practically seeping out of her pores. 'He pulled me for a chat last night. Saying we should be together, that I should cancel the wedding, that fate had brought him here, and it was a sign. That if I didn't call off the wedding, then he would find a way to do it for me.'

'OK, first of all, fate didn't bring him here,' I insist. 'It was a combination of me being ditzy and your ex and your second-best friend having the same name.'

'*Third*-best friend,' Van corrects me.

'Sorry, third-best friend,' I say. 'Oh, Di, is this why your reflux is back? Because he's stressing you out?'

'Yep,' she replies. 'He'd hinted earlier in the day that he was going to make trouble for me, but then last night he confirmed it.'

'Are you sure?' Van asks. 'That just doesn't seem like him? Not the new, rich him who can have any girl he wants.'

I'm a little taken aback – albeit it pleasantly – by Van's shift in mood. Not only does she usually use smutty jokes to diffuse difficult situations, but it's not like her to speak up for Alex.

'I'm sure,' Di replies.

'Are you sure you want to get married?' Van asks her. 'You're not looking for a way out or...'

'I want to marry Charles more than anything in the world,' she insists.

Van's phone makes a noise on the blanket next to her.

'OK, speaking of your forthcoming nuptials, I have to go and do a little bit of scheming for tonight,' Van announces. 'I'm going to leave you in your sister's very capable hands and go get things ready for you.'

'OK, see you later,' Di says with a smile. She quickly wipes away the tear that has escaped one of her eyes.

'See you later, boys,' Van calls out before she disappears up the pathway back to the house.

The three of them shout goodbye to her before getting back to their conversation.

'Di, I feel so guilty,' I admit. 'I'm so sorry I brought him here.'

'You have nothing to be sorry about,' she tells me with a

squeeze of my hand. 'I'm just going to do my best to ignore him – he can say he'll try and ruin the wedding all he wants, but he can't, can he?'

'Of course he can't,' I reply. 'Charles would never let him.'

'That's what I thought,' she says. 'Still, I'm terrified he'll cause trouble.'

'You just worry about making sure this wedding is everything you want it to be,' I insist.

Di puffs air from her cheeks.

'Yeah, you're right,' she says. 'I just need to ignore him. He'll get bored, realise he's wasting his time and leave me alone.'

'I'll make sure he does,' I reply.

Poor Di. I should have known something was up when she seemed so stressed out. I knew it was more than just wedding jitters, but I had no idea it was for this reason.

'Please don't say anything to him about it,' Di insists. She sounds a little panicky now. 'I don't want it to be a thing.'

'Of course I won't,' I promise. 'I can make sure he doesn't ruin your wedding, without saying anything. I'll just keep a close eye on him.'

'Thanks, sis,' she says.

Despite what I said to Matt last night, now definitely doesn't seem like the time to be reminding her of how good things were with Alex. He's still a dick, it turns out, just like all the others. I'll just have to find a different way to get her to think about what she's doing, but now I'm worried that Alex trying to come between her and Charles has only pushed them closer together. Which is going to make my job even harder, but who knows, perhaps none of us will survive Van's party. And then none of this will matter...

27

I thought it might take some time – even if it was only minutes – for Vanessa's party antics to shock me, but pretty much from the second I walked downstairs, I was immediately taken aback.

Once again, I have borrowed one of Van's dresses – well, the last one was a big hit – but this one requires a lot more self-confidence to style out. It's a clingy, strappy red thing with a split so high up in the front of one thigh I'm worried you can see something you shouldn't, like my underwear, or my ovaries. Still, Van told me I looked amazing. She gave me vampy make-up and deep-red nails to match, before buzzing off to get on with her party prep, leaving me to do my own hair.

I sectioned it off before curling it with Van's amazing cordless straighteners that are honestly game changers. I painstakingly dragged them through every piece of my hair until I had big, bouncy curls. Once they cooled, I brushed them out a little before smoothing them all down with serum. By the time I found my dry shampoo, to give my roots a boost, I started to wonder if I might be stalling because I felt so nervous.

I suppose I'm a little bit more self-conscious in this dress than I thought I would be, and I'm not exactly sure why because I'm comfortable with my body, and I think it looks great – and everyone here has seen me in my swimwear by the pool, anyway. I think it's more about what the dress means, than how it looks. I'm dressing to impress (although I'm not exactly sure who yet), and I'm dressing to compete (with basically every woman here, and everyone else is gorgeous).

So, when I arrived downstairs to the party a moment ago, which seems to be spanning the entire ground floor, inside and out, I was shocked to realise that there are far more people here to impress and compete with than I anticipated.

Van hurries to meet me at the bottom of the stairs. She's carrying a tray of shots with the careless confidence of someone who has already had a few.

'My favourite cousin,' she announces, glancing from side to side theatrically to make sure Di isn't around to hear it.

I laugh.

'Van, who are all these people?' I ask.

'Oh, they're my new holiday friends,' she says. 'What's that face for?'

I didn't realise I was making a face.

'I guess I'm just a little confused about where your holiday friends have come from,' I say. 'Given that we're the only ones here.'

'Oh, I see what you mean,' she says. 'These are all friends I've made on the resort side of the island. I've been popping over to use the facilities, and I've got to know all sorts of new people, from guests to staff.'

I did wonder what she was doing to keep herself amused while I've been stuck on my fake dates with Matt.

'You've made a lot of friends,' I point out, kind of pointlessly. Obviously she can see the room is full.

'Let me introduce you to some,' she says. 'But first, drink this.'

She hands me a bright yellow shot of something. At this stage, it's probably easier just to drink it.

Van sinks one too before placing the tray down, taking me by the hand and running me around her favourite new friends.

'So, this is Massimiliano. He works at the resort,' Van tells me as she practically shoves me into a handsome young Italian bloke.

'*Ciao*,' I say.

'*Ciao, bella*,' he says with a smile.

I think my vague stabs at the Italian language are sometimes amusing to the locals. Well, it's a beautiful language, but my Northern accent doesn't exactly do it justice.

'He's here with, erm, a girl called Zoey and another fella called Matteo, but I figured this one is just your type.'

As Van says this, she winks, not subtly at all, raises her hand up and points to Massimiliano behind it. Obviously he can see what she's doing. He just laughs.

'Sorry,' I mouth at him as I steer Van away. 'Go on, who else do we have?'

'Let's see, who else do I even remember?' she wonders out loud. I watch her crazy eyes dart around the room. 'Over there we have Liam and Rebecca – Australian couple, here for the couples counselling, like a make-or-break-their-relationship kind of holiday. Do you want to meet them?'

I glance over at two people who you can tell from the looks on their faces and their uncomfortable body language could not be less stoked to be here, or around each other for that matter.

'Maybe I don't need to meet everyone,' I tell her.

'That's a shame,' she replies. 'There's a lovely couple – Emma and Carly – who are from Bridlington. Small world! Oh, there is someone you should meet though.'

Van is going at a million miles an hour. Usually she's a little cooler than this.

We weave in and out of people – seriously, this place is packed like a nightclub – while Van finds me whoever it is I should meet. There is music playing, the drinks are flowing, and while the room might be busy, it's actually a really nice atmosphere. Still, other than Van, I haven't seen anyone I know yet.

'This is September,' Van says, introducing me to a young woman in a dress not unlike my own (well, technically Van's), only in hot pink.

'Is this her?' September says excitedly.

'It is!' Van replies.

'So great to meet you,' September tells me as she hugs me. 'I've heard so much about you from Vanessa.'

'Oh yeah?' is about all I can say. I don't quite know what to do with that information.

'She told me to tell you to shag Big Ben – whatever that means,' September says casually.

'Wow,' I reply, before a swift subject change. 'I love your dress.'

'Great minds, right?' she says in her strong East London accent. 'Top tip – mine looks much better on me since I had these babies put in.'

She points at her breasts with her index fingers, but to be honest, they're that huge, they don't exactly need pointing out.

'If you want a pair, I'll give you my Insta – I've got a referral code on there for a discount with the surgeon I used.'

'Oh, thank you,' I reply, as casually as I can, given what she's saying to me. 'Very kind of you.'

'Just let me grab one of those drinks,' she says. 'Back in a min.'

'Van, did you desperately want me to meet this person so I could get a discounted boob job?'

She snorts.

'Of course not,' she says. 'I met September at the resort today. She's here with a guy – it's him I want you to meet.'

Van manoeuvres me by the shoulders so that I'm facing a man not too far from where we're standing. He's sipping away at a big shot of whisky while he commands the attention of everyone around him. What's most surprising of all though, is that I know him.

No, don't worry, he isn't another one of my exes. I only know him because he's famous.

'That's...'

'Didn't you have the biggest crush on him ten years ago?' Van says.

'God, did I ever!' I reply. 'I still had his posters up on my bedroom wall until Dad ripped them down to redecorate the second I moved out.'

The man in question is Dylan King, who used to be the frontman of a band called The Burnouts, who I was *obsessed* with when they were huge in the early twenty-tens. He must be in his late thirties now, maybe early forties even. He still looks like a rock star. I still feel weak at the knees, being in the same room as him. 'Robbie Williams-style good looks' is what everyone used to say about him. I was never quite sure what that meant – I thought Robbie was gorgeous too – they definitely have the same cheeky, bad-boy look about them.

'Oi, Dylan', Van calls out.

'Oh my God, you can't "oi" Dylan King,' I say under my breath.

'Hey, is this your cousin?' he says. 'The famous Peach?'

'It is,' Van replies.

How has she managed to become best friends with these people in a day? I wish I had that talent (no, we don't count Matt, because we didn't actually become anything apart from a mistake, and now briefly partners in crime).

'Hi,' I say. A simple, classic, cool response – but in reality the only one I can muster.

'Peach has told me all about you, and about Di.' He leans closer. 'And she let me in on a few little secrets about the boys too.'

'Oh, did she?' I say with a faux politeness.

I am simultaneously mortified and kind of angry. I finally meet Dylan King – which I never ever thought would happen – and now he obviously knows some things about me, things that can't be good. I could strangle Van. Why would she tell him?

'Dylan is going to help us screw with them,' Van says.

'Do, er... do we need to screw with them?' I reply.

What is going on with her?

'Don't you want to show your exes that you don't give a fuck what they think?' Dylan asks. 'Any of them?'

'I can't believe Dylan King is talking to me about my ex-boyfriends,' I say, without a flicker of emotion, because in an odd way this suddenly feels so on-brand for this holiday.

Dylan just laughs.

'We're going to play some kissing games,' Van announces excitedly.

I turn to Dylan.

'Aren't you here with your girlfriend?' I ask.

'September? Not my girlfriend,' he says very casually. 'This is sort of our first date, this holiday.'

'Ah,' is about all I can reply.

I don't read so much about Dylan in the news as I used to. Only ridiculous headlines spilling the details of his private life, but nowhere near as frequently as back in the days when he was still touring, or after when he did loads of reality TV. The thing I remember the most though was the antics he was famous for. This sort of thing sounds right up his street. But I'm not sure these kinds of games are Van's usual style though.

'September is in on it too. Come on,' Van says. 'Let's grab some drinks, I've assembled the gang on the outdoor sofas, by the firepit.'

I follow Van to the bar where she grabs bottles and I get the glasses.

'Are you OK?' I whisper.

'Yeah, why?' she replies.

'You seem a little... uptight,' I reply. 'And yet somehow *very* easy-going. You seem like you're... I don't know... up to something.'

'It's been too long since the last time we hung out if you think this is out of character,' she points out with a laugh.

'it's not that it's out of character,' I reply. 'You just don't seem yourself. Maybe I'm imagining it...'

Vanessa is a party girl, and she always makes an effort to have fun, but it weirdly feels like she's trying too hard.

Still, the atmosphere at the party is great. There's music, food, and the drinks are flowing. Everyone has a smile on their face. There are little clusters of people all over, all having fun, I really like the vibe. Stag and hen parties always come across as debauched craziness, but this feels so civilised. Well, apart from Van being a woman on a mission, whatever that mission is...

'I just want to mess with the boys,' she says. 'Keep up, P.'

I suppose it's sweet that my cousin seems willing to go to war for me like this, but it seems like her heart is *really* in it.

Outside, sitting on the sofas around the firepit, there's Di, Charles, Matt, Ben, Lex, Chris and Alex. The whole gang.

'Right, we're here, ready to play games, and we've brought some new friends to play too,' Van says. 'This is September, she's an influencer – very cool girl. And this is Dylan.'

Everyone just stares. Clearly Dylan needs no introduction.

'September, Dylan, over there you have Charles and Di, the happy couple. Then Matt, Charles's friend. Charles's cousin Ben. Lex is a friend of the bride, and Chris and Alex are old friends. From back in the day.'

That's a nice way to say 'exes'.

'I've heard so much about you all,' Dylan says. 'Psyched to play party games with you. Congratulations, by the way.' He raises his drink to Di and Charles.

'Erm, thanks,' Di blurts.

I can't help but notice how tightly wound Di looks too. Sure, she's stunned Dylan King just waltzed up to her at her hen party, but she seems stressed. She's dolled up in a long floaty dress, with her hair and make-up done, but she's not exactly dressed for a night of partying, more like a day at the beach. I know my sister and this isn't how she dresses when she's going out-out. Something just seems off with her too. The Alex stuff must be on her mind – I wonder if he's said anything else. I know I promised not to say anything to him, but I need to get him to back off.

'Yeah, cheers,' Charles replies. 'Remind me to sort you out with a wedding invitation before you go.'

'Sounds great,' Dylan says. 'I love a good wedding.'

'OK, so, sit down,' Van demands, 'and we'll get started with the games.'

'Actually, I think I'm going to go to bed,' Di says.

'What?' Van shrieks, so high-pitched I swear the glasses I just carried through vibrate, like they're about to smash. 'It's your hen party, you can't!'

'I'm really not feeling well,' she says as she snatches up the antacid packet from the table in front of her. 'I think I just need to go and relax, try and shift this reflux – I don't want it to ruin the wedding.'

I give her my best reassuring smile. Poor Di. The saddest thing is the more she stresses about it, the worse it usually gets. I don't want her to miss her own hen party, but it's more important that she feel better for her wedding day. Relaxing is the best thing for her. Whatever Van has planned for now will be anything but.

'But I want you all to stay here and have fun,' she insists. 'You too.' She points at Charles.

'Me?!' he says in disbelief. 'Not a chance, I'm coming with you.'

'Don't miss the party – I'll feel awful,' she replies.

'Di, we're about to formally start the rest of our lives together,' he says. 'Why would you think I didn't want to start right now?'

Various 'aww's and 'ohh's come from the group. Everyone just laps it up. Even I'll admit, that is pretty sweet.

'Promise you'll come back if you feel better?' Van demands.

'Of course,' she says. 'See you all later. Sorry again, thanks for coming.'

'Right, let's not let this ruin a perfectly good night,' Van says. She really is like a woman on a mission. 'Everyone spread out around the table.'

Van fixes everyone various drinks from the bottles she just carried over. Then she takes one of the empty ones and places it in the centre of the table.

'Spin the Bottle,' she says. 'Movie edition.'

'Oh, God,' I can't help but blurt.

'Yeah, I'm not playing that,' Alex insists.

'No?' Van says. 'Good riddance then. Everyone else, get comfortable.'

Comfortable sounds like the last thing this is going to be.

I'm not sure what has got under Van's skin, but there's no stopping her now.

'Chris, you go first,' she announces excitedly. 'You're at the top of the table, then we'll work our way around.'

Chris spins the bottle so meaningfully it seems like it might never stop twirling but eventually it slows down and lands on Van.

'Someone call out a movie,' Van says as she makes her way over to Chris.

'*Spider-Man*,' Dylan calls out.

'*Spider-Man*?' I squeak. 'The upside-down one?'

'Let's start as we mean to go on,' he replies with a cheeky grin.

'Oh, wow, how are we going to do this?' Van says with an undeniable giddiness in her voice as she glances around for inspiration. I don't think it's that she's excited to kiss Chris, specifically, more that she's just so into the game.

'Well, I suppose Ben could dangle him by his ankles,' I joke.

Ben cocks his head thoughtfully.

'I could do that,' he says, like it's no biggy.

'Oh my God, do it,' September demands. 'That would be so funny.'

I look over at Matt and pull a face, as if to say, 'What the fuck?' as Ben grabs Chris, turns him upside down and sort of hooks his knees over his shoulders so Chris hangs inverted. Van gets down on her knees so that she's at the right height, and they recreate that iconic Spider-Man half-upside-down kiss.

Matt has his hand over his mouth, as though he's in shock, but I can see him laughing underneath. I suppose it is pretty funny.

'I feel kind of weird just watching,' Alex says. 'I'll go get a drink and be back for the next game.'

'No worries,' I reply. I suppose this must be weird for him if he's pining for Di. I thought it would have been weird for me, watching my cousin kiss my ex, but I honestly don't feel a thing for him. It's been nearly a decade since we were together, and it is just a game, right?

'Wehey!' Van says once she finally comes up for air.

Ben lowers Chris back into his seat.

'Wow, the room is spinning,' Chris says with an uneasy laugh.

'I have that effect on men,' she jokes with a grin as she reaches for the bottle.

'Dylan, you're up,' Van says.

Every time she speaks to *Dylan King* so casually, I feel my guts twist.

Dylan playfully raises the bottle to his lips, as though he were making sure we're not wasting any. Then he spins it, and when it lands on me, I turn to stone.

'Peach,' he says. 'Let's do this, what have we got?'

'I'm thinking *Ghost*,' Van suggests. 'The pottery-wheel thing.'

My eyes widen and for some reason I look over at Matt. He gives me a shrug and a smile. It's just a game, right?

'Erm, OK,' I say with a nervous giggle. 'How does that

work?'

'Scoot forward,' Dylan suggests before he hops behind me, his body suddenly so close to mine. He wraps his arms around me and holds my hands. I turn around to kiss him with the same sort of timid awkwardness Demi Moore has in the movie. After a few seconds, Dylan picks me up and we kiss a little longer. It's nothing quite as sloppy as Van and Chris's kiss, thankfully. It is made all the more bizarre by the fact that everyone around us is singing 'Unchained Melody'.

It's strange. When I was younger, kissing Dylan would have been like a dream come true, but I don't actually get anything from it. It's fun, and it's silly, but it's just a kiss.

Everyone cheers us afterwards. I feel like Matt's enthusiasm is a little muted, but I think he feels that little niggling sensation of awkwardness that I do too.

September spins the bottle next. It lands on Chris again before the two of them share a *Dirty Dancing*-style kiss, where she crawls across the table to kiss him.

Next up is Ben. The bottle spins and spins and then it stops on me.

I laugh awkwardly.

'Looks like it's us,' he says, walking around the table to sit next to me.

'What about *Titanic*?' Lex suggests.

'I'm going to get a stiff neck,' I joke, recalling when Jack and Rose kiss on the deck of the ship.

'OK, stand on the little step by the pool,' Ben says. 'I'm way taller than you.'

I do as I'm told, and Ben stands behind me. I'd be lying if I said I hadn't wondered what it would be like to kiss Ben, but, again, there's just nothing there. At least with Dylan I've had a sort of lengthy relationship with him in my head, in that way fans often fantasise about their celebrity crushes, but with Ben I feel even less. And it really does make my neck ache, having to turn around again. They always look so romantic in the movies, don't they?

We exchange glances immediately after. I don't think Ben is overly blown away by our interaction either. He seems more excited about getting on with the game.

We barely have a moment to get back in our seats before the game moves on. We're even starting to draw a crowd around us now, of other partygoers, looking for some entertainment. It's so weird that Di and Charles aren't even here, when it's their stag and hen party, but I'm kind of glad my sister isn't spectating this, to be honest.

'My turn,' Van says as she rocks back and forth in her seat.

She spins the bottle and – would you believe it? – it lands on me.

'*Cruel Intentions*,' Ben calls out, practically bursting with delight at his own idea.

I flag his suggestion of a girl-on-girl kiss by raising an eyebrow at him.

'I mean obviously I'm her cousin,' I point out. I can't believe it needs saying.

Ben doesn't look put off, which is kind of gross. I'm really starting to see his true colours today and I don't think I like them.

'She gets a family pass,' September says, like it's a normal thing to have to say, but I am grateful.

'Thank you,' I reply – and I can't mean it enough. Even talking about kissing my cousin is completely gross.

'I'll do it,' September says, like it's no big deal, like she's offered to take in a parcel for me or something.

Let me tell you, I have seen my cousin do some wild things in her time, but watching her lock lips with a girl she's just met, in front of a captivated audience, is certainly a new one.

Afterwards, the game calms down for a second, but only until Matt's spin lands on Dylan. Somehow, Van manages to talk them into a kiss-of-death-style peck, like the one in *The Godfather II*. All in the spirit of the game, of course, although most men find *The Godfather II* to be such an important film, so this is surely an offer they can't refuse.

'My turn,' Lex says. Even she seems really into it. I wouldn't have thought this was her scene at all.

The only thing that knocks me back more is when the bottle lands on Matt, because I care, I really care. There's a voice in my head, telling me to find a way to stop her.

'*My Girl*,' Van calls out quickly, her mouth twisted into a grin. 'Do *My Girl*.'

'I don't know that one,' Matt says.

'I do,' Lex replies as she suppresses a scowl. 'You just need to close your eyes.'

Good old Vanessa, giving Lex and Matt the briefest kiss in movie history.

Lex, although unhappy with the pick for her and Matt, embraces it. She counts down before planting a light, quick peck on Matt's lips.

It's such a fleeting peck that it barely registers as a kiss at all – and yet I am boiling mad inside. I'm not mad at Lex for kissing him, or Matt for letting her, I'm mad at myself, at the jealousy surging through my veins.

'*Honey*,' Vanessa says, in a way that makes me think I might have missed the first few times she said it. 'You're next.'

'Oh, right,' I reply.

Suddenly this game doesn't seem quite so fun any more. It was light-hearted at first, but after two underwhelming kisses and a near miss with my cousin, it's just left me feeling kind of deflated. I didn't feel too bad, until I saw Lex and Matt kiss, and now I'm just ready for it to be over.

I swallow hard before spinning the bottle. Now that I know you get a free pass with blood relatives, I wonder who would be the worst person to kiss: my ex, Chris, or my nemesis, Lex. I'm lucky they're not sitting next to each other because, knowing my luck, it would land between them, and I'd be peer-pressured into kissing them both at the same time, à la *Spring Breakers*.

The bottle goes around and around, and then it slows down. Finally it grinds to a halt, and the person it is pointing at is Matt, without a doubt, straight at him.

In a way this should put me at an advantage because I've kissed Matt before, recently, so I know what to expect. But at the same time I'm so annoyed at him for sleeping with me and then bailing on me, and being kind of cool with me about it ever since, and the fact that I just watched him kiss someone I don't like and felt so much jealousy, I'm not even sure I can stomach his lips on mine, as much as I can't stop myself from thinking about them.

'You don't have to kiss me,' Matt says, but this only puzzles everyone else.

'I had to kiss you,' Dylan reminds him. 'So she definitely does.'

'Yeah, no, that's fine, of course I will,' I babble in an attempt to seem as normal as possible – well, as normal as I can be, playing kissing games at my sister's hen party, which she isn't even at. 'It's just a game.'

Van points at me before moving a thumbs up in a circular motion – she's asking me if I'm OK.

I gesture towards myself with the flat of my hands before a double thumbs up back, letting her know I'm fine with it.

Dylan narrows his eyes at us.

'Either I'm really drunk or you're talking in a secret code,' he observes.

'*In that case...*' Van signs, before switching to speaking. 'You should do *Romeo and Juliet*. The one in the pool.'

'You want us to get in the pool?' I say to her.

'Just the shallow end, you baby,' she replies.

It's not the pool that makes me nervous. I glance over at Matt. He gives me a reassuring smile. One that says: 'I'll go along with whatever you want.'

'OK, fine,' I say, trying to sound all cool and casual. 'After you, Matt.'

Matt hops to his feet and climbs into the pool, fully clothed, like it's the most normal thing in the world.

I'm a few steps behind him.

I never thought I'd be in my thirties and still feeling the overwhelming command of peer pressure. This house party is very much like a teenage house party. I'd be lying if I said I didn't want to kiss Matt again, but I'd prefer not to have an audience, obviously.

'Oh my God, it's freezing,' I shriek as the cold water instantly soaks through my dress.

'It won't be for long,' Van calls back.

'You have to fully dunk underneath,' September shouts. 'Make it authentic.'

'Oh, well, if it has to be authentic,' Matt says with a cheeky grin, right before he ducks under the water for a few seconds.

'I can't believe I'm doing this,' I laugh.

I keep a tight hold of my nose and squeeze my eyes shut while I duck under. The funny thing about not being a swimmer is that, when I want to float, I can't. Now, when I'm trying to duck under the water, I feel it pushing me back up.

So here we are, both soaking wet, in a swimming pool, in the middle of a party, with a gang of oversized horny teenagers and an ever-increasing crowd of spectators staring at us from the side.

'Do you just...' I start.

'I guess,' Matt replies. 'Here...'

Matt moves towards me and holds his lips just millimetres away from mine for a second or two. Then he kisses me, ever so lightly and impossibly gently. Just seconds of the slightest touch of his lips on mine, and I feel myself melting. *This* is what a kiss is supposed to feel like.

Matt places a hand on my face and kisses me passionately, and I kiss him back – I mean *really* kiss him back. He wraps his arms around my body and I hook mine around his neck. It's like his body is drawing me close, keeping me there. I can't stop – I don't want to.

We kiss and we kiss and we kiss until...

'Oi,' Van calls out.

We quickly break apart and stand there in the water, staring up at them, like a couple of naughty kids who just got caught out.

'You didn't kiss me like that,' Dylan says, sounding as though he feels like he's been short-changed.

I've never kissed anyone like that. Well, apart from Matt, the first time we kissed, but I did wonder if all the wine I had that night made me remember things differently. I've hardly touched a drop tonight so, believe me when I say, that's the best kiss I've ever had, by a lot.

'You two should go get dried off,' Van suggests. 'Come join us after, yeah? We'll play Truth or Dare.'

As Matt and I wade towards the pool steps I whisper to him.

'Let's absolutely not do that.'

'I'm with you on that one,' he replies.

28

Sometimes, the more awkward you feel, the harder you try to pretend you don't feel awkward at all. That's peak awkwardness, and it's the most obvious kind.

Matt and I head upstairs, laughing and chatting about what just happened, but talking about everything apart from our kiss. That's fine by me though. It's nice, to be on friendly terms and to be joking around with each other.

'I can't believe *Dylan King* was here,' I say. 'And that I got to kiss him. My younger self is doing a happy dance right now.'

'*You* can't believe you kissed him?!' he replies. '*I* can't believe I did.'

'Oh please, he gave you a long peck on the lips, for about three seconds tops,' I reply with a smile and a roll of my eyes. 'He slipped me the tongue.'

'Vanessa is really going for it tonight,' he says. 'She seems like she's having the time of her life.'

'Yeah, but she's usually more subtle than this,' I reply, unsure if Matt will know what I mean by this, but I do. It's like she's trying too hard. 'I'll have a word with her, make sure she's OK.'

As we approach the corridor where our bedroom doors are, it's time to go our separate ways. We reach my door first and, truthfully, I've never had such an overwhelming urge to pounce on someone. That kiss was just amazing, incredible, next-level perfect. Yes, even with the water in my eyes and an audience. I want Matt so badly, but I want more than just another night with him in a bed that isn't mine. I can't settle for that. I need to force myself to resist him.

'Well, we'd better hurry back to the party,' I say. 'Just, maybe not to where the games are.'

'Yeah, I think I've hit my limit as far as games go this week,' he replies, taking a step towards me.

I have to resist him. I have to resist him.

I shift towards my door.

'See you back down there,' I reply.

'OK.' Matt backs way again. 'See you there.'

The second I step inside my room and close the door behind me, I regret it. Why can't I just sleep with him again, even if it won't go anywhere, just because I want to? It's because I want more, I suppose. As incredible as it would be to sleep with Matt again – especially after the warm-up we just had – it's never going to be enough.

I tick myself off as I kick off my shoes. I shoot myself a dirty look as I pass the full-length mirror. But then I open the bathroom door at the exact same moment Matt opens his, and it feels like I've been given a second chance. He knows it too, I can tell from his smile.

We hurry towards each other, meeting in the middle of the bathroom where we start kissing again, only this time we start tearing off each other's wet clothes.

Matt sits me on the countertop, next to the sink, leaning me back against the mirror. I lock my legs around his waist and in little more than a second he carries me over to the chaise longue, laying me back before pressing his body down on top of mine.

I know what you're thinking, I said I was going to resist him, but I can't. Being with Matt just feels right and, well, if he takes off in the morning, that's a problem for future Peach, not me.

I let out a little groan as Matt pins my hands above my head and kisses my neck.

Yep, I'm sure future Peach will forgive me for this one. And if not, well, it was worth it.

29

The last time Matt and I *got together* I was so over the moon immediately afterwards I dropped off straight away, drifting into the deepest, most contented night's sleep I've ever had. Or maybe that was because I'd polished off the best part of a five-thousand-pound-bottle of wine. It was probably a bit of both but, the point is, I was so deliriously happy.

Sleeping with Matt again (or not, as it's playing out) was even better than the first time. The only problem is that this time I'm too scared to close my eyes, even for a second, because if history repeats itself, he'll currently be figuring out the right time to take off. I suppose it's better this time – we're on an actual island, so there's nowhere for him to go. But perhaps that's worse, him trying desperately to avoid me in such a small space.

So we're just lying here, on the chaise longue together, covered with a towel because we're still both damp from our dip in the pool. Being squashed on here with him means we're very close together – awkwardly close, perhaps, depending on what happens next. We haven't moved a muscle, or said a word yet, and I don't think either of us wants to be the one to go first.

I chew my lip thoughtfully. I know I should probably feel like this was a mistake, but I don't, I don't at all. I've never felt such a strong attraction to anyone – not just a sexual attraction either. I knew from that first evening we spent together that Matt was the one for me, and just because he has whatever issue he has that makes him bolt, well, I'm not going to feel bad about it. It's his loss.

Lying here with my head on his chest, I can hear his heartbeat thudding in my ear. I swear, it's getting faster and faster until...

Matt slinks out from under me and stands up. He walks across the room, but I don't let him get far before I call him out.

I'm not going to feel bad. I am going to feel pissed off though.

'Leaving so soon?' I say.

Matt stops and turns around quickly.

'Sorry, I thought you were snoozing,' he says. 'I was just going to run us a bath. Your hair is still wet, and it's starting to feel cold. I could do with warming up myself – uh, my eyes are up here.'

His joke, designed to distract me from looking at his cold naked body, makes me feel a bit better, but only for a second.

'I thought you were sneaking out,' I say softly. I'm not ruling it out, just because he's being cute.

Matt scratches his head.

'Well, I'm walking towards the bath, and not the door,' he reasons.

Ah, there is that.

'A bath sounds great, thanks,' I say sheepishly.

'This bath is so big, we could both be in it, and not feel like we were in the same room, so I'll forgive you for thinking I was heading off,' he says with a laugh. 'Unless you'd rather be alone...'

'No, I'd like the company,' I reply before I've had a chance to think about it.

Once the bath is ready, Matt hops in.

'This is going to sound absolutely pathetic, but can you not look for a second?' I say.

Matt meaningfully grabs a handful of bubbles and playfully places them over his face.

I like that he just did it, without asking me why, or trying to convince me I didn't need to feel awkward, because no amount of reassurance makes being naked around someone feel less weird, especially when you haven't been naked around another person for all that long in a while, and being naked when you're having sex, and just being generally naked are completely different things. Why am I overthinking it? He's smothering himself under a cloud of bubbles so I can get in the bath without feeling uncomfortable.

The water is so warm and the bath products give the water such a slick, silky feel. I love the way it feels on my skin. I lie back and relax. All I can hear is the sound of the bubbles lightly popping. It's glorious.

'OK, you're safe,' I tell him.

I cup the warm water in my hands and pour it down over my hair, just to warm it up a little. I'll need to wash it properly, obviously, but the only thing Matt needs to see less than me making a naked dash across the bathroom, is me going at my long locks with a detangling comb and half a bottle of conditioner.

'Phew,' he says with a smile. 'So, did you think I was going to get revenge this time?'

'Revenge?' I reply.

'Yeah, after what happened last time,' he says as he plays with the bubbles. 'I promise you, I'm not that kind of guy. Revenge just isn't in me – plus, I was going to invite your ex on this holiday, but someone beat me to it, so I just gave up.'

I laugh, but I'm confused.

'Sorry, are you talking about when we were at Mote?' I ask.

'Obviously,' he says. Now it's his turn to laugh awkwardly.

'That was like next-level ghosting,' I tell him. 'Like, there one minute, gone the next. Like an actual ghost.'

'Please don't beat yourself up about it, Peach.' Matt takes me by the hand and looks into my eyes. 'I've had a lot of time to think about it and I wouldn't have called me either.'

I snatch my hand away for a second.

'Wait – called you?'

'Yeah, I get it,' he insists. 'I promise you, I tried a few times to wake you, but you were fast asleep. I thought the note was fine, under the circumstances, but clearly I am absolutely crap with women.'

'Who do you think ghosted who?' I blurt, cutting to the chase.

'Well, I'm not really interested in assigning blame, but I suppose technically it was you who didn't call me,' he says.

I dip my hands into the warm water and wipe underneath my eyes – which are surely a mess of smudged make-up – as I put the pieces together.

'I never found a note,' I tell him, through a smile, for some reason. 'I woke up, you weren't there, I assumed you'd taken off.'

Matt's face falls so far I'm surprised he doesn't swallow bath water.

'Oh my God, Peach, no, I'm so sorry,' he says, fumbling

around under the water to take me by the hands again. 'Just to be clear, that was one of the best nights of my life. My phone woke me up the next morning – it was my mum to say their bathroom was leaking into their kitchen. I tried to wake you, but you are a *seriously* deep sleeper. So I wrote you a note explaining what had happened, and I left you my number so you could call me. When I didn't hear from you, I just assumed you weren't interested.'

'I didn't see a note anywhere,' I tell him. 'But I wasn't looking for one, and I was rushing, I suppose. Shit, I've been so mad at you all this time.'

The colour drains from Matt's face.

'I'm sure this goes without saying, but remember a few days ago, when I said I didn't tell anyone about that night because it was "nothing to brag about"? I meant because you weren't interested in me after, that's all. I definitely wasn't talking about the sex, that was great – look, I'm in a bath with you.'

I laugh.

'I've been such a bitch to you,' I tell him. 'And I told Van you shagged me then snuck out on me, so she's been a bitch to you too.'

'Van hasn't been a bitch to me.'

'Oh, trust me, she has,' I say. 'But I'll tell her to stop.'

'Oh, OK, thanks,' he says with a big, dumb grin on his face. 'Sorry, I'm just feeling pretty pleased with myself now.'

'How so?'

'I thought I'd done something wrong,' he says. 'Something to make you not want to call. Now I think you might like me as much as I like you...'

'Don't go mushy on me – I thought we were supposed to be ruining a wedding,' I say quickly, but then I soften. 'But, yeah, I think I might like you too.'

'On the subject of the wedding, I did think of something that could potentially kneecap it,' he says. 'But now I'm starting to think that, I don't know, maybe you can fall for someone in a week.'

I smile. I think I know what he's getting at. And I might just agree.

'Yeah, I'm slowly coming around to the idea,' I reply. 'But I'd be curious to know what you were going to tell me.'

'OK, but this is just between us,' he starts. 'Promise?'

'Of course, I promise,' I say. 'Spill!'

'Has Charles mentioned that he lived in Canada for a while?' he asks.

'Oh, yeah, only five or six times,' I joke. 'Didn't he go there and swallow up a poor small business?'

'Well, it's not really important to the story, but the company they bought into had actually developed – I'm not going to pretend I know exactly what it is, so forgive me – some kind of vacuum cleaner for the sea that removes litter from the water. His dad's company funded it.'

'OK, that's a different picture to the one I had in my head,' I admit.

'But while he was there, he was painting himself as a sort of Z-lister – keep in mind, across the Atlantic, everyone from England sounds like Prince William, even a Yorkshire lad like Charles. Long story short,' Matt says, mistaking my eagerness for the tea for boredom, 'Charles has been married before.'

'What?! He's already married?' I ask.

'No, no, he's not married any more – he got it annulled,' Matt reassures me. 'He was only married for a matter of days.'

'Right, you're going to have to tell me everything,' I insist. 'This sounds insane.'

'He was on a reality-TV show,' Matt says. He makes a face, like he's expecting this to explain everything. I suppose it does.

'A Canadian show called *Just Married* – it's their equivalent of *Married at First Sight*,' he explains. 'Charles was on that.'

'So, he was one of the ones that didn't work out?' I ask, although that seems obvious.

'Actually, it was a little more than that,' he says. 'Charles is kind of one of the most hated men in Canada.'

My eyes widen so much it hurts. The only thing wider is my grin.

'Just keep talking until I know everything,' I say with a laugh.

'Basically, you get married on the first day – he wanted me as his best man, so I flew over. He met the woman he was marrying at the altar – a really nice, really attractive woman called Ellen – and everything seemed great. But then, at the reception afterwards, he found out from someone else that Ellen already had a son from a previous relationship. Charles freaked out, said he didn't want to raise anyone else's kid, and pulled the plug on the whole thing. He was the villain of the show. People make memes about him.'

'What a bastard,' I say through an amused grin. 'Is there somewhere I can watch this?'

'You just want to watch him make a fool of himself on TV, don't you?' Matt says with a smile. 'Well, there are a ton of clips on YouTube, if you're looking for them, otherwise no one back home has heard about it. Shall we get out?'

'Yeah, sure,' I reply.

Matt gets out first. He grabs a towel and wraps it around his body before bringing one over for me. He holds it out for me and, without making a big deal, doesn't stare at me.

'So, I take it Di doesn't know?' I say as I climb out.

'No,' he replies. 'And, for what it's worth, Charles knows that it wasn't his finest hour and he isn't that wannabe any more. I think it knocked some sense into him. With Di, I think he knows what he's doing.'

'I didn't expect him to go to bed early with her when she wasn't feeling well,' I say.

'No, that's not usually his scene so... I don't know, why don't you go talk to him in the morning, call him out about inviting Chris here – he'll respect that,' Matt suggests.

'You know, I think I'll do that,' I say. 'And we'll keep the *Just Married* thing to ourselves.'

'I think that's for the best,' Matt replies. 'So, what now?'

'I guarantee Van won't be sleeping in her own bed tonight,' I say. 'She just won't be sleeping at all. That girl will party and party when she gets going. Do you want to stay in my room? It will give you a break from Alex...'

I don't know why I'm trying to incentivise it.

'Yeah, sounds good to me,' Matt says.

'I'm going to wash my hair quickly first,' I tell him. 'Or I'll have to cut it off tomorrow, it will be so knotty.'

'OK,' Matt replies. 'I'll see you in there.'

Before he goes, he grabs me and kisses me and the fireworks are still there.

I think Matt is right – and therefore Di and Charles are right. Perhaps you can fall for someone in a week. Now I just need to clear the air with Charles, and then perhaps I can get on board with this wedding after all. Wouldn't that be nice?

30

This morning, I woke up in bed with Matt for the first time, and it felt amazing. Honestly, I feel like everything has clicked into place, now that we've cleaned up the misunderstanding at Mote. I think the thing that makes me feel the most certain that I'm doing the right thing is that Matt has always felt the same way as I have, in more ways than you might think.

Obviously we both really like each other, but that's not what I'm talking about. What I mean is that, when we both thought the other person had ghosted them, we were both upset. When we saw each other again, we were both annoyed at each other. When we've needed each other, we've put our differences to one side. And last night, when we could deny our feelings no longer, we were both willing to give the other person a second chance, even if it meant getting hurt. We are always, always on the same page. We're going to be one of those adorable couples who finish each other's sentences, and sandwiches, unless those sandwiches have something in them that a fussy eater won't touch.

Well, I say couple, we haven't exactly had any kind of talk

about what we are yet, but I have a good feeling about this. Not to take a leaf out of my sister's book – I'm not going to marry him next week – but perhaps it's true: when you know, you know.

This morning Matt gave me Charles's number so that I could text him and ask him to meet me in the garden for a chat and he said he would be happy to talk, so that feels like progress already. I'm going to do my best to clear the air with him and just hope that I am able to see in him what Matt and my sister do.

I'm currently in the bathroom, putting the finishing touches on my make-up before I head outside. No, I'm not getting dolled up for Charles, it's because afterwards Matt and I are going to head over to the resort side of the island and get lunch together. I reminded him we could eat lunch here, but he was insistent that he wanted to actually buy me lunch himself, because so far, despite all the meals we've had together, neither of us have paid for any of them.

'Your phone is ringing,' Matt calls out. 'It's a mobile number.'

'Is it Charles's?' I call back, worried he's changed his mind about meeting up to talk. 'Answer it on speaker for me – I'll be through in a second, I'll just dry my hands.'

'Hello?' I hear Matt say.

'Oh, hello, is that Matthew?' I hear a woman reply.

'Erm... yes,' Matt says.

I suddenly twig. Shit, shit, shit. I dry my hands at warp speed, but it's too late.

'Matthew, lovely to finally speak to you,' the voice says. 'This is Annette calling from The Chadwick Hotel. I just wondered if you and Penelope had given any more thought to having your wedding here, as we do have another couple interested in the same date as you.'

By the time I get to Matt, he's just staring at the phone with his mouth open. I take the phone from him so he stares at me instead.

'Hi, Annette, it's Penelope here,' I say, taking charge of the situation. 'Sorry, we're just in Italy at a wedding at the moment. Can I call you when we get back home?'

'Oh my goodness, I am sorry,' Annette says. 'Of course, speak to you then.'

'Thanks, bye,' I say. I don't wait a second after I've hung up before I start explaining. 'Right, so—'

'Your family don't waste any time at all, do they?' he says with a smile.

God, he looks so good, lying back in my bed, the covers pulled up to his waist but still low enough to drive me crazy.

'No, it's just... Wait, why aren't you panicking?' I ask.

'Why would I panic?'

'Because...' I'm about to launch into an explanation about why he should be panicking, but an explanation about the call is probably sufficient because, after his initial surprise at hearing his own name, Matt doesn't seem freaked out at all. 'Basically, like the mystery visit at Mote, I also do mystery visits where I go to hotels and check out their wedding facilities. That's all. Matthew Hemsworth is the name of my fake fiancé.'

'An excellent choice,' he says with a smile. 'Perhaps I could go to a few with you – we killed it at dinner, at Mote.'

'We really did,' I say. 'Wow, you really are too good to be true – what's wrong with you?'

'Get out of here,' he says. 'Go try and get Charles on side. But give me a kiss first.'

I crawl across the bed, on top of Matt, and plant a kiss on

his lips. He pulls me closer, and all I want to do is get back in bed with him, but I've got to do this for my sister.

'Get dressed and meet me downstairs,' I tell him. 'I'm looking forward to lunch.'

'I'll be ready in minutes,' he tells me. 'Promise.'

As I head downstairs, I genuinely can't keep the smile off my face. It's so stuck on there that by the time I find Charles in the garden, standing next to the pretty ornamental pond, I look almost pleased to see him. Well, it's usually pretty, but the party clean-up is still taking place, and I can see a couple of empty bottles in there, which is horrible. Charles must catch me looking at them.

'I've already fished a few out,' he tells me. 'The gardener is coming with a net to get the others.'

'Oh, good,' I reply.

I'm instantly reminding myself of all the good Charles does with his job, and I feel myself softening by the second.

'You're late,' he tells me. 'I thought it was some kind of trap – I've been looking up for large objects suddenly plummeting down on me from the roof.'

'Nah,' I reply. 'It's worse than that. I want to talk.'

Charles gives me a slight smile.

'I'll give it a go,' he says.

'OK, well, I'm just going to say it. I know you. I remember you. I remember everything that happened and I think you do too,' I blurt.

Charles runs both hands through his hair and puffs air from his cheeks.

'OK, yes, fine, I remember you,' he says. He paces back and forth a little. 'I panicked when I saw you. Obviously I didn't expect to see anyone I knew – never mind someone I'd slept with before – and I couldn't think of anything better to do on the spot. *Why* are you smiling?'

'Because you just said you slept with me,' I tell him. 'You said the opposite, so many times, back in school that it's nice to hear you tell the truth.'

'Put yourself in my shoes,' he says. 'I am head over heels in love with Di, all I can think about is marrying her, and then there you are, and I'm terrified it's going to mess things up.'

'Which is fine – I didn't exactly say anything myself – but then everything that's happened since...'

'I was going to talk to you when you got here,' he insists. 'But then you turned up with Alex and I thought you were playing dirty. So I knew I needed to fight back.'

'Alex was an accident,' I tell him. 'Lex's real name is Alex, and I just wasn't thinking.'

'It's easy to see that now,' he says. 'But I just – I can't say this enough – I love Di so much, and I'll do anything to marry her. If you want me to tell her, I'll tell her. I'll go do it right now. But please, know that I'm aware how badly I messed up pretending I didn't recognise you.'

I get why he panicked. I did the same. Suddenly I feel like I'm seeing a different side of Charles. A softer side, and it makes me more gentle – hell, I actually feel sorry for him.

'Don't be too hard on yourself,' I say. 'It must have been weird. You won't have thought of me in years.'

'That's not true though,' he says, stopping suddenly. Charles faces me, places his hands on my shoulders, and looks me square in the eye. 'I have thought about you. I would think about you all the time. I was horrible to you back then – just the absolute worst you can be to another person – and I don't have any excuses for you. I was a horrible, horrible teenager, and I messed up. I'm sorry. I'm so sorry. Every time I would start seeing someone new, I would think about it each night when I got in bed and closed my eyes. But when I met Di, it just felt like everything fell into place, and then when I walked into her parents' house and you were there, well, in an odd way it felt like my punishment. Life reminding me that I don't get to be happy, because I made someone so miserable.'

Charles seems genuinely cut up about everything that has happened. I can tell because he's stripping back the bullshit, the showing off, the theatrical way of talking. I can see a tear in his eye that he thinks he's keeping under wraps by squinting. I can see the corners of his mouth being tugged downwards. I can practically see the lump in his throat.

'I don't think we should tell Di,' I tell him. 'I don't see the point. You're clearly not that sixteen-year-old from back then. And I really appreciate your apology.'

'I'm sorry for inviting Chris too,' he says. 'I just wanted to scare you into backing off.'

'Oh my God, there you are,' Van calls down from the terrace. 'Wait there, I'm coming down.'

'By the way, Van knows about what happened between us at school, but she won't say anything,' I tell him. 'We just want Di to be happy.'

'Well, I promise to spend every day of my life doing everything I can to make Di happy,' he says. 'And if I ever step out of line, please, tell her whatever you want.'

'That's OK,' I tell him. 'I trust you. And if Matt trusts you, that's good enough for me.'

'You know, I think Matt might like you,' he says through a smile.

'Oh, buddy, you're way behind on that one,' I reply.

Eventually, Van joins us.

'You son of a bitch,' she practically spits at Charles.

'Van, it's OK, we've made up,' I reassure her, taking her by the forearm, which is just supposed to be a reassuring gesture, but now I think I might be holding her back.

'What happened in Canada?' she asks him.

My heart sinks.

'What do you mean?' I ask her, but I know damn well what she means.

'I just went to check on Di, to see how she was feeling today, but when I walked into her room, I couldn't find her. But I did find this note.' She thrusts a piece of paper at me.

I know what happened in Canada. The wedding is off – don't try to find me.

'OK, obviously we need to try and find her,' I say.

'Shit,' Charles says weakly. 'Shit!'

He kicks a potted plant, which thankfully is in a plastic pot, meaning he boots it into the pond as opposed to shattering every bone in his foot, before dashing off, through the trees in a direction that doesn't lead anywhere that I know of, other than deeper into the island.

'OK, I watched *Lost*, so I know that's a mistake,' I say. 'I'm going to go and find Matt and tell him to go after Charles. I'll swap numbers with him, so we can coordinate. Then you and I can try and find Di and talk some sense into her.'

'What do you mean?' Van replies. 'Do you know what happened in Canada?'

'Yes,' I say as I hurry back indoors. 'I'll tell you when I get back.'

Shit, I can't believe it, for days all I've wanted is for this wedding to be called off and, now that it has been, all I can think about is getting it back on track.

31

'Peach, can I have a word with you?' I hear Chris call out from behind me.

'Urgh, just keep walking,' Van says, practically dragging me onto the boat that takes us to the resort.

'Peach, hang on a minute,' Chris calls again.

We take our seats, but it only takes him a few seconds to catch us up and plonk himself in the seat in front of us. He turns around to talk to us, like an annoying boy on the school bus.

'Hi,' he says.

'Hi,' I reply. 'Sorry, Chris, we're kind of in the middle of something.'

'I just really need to talk to you,' he insists. 'It's important.'

'I promise you, I'm dealing with something a lot more important. Can we talk later?' I reply. If I'm being honest, I'm fobbing him off. Yes, I do have a real emergency now, but I don't want to talk to him later either. He's going to try and get back with me and that's the last thing I want. Genuinely, I would rather be stuck in a perpetual game of Spin the Bottle than ever have a relationship with him again.

'Fine,' he says, turning around in his seat with a huff.

I turn to Van to sign to her.

'*He's a psycho.*'

'*Yep,*' she replies.

I explained to Van, in the briefest of terms, what happened with Charles in Canada as we were walking from the house to the boat. She called him a stupid bastard but agreed that the two of them can figure it out if they talk about it. We can get this wedding – which is tomorrow, by the way, but let's not panic yet (because relative to the length of the engagement, a day to sort this out is *ages*) – back on track.

Once we're off the boat at the private dock, we quickly leave Chris in our dust, hurrying through the resort to find Di, weaving in and out of all the loved-up couples who are largely oblivious to everything going on around them. I sigh. I was supposed to be here having lunch with Matt right now. Our first actual proper date. We'll just have to do that some other time.

'She'll be heading home,' I say. I glance around and see that there's no boat to the mainland at the resort dock, and no boat in sight in the water heading either way. I check the timetable on the wall. 'I don't think there's been a boat off the island for a couple of hours, so she must still be here.'

'This way,' Van suggests. 'There's a waiting room.'

We hurry up the path to the hotel lobby. San Valentino, on the resort side, is like its own little town. There are large villas sitting at the top of the hill, smaller ones on the way down, and then here, where we are, is the bit with the shops and the restaurants. The main hotel is here, next to the dock, and it seems like it acts as a sort of general hub for all the guests.

The hotel lobby is just as luxurious as I imagined, although I had no idea how beautiful it would be. It's enormous, with gleaming marble floors and impossibly high ceilings. It somehow oozes luxury while still having a really earthy, outdoorsy vibe. The huge windows that flood the place with light and all the vividly green plants that are absolutely everywhere could almost convince you that you were outdoors. They've somehow got this cool breeze that passes through, which makes it a lot more pleasant to be in than the sticky midday heat right now.

Just off the lobby, there is an espresso bar that doubles up as a seating area. More of the same decor as the lobby with added Instagramable cups, delicious smells... and my heartbroken sister, sitting alone at a table, cradling an iced drink.

When Di spots us, she rolls her eyes and groans.

'Hey,' I say softly as I sit down next to her.

Van sits down at the other side. I don't think she's officially flanking her but it would be impossible for Di to run away again.

'I'm going home,' she says first and foremost.

'Yeah, that's fine,' Van says. 'We're just here to check on you.'

Di grabs her drink and aggressively slurps it as fast as her dwindling paper straw will allow.

'What are you drinking?' I ask. 'It smells amazing.'

'It's like a Slush Puppie,' she replies. 'But it's mint flavoured.'

'Right, we're getting a couple of those,' Van tells me. 'Back in a sec.'

'Did you see my note?' Di asks.

'Yes,' I reply. 'And Matt told me all about what happened. I know it seems like a big deal, that Charles has been married before, but honestly it sounds like it barely counted. It was annulled so quickly, and he was just doing it to get on TV –

Matt says it cured him of his rising Z-lister status – he's not interested in any of that now.'

'It's not so much that he didn't tell me,' she explains with a big sniff, 'although I wish he had – it's the reason why he bailed on his stupid TV marriage that upset me.'

'Look, I know you want kids, but he freaked out because he'd just married someone on TV who already had one,' I reply. 'And you know how much they manipulate reality TV.'

'The idea of raising another man's child was just too much for him,' she sobs.

'I guess some people are like that,' I reply with a squeeze of her hand. 'Charles loves you so much. So unless you've got a kid somewhere I don't know about...'

I say this with a playful chuckle until I notice what little colour Di has right now drain from her face until her skin is the same colour as the silvery-grey slush in front of her, and then it hits me.

'Oh my God, are you pregnant?' I ask in what I think is a whisper, but Di quickly shushes me.

Van, who has just appeared behind Di with two drinks, freezes on the spot for a second, a look of pure horror on her face. She quickly turns around and walks off again, our drinks still in her hand.

'Can you say it a bit louder, please? I don't think everyone heard you,' Di whispers angrily.

'Sorry, sorry,' I say quickly. 'It's just...'

Hang on a minute. I'm not a maths whizz, and I don't have a calendar with me, but I know how cycles work, and if she thinks she's pregnant now, then she must be late, and if she's late, well...

'Ah,' is about all I can say.

'So yeah, obviously I'm freaking out, because Charles isn't

going to marry me if he thinks I'm having someone else's baby. And if I don't tell him that I might be pregnant and he finds out after, we know how that goes too.'

'I think you need to give him a little more credit,' I say and, no, I can't believe what I'm saying either. 'Charles loves you. You're not someone he doesn't know on a TV show.'

'No, I'm someone he met at a wedding a fortnight ago,' she corrects me as she places her head in her hands.

Van reappears. She places three drinks down on the table. Di looks up.

'I already have one,' she says.

'Yeah, well have another,' Van replies. 'You're going to need all the pee you can get. There's a pharmacy, just down the street – they'll sell pregnancy tests there.'

'Oh, God,' Di cries. The reality of taking a test – and getting results – must be freaking her out.

'I know what you're thinking, but it's better to know,' I tell her. 'If we know what we're dealing with, we'll know how to tackle it. Look, wait here, and I'll go get you a test, OK?'

Di just nods.

'Van can keep you distracted in the meantime – she can tell you all about last night,' I say with a wiggle of my eyebrows.

'I'll tell her what I can remember,' Van says with a wink.

I hurry down the road to the pharmacy, hoping that once I'm there, I'll be able to find what I'm looking for. Sadly, that's not the way *la farmacia* works here. You have to ask for the things you want.

Luckily, there are two men working behind the counter and no other customers in right now.

'*Ciao*, can I get a pregnancy test, please?' I ask in little more than a whisper.

The two men look at each other and then back at me. Neither of them says a word – they better not be judging me.

'*Scusi, non la capisco*,' one of them eventually replies.

Now, I don't speak Italian, but I'm going to hazard a guess that means he doesn't speak English.

'English?' I reply. '*Anglais*?'

Nope, I don't think that's right. Neither do they – clearly, they have no idea what I'm talking about.

'Uhh... *uno secondo*,' I reply, another genuine stab in the dark. I can't believe the first people I've encountered here who don't speak English are the ones I desperately need to be able to communicate with. '*Per favore*.'

I grab my phone from my bag and begin searching for the right words online. I find a page with pregnancy-related phrases in Italian and I've no sooner skimmed over the first one when my battery dies. Well, I was a little too distracted to charge it last night, wasn't I?

What are the chances that the first phrase I read was the one I needed?

'*Io rimarrò incinta stasera*?' I say, repeating the first phrase I saw without a pinch of confidence, in fact it sounds more like a question.

The pharmacists' eyes widen. One of them disappears before returning with a box of condoms.

'Oh, no, not those,' I say with an awkward laugh. 'It's a bit late for those. I need a test. *Test*.'

Yep, saying it louder will make it clearer. Great job.

The first man continues to stare while the second man disappears again.

'OK, look...'

If English isn't getting me anywhere and my Italian doesn't exist, it makes sense for me to try sign language, right? After all the sign for weeing and the one for pregnant are pretty self-explanatory, even if you don't know British Sign Language.

I honestly don't know who finds my signing funnier, the first pharmacist who hasn't done much apart from stare at me, or the one who returns with a pregnancy test, right as I'm signing having a wee and my belly getting bigger.

He hands me the test and I notice that on the box it says '*test di gravidanza*', which means they knew what I wanted the second I said 'test' in English, but at least I made them laugh with my charades, I suppose.

Red-faced, I pay for my sister's pregnancy test, and make a play for the door. I'm only outside a few seconds when Chris appears, stopping me in my tracks.

'Peach, can we talk now?' he says, stepping in front of me.

'Chris, I can't – I need to get this to Di,' I say, brandishing the brown paper bag.

'What is it?' he asks nosily.

'It's more of those Italian Rennies she's popping like Smarties,' I reply. 'I really can't talk.'

'But it's important,' he says, as though that's going to help his case. 'If you hear me out, you'll understand.'

'*Mi scusi, signora*,' one of the pharmacists interrupts. He hands me my debit card.

'Oh, thank you,' I reply. '*Grazie*.'

He still has that same amused look on his face. He'll be going home and telling his wife all about the woman who came into the pharmacy and mimed a pregnancy test.

I purse my lips and nod my head, as if to say, 'OK, OK, I get it, it was funny.'

The pharmacist repeats my signs back to me.

'Yep, very funny,' I say with a big fake smile. 'Hilarious. I need to go now.'

'Peach, wait,' Chris says, grabbing my forearm as I try to take off.

'Oi, get off me,' I say, snatching it back. 'Chris, look, I'm sorry, but I really don't want to get back with you. In fact, I'm kind of seeing someone, so just let it go.'

I don't give him a chance to say anything else before I shoot off. By the time I get back to Di and Van, I am sweating my skin off. I pass Di the test and grab my drink, which thankfully is still nice and cold. I take a big sip before swiping the cold, wet plastic cup across my forehead.

'That was horrendously embarrassing,' I tell her. 'Whatever you do, don't mess this one up – I can never show my face in there again.'

'Sorry,' she says. 'I've got myself in such a mess. I'm so, so sorry.'

Di starts crying, and I feel my heart sink. She must be so scared.

'Nip into the loos and do it now,' Van suggests. 'Just stuff it in your pocket and come out here and wait with us, OK?'

'Oh, God, OK,' she replies. 'I'll be right back.'

I watch until Di is safely through the door of the ladies.

'OK, I didn't see that one coming,' I whisper to Van.

'Neither did I,' she replies. 'Do you know who the father could be?'

'Not a clue,' I reply. 'She hasn't mentioned being involved with anyone for ages.'

'Oh, that must be why she stopped drinking,' she replies. 'And why she ducked out of the party.'

'Anyone with a brain would have ducked out of that party,' I reply with a smile.

'I don't know, from the smile I saw on your face earlier, I'd guess it worked out pretty well for you.'

'I wasn't smiling when you saw me earlier,' I reply.

'You were at five this morning when I came to bed and found you snuggled up with Matt,' she replies with a knowing grin. 'Don't worry, I crashed somewhere else.'

I daren't ask where.

'It turns out, back when we met, after we slept together, he had an emergency and had to leave, so he left me a note,' I explain. 'Obviously I didn't even look for a note, I just assumed the worst in him. So when he saw me again, he felt the same as I did – hurt, upset, angry.'

'So you've been on the same side of this argument this whole time,' she says. 'Ah, well, at least this week is going to work out well for one of us.'

'Oh, don't say that,' I reply.

'What if she is pregnant?' Van says. 'Do you really think Charles is going to stick around? It's obviously not going to be his – she hasn't known him long enough.'

'I have no idea,' I reply. 'I like to think he will, but seeing him as a good guy is a relatively new sensation for me.'

Di reappears and sits down at the table. She has her test tucked under her hand discreetly.

'Just a couple of minutes to go,' she says. 'I don't think I can look. I feel sick – which is making me think I must have morning sickness.'

'It's OK,' I insist softly in an attempt to calm her down because she's starting to panic again. 'You always feel sick when you're stressed. Try not to worry.'

'You know we've got your back,' Van reassures her. 'No matter what. I will move back to England and raise this baby with you myself.'

'Van would actually make a better dad than pretty much any of the men we know,' I point out. 'And if she's willing to

move back to England for you, then she must care – she hates
England.'

'Actually, I'm thinking about moving back home,' she says.

'What, really?' I reply.

'Yeah, well, I'm not sure there's much for me in LA at
the moment – apart from the sunshine and the gorgeous
men and the amazing restaurants,' she brags, but then she
dials it back suddenly. 'But I've been feeling kind of lonely
lately, and being here with you guys has just been so
much fun. I think I need to be around my family for a
bit.'

'Well, that's actually great news,' I reply. 'I'm so, so happy.'

'I'll go get some champagne,' she says. She's only just on her
feet when she realises. 'Oh.'

Di peeps at her test then looks back up at us.

'It's negative,' she says simply.

'OK, I'll definitely get the champagne then,' Van says
excitedly.

We both shoot her a look.

'Not that I think we should celebrate you not being knocked
up,' she insists, although her use of the phrase 'knocked up'
kind of suggests otherwise. 'But this means you don't have to
worry about Charles not wanting to marry you.'

'You should just do whatever you think will make you
happy,' I tell Di once we're alone. 'If you don't think you can
trust Charles, well, that's no way to live. But you could try
talking things through with him before you take off.'

'I do love him,' she says. 'I love him so, so much. But this
really gave me a scare.'

'I'm not surprised,' I reply.

'I've just been so stressed,' she continues with a lump in her
throat. 'That's probably why I'm late. But I just couldn't stand

the idea of Charles dumping me over this... Especially if he found out...'

'If he found out?' I say.

'If he found out who the dad was – or would have been, rather,' she replies.

'Is it someone I know?' I ask. 'You don't have to tell me, obviously, but you can if you want.'

'Let's just say there's a reason I'm so freaked out about my ex being here,' she says quietly. 'It was just one stupid night, after we bumped into each other, drunk, at the pub. And now he's trying to get me to leave Charles for him, if he knew...'

'You just leave Alex to me,' I reassure her.

'Please don't say anything to him – if we provoke him, he might still make a scene,' she replies.

'Don't worry. Like I said before, I'll keep an eye on him. I won't let him do anything, I promise.'

Di doesn't look convinced.

'Here we are, ladies, a bottle of champagne and three glasses,' Van announces upon her return. 'We'll sink these then head back to the villa to sort things out.'

'Your dress fittings are supposed to be this afternoon,' Di tells us. 'If the wedding is still on...'

'Well, that's why it pays to leave things to last minute,' I joke. Di smiles.

'It was the only day the designer had free,' she replies. 'I wanted you to have dresses from the same place as me.'

'I can't wait to see your dress,' I tell her. 'You're going to look amazing – if you still want to get married, that is? If you do, we're right here. If you don't, Van will hijack a boat for you before you've finished your drink.'

'Give me an extra five minutes and I'd make it a helicopter,' Van jokes.

'Do you think Charles will still marry me?' Di asks.

'Are you kidding? Of course he will,' I reply. 'He'll be the one begging you to forgive him for the Canada stuff. You know, I recently found out all about the work he did there, and he was sucking litter out of the ocean.'

I don't know if it's because I've been watching her cry, but I swear Di smiles the biggest smile I've ever seen.

'I was worried you didn't like him,' Di says. 'But now... I feel like I have your approval. I feel like I can do it now and be happy.'

'You definitely have my approval,' I tell her. 'Now let's neck these and go get your man.'

'And our dresses,' Van adds excitedly.

'Oh my God, I'm really doing it,' Di says. 'I'm really getting married tomorrow.'

'Yes, you are,' I tell her, because I am going to make sure of it, and just you watch what happens if Alex tries to get in the way.

32

As the three of us approach the villa's front door, slightly tipsy from our bottle of champagne, there is a general sense of nervousness about what happens next. Di is going to talk to Charles about Canada and why she took off this morning. I don't know if she'll tell him about taking the pregnancy test but, like I told her on the boat, pretty much anything that happened before they met should be forgotten about. They say marriage is the first day of the rest of your life, so what's the sense in worrying about the ones that came before it? I do feel guilty, not telling her about what happened between me and Charles, even though it happened over a decade before they even met, but what's the point dragging it up now? All it would do is ruin her happiness. This is going to be a fresh start for both of them.

Di stops just before we reach the front door.

'Peach, will you do me a big favour, please?' Di asks. 'Go in, see if Charles is there, and if he is, see if he's mad at me?'

'Of course I will,' I tell her. 'You two wait here.'

I'm only just through the front door when I find Charles. He's sitting on the sofa, looking pretty stressed out.

'Peach, did you find her?' Charles asks the second he claps eyes on me.

'I did,' I reply.

'Oh, thank God,' he says. I can practically see the wave of relief wash over him. 'Is she OK?'

'She wants to talk to you, but I think she's a bit worried you're going to be upset with her,' I tell him.

'No, no, I'm just so relieved she came back,' he says, a strange combination of excited and devastated. 'Can I talk to her?'

'She's outside with Van,' I say.

Charles is on his feet in an instant. He runs outside and the second he sees Di he runs to her, grabs her, picks her up and twirls her around. From the look on Di's face, I think that's all she needed to confirm she's doing the right thing.

There's an iPhone charger in the living room, so I plug my phone in. Eventually it springs to life, and I see that I have messages from Matt, so I give him a ring.

'Hello,' he says. 'Did you manage to find her?'

'I did,' I reply. 'And I think it's all going to be OK. They're going to have a chat and figure things out but... oh boy, if you could see them kissing right now.'

Di and Charles's hug has turned into something less sweet and more passionate. They're kissing as an almost disturbed-looking Vanessa watches on. I laugh to myself as she edges away from them and looks off into the distance.

'Ahh, that's great news,' he replies. 'It sounds like you saved the day.'

'It was touch and go,' I say. 'But I think it's going to be OK.'

'Well, how about that lunch we said we'd have? I'm at the resort now, I came looking for you.'

'Oh, I just got back from there,' I tell him. 'Lunch would be wonderful but I think I have my dress fitting at some point this afternoon, and the family are arriving at some point soon, so let me just check the times – I'll have to leave my phone here on charge, so give me two seconds, OK?'

'Sure, take your time,' he replies.

I make my way outside and head over to where Van is standing. She's put even more distance between herself and the happy couple now.

'I'm happy for them but it's gross to watch,' she tells me.

'Erm, less than twenty-four hours ago you had us playing kissing games for your amusement,' I remind her.

'Yes, but it's fun when it's fun. When it's mushy, it kind of makes me feel sick,' she says. The wrinkle in her nose proves her point.

'Well, speaking of mushy, Matt wants to meet me for lunch,' I tell her. 'Do you know what time the dress fitting is? I'd ask Di but...'

We both look over at Di and Charles. They're *still* kissing.

'... Her tongue is busy,' Van says, finishing my thought for me. 'I don't think it's for another couple of hours but, listen, there's something you should know.'

My breath catches in my throat.

'No one ever follows a sentence like that with anything good,' I say softly. 'What's wrong?'

'Well, I was talking to Di while you were inside getting Charles, and curiosity got the better of me, so I asked her how she found out about Canada,' Van explains.

'And?'

'And she said Matt told her,' she tells me as gently as possible, but it's not enough to stop it hurting.

'He told me he wasn't going to,' I tell her. 'He said he didn't want to sabotage their wedding with it.'

'Well, I don't know, looks like he might be a double agent or something,' Van says. 'Because he told her.'

'Oh.'

'Peach, I'm sorry,' she says as she pulls me close for a hug. She squeezes me so tightly I feel worse – she must feel so sorry for me.

'Well, I've got him on hold, so I'll just go tell him I can't make lunch,' I tell her, my brave face well and truly engaged. 'Back in a sec.'

I make my way back inside and pick up my phone.

'Hey, sorry, the dress fitting is soon, so... Can't make it, I'm afraid,' I say.

'Oh, OK, well maybe we can meet after?' he suggests.

'Hmm, yeah, not sure about that,' I say casually. 'I told Di I'd help her with some wedding things and my parents will be arriving so...'

'Is everything OK?' he asks.

Perhaps I'm being too casual – he can tell something is up.

'Oh yeah, everything is *fiiine*,' I say, a little too far the other way. 'See you later.'

And with that, I hang up. With one push of the button, I end the call and any chance of anything happening between me and Matt ever again. Some people, like Charles, are worth giving a second chance. Others, like Matt, will only ever let you down.

Well, he's not going to get a third shot with me. It's one thing to mess with me, but to mess with my sister, after we agreed it would be a bad idea... That's just too far. He's totally blown it this time.

33

About ten seconds after I woke up this morning, I pulled my reluctant face into the biggest smile I could muster and I haven't let it slip for a moment since. Despite how I'm feeling, this day is all about Di, and I'm not going to do anything that might make it anything less than perfect.

This means, despite how crappy I am feeling inside, I need to put on a brave face and pretend that everything is fine, even though it isn't. This also means that, no matter how annoyed I am at certain people, there can be absolutely no confrontations today because any kind of drama will ruin Di and Charles's day.

Today is about love. Today isn't about kicking off at the people you hate, no matter how good a reason you think you have.

The wedding guests – the immediate family and close friends who were able to make a wedding at short notice, that is – arrived on the island last night. Luckily (well, it's more about money than luck really), because Charles knows the owners, he was able to book out villas on the resort side of the island, so there's plenty of space for everyone. Last night, me, the happy couple, Mum and Dad, and Charles's parents got together for dinner, which allowed us to not only feel more like a family coming together, but it gave me the perfect excuse to avoid Matt. That phone call yesterday was our last proper conversation before I slammed the breaks on again. I've fobbed him off a couple of times since, and I think he's got the message now because he's giving me space. I just need him to stay out of my way today because I will do anything to make sure Di has the perfect wedding day.

Looking on the bright side, the potentially dangerous bridesmaid dress fittings yesterday – less than twenty-four hours before the wedding – went without a hitch or a stitch. Our dresses fit us perfectly and, I have to say, I am rather in love with mine. It's short, the perfect shape for my frame, and in a gorgeous shade of millennial pink.

To thank me, Van and Lex for being her bridesmaids, Di presented us each with a box containing a pair of glittery Christian Louboutin heels to wear today. I definitely had a bit of a Cinderella moment when I put them on because not only did I feel excitement in a way that only someone who couldn't afford them would, but they fit like a glove, as though they were made just for me.

We're at that point in the morning where it's finally time to get Di into her dress. Her hair and make-up look flawless, her bridesmaids are all good to go, and our dad is waiting downstairs to walk her down to the beach where the ceremony is taking place. The only problem is that, no matter what we say to her, she just doesn't seem to want to put her dress on, and we're all skirting around the issue because no one wants to stress her out. Something is going on though.

'Right, let's get this dress on you,' I say, with a meaningful clap of my hands, cutting to the chase.

'I think I need the loo again,' Di says.

She's been to the loo three times in the past hour.

'OK, nip to the loo, then I'll help you on with your dress,' I tell her, my smile still firmly in place. She's starting to stress me out a bit now though.

'Erm, OK, I'll be right back,' she says. She tightens her dressing-gown belt before disappearing into the en suite.

'Is she OK?' Van asks me quietly.

'She's definitely being strange,' I reply. 'I should try and get it out of her, shouldn't I? Do we have time?'

'Well, time doesn't matter if she doesn't put her dress on, does it? Unless we move the wedding in here and she doesn't mind being in her dressing gown.'

'I'll float that by her,' I joke. 'Can you clear the room for me?'

'Of course,' she replies.

When Di eventually emerges from the bathroom, it's just the two of us. She glances around the room and, upon realising it's just the two of us, starts to panic.

'What's happened?' she asks. 'Is everything OK?'

'Everything is fine,' I insist. 'Come and sit with me.'

Di seems almost sheepish as she skulks over and sits on the bed next to me.

'What's going on?' I ask, getting straight to the point. 'Why won't you put that beautiful dress on?'

'Am I doing the right thing?' she asks quietly.

I wrap an arm around her and give her a squeeze. 'Only you can answer that,' I tell her. 'Do you still have your doubts about Charles?'

'They're more about myself than they are about Charles,' she admits. 'What if I'm not right for him? If I'm not good enough for him?'

'Di, of course you're good enough,' I tell her. 'You're amazing. I love you so much.'

'You're too good for me too,' she insists. 'Being here at a moment's notice, with all the people here you don't get on with, and you're not complaining.'

'You'll have to do the same for me one day,' I reply with a smile. 'Maybe. Hopefully. Not for ages, so don't worry about it.'

'I think just... the scare, and the ex causing trouble, and just wanting things to be perfect. I'm terrified. I do really, *really* want to be married, but I can't face getting up in front of all those people and fucking up. I can't do it. I can't.'

'All of it?' I ask.

'Just the ceremony,' she replies. 'I can't stand the idea of everyone watching me.'

Not only is Di freaking out, but she's dangerously close to tears, and there's no way I can fix this make-up, so I need to do something.

'Van joked about you getting married in here,' I tell her with a laugh.

'That would actually be great,' she replies, forcing a smile.

'Hmm,' I say to myself. 'You want to be married, but you don't want to do it in front of everyone. Leave it with me.'

'Really?' she says. 'Do you have an idea?'

'I do,' I tell her. 'Do you trust me?'

'With my life,' she replies.

'Then get that dress on and leave the rest to me,' I say as I jump to my feet, springing into action with a plan I came up with about twenty seconds ago. I think it can work – well, I know it can, but I'm going to need help. I'm going to have to swallow my pride and put a lid on my anger and call him.

'Hi Matt,' I say when he answers.

'Peach, hi,' he says, sounding pleased to hear from me, until he gets down to business. 'Is everything OK? We're all on the beach waiting. Has Di changed her mind?'

'No, no, everything is still going ahead, there's just been a slight change of plan,' I say. 'I'm going to need your help though.'

I can hear myself being bizarrely formal with him, in a way that he must pick up on, but he's ready to tackle the task at hand.

'Sure,' he replies. 'Just tell me what you need.'

'OK,' I reply. 'But you need to be sneaky...'

34

At 11.48 a.m., eighteen minutes later than they were supposed to, Di and Charles tied the knot in an ultra-private beach ceremony, surrounded by only their closest family and members of the wedding party.

We're already on a private island, so it was already a relatively exclusive affair, but after Di's cold feet about tying the knot in front of people, I set about putting the wheels in motion for her to get married on a different bit of beach, with only her very nearest and dearest watching.

I told Matt, who told Charles, who said that all he wanted was to be married to Di and he didn't care how he did it (it sounded more romantic when he said it, I promise). The two of them set about sneaking the parents away from the original ceremony location, ushering them to the new one, and I made sure I took the girls to the right place.

The private ceremony was everything Di and Charles wanted it to be, and I love that because that's all that matters. That they are happy with it. And sure, you might think that everyone else (not immediate family and less close friends) would be upset to have missed it, but they weren't, because it meant they got to start the reception sooner. So long as people get some food, drink and the chance to party, they're not going to mind that they didn't get to spectate the actual 'I do's.

It's party time, now that we're all at Grotta Biancofiore, but it looks a little different to the last time I was here. When Matt and I were here tasting food, it was set up in its usual restaurant arrangement, but now it looks even better, all dolled up for the wedding. I can't wait to see this place at night, when it's dark outside, and we have all the lights on. This really is a dream wedding location.

All the guests are currently mingling with glasses of champagne and delicious canapés – mini *panzerotti*, which are these amazing closed deep-fried pizzas – while we wait for the happy couple to arrive after having their photos taken.

I'm currently chatting with Van, Uncle Mike and Auntie Jane. Van is recapping the events of the last week for them, but a parent-friendly version that is missing pretty much every event you could call interesting.

'Hey,' Matt says are he joins our group.

When we're chatting with my uncle, we speak and sign everything, so that he's always included in the conversation.

'This is Matt, the best man,' Van says/signs. 'Matt, these are my parents, Mike and Jane.'

'Nice to meet you both,' Matt says, as he makes the sideways thumbs-up gesture he remembers Van making at him when they met.

'*Did he just tell me to piss off?*' Uncle Mike asks with his hands.

'*He's been learning sign language from your daughter,*' I reply. 'Matt, let's go get a drink.'

I say goodbye for us and usher him away.

'I just said something offensive, didn't I?' he says. I can tell how hard he's cringing through the change in his voice.

I lead Matt over to the railings. It's funny, the sea is the only thing you can see from here, and during the day, the view hardly changes, and yet it's just so mesmerising. I can't wait to be looking out here later when the sun is setting, I bet that's a sight to behold.

'Ladies and gentlemen, can I have your attention please?' Charles's dad says through a microphone. His dad looks just like a middle-aged version of him, with big rich-guy energy, which makes me feel like he's the kind of person who shouldn't have a mic, but always ends up with one. 'Please allow me to introduce, for the very first time, Mr and Mrs Blake.'

All of the guests cheer and clap – and I do feel a huge wave of relief wash over me when I realise that people really don't mind that the ceremony took place without them. This is the bit that matters. This is how we celebrate together.

Di looks beyond beautiful in her dress. Genuinely, if I look at her for too long, I get a tear in my eye and a lump in my throat. Charles looks great in his suit – so does Matt, but I'm trying to ignore that fact. I'm also trying to ignore how good his hair looks, how he's trimmed his beard a little shorter than usual, and how much I want to rip his clothes off him. It's a cruel irony when, the more someone does to piss you off, the less you like them but the more you want to pounce on them.

Di and Charles do the rounds, thanking people for coming, being hugged and kissed and congratulated again and again and again. Eventually the two of them are separated by the hordes – at least they'll cover more ground that way, and then we can eat.

'Right, I'd better go see if Di needs a hand,' I say. 'See you later.'

'Will you see me later?' Matt asks.

'Hmm?'

'Will you see me later?' he repeats. 'Will *I* get to actually see *you* later? I can tell you're avoiding me.'

'It's my sister's wedding, I'm busy,' I tell him, although for someone who is trying to shut this down, I can't actually muster up all that much politeness.

'Yeah, but that's the thing. You weren't busy until you were,' he points out.

'That makes absolutely no sense,' I tell him.

It does though. He's not stupid – he knows I'm avoiding him.

'You couldn't even look at me during the vows,' he points out. His voice gets the tiniest bit louder as his frustration grows.

'Keep your voice down,' I insist firmly. 'It wasn't our vows, was it? I didn't have to look at you.'

'You can hardly look at me now,' he points out. 'You're looking out to sea. What's going on?'

To tell him that I was thinking about throwing him in it would be counterproductive to the no-drama vibe I'm going for today, but I don't think I'm going to be able to get him off my back until I say something.

'You're determined to do this, aren't you?' I reply. 'Fine, I'll tell you what's wrong, but then you have to leave me alone, OK?'

Matt takes a couple of steps back. I don't think he was expecting me to say something like that.

'I know it was you who told Di about Canada,' I tell him. 'After we agreed we wouldn't, you went ahead and did it anyway, and it nearly ruined the whole thing.'

'How do you know that?' he asks. The sort of soft, worried

look on his face has tensed up into something much harder. He looks almost angry.

'Because she said she wasn't going to go through with it, until I talked her back around,' I explain.

'No, how did you know it was me who told her?' he asks again.

'Because she told me,' I reply. 'So you can stop playing dumb with me.'

Matt just laughs to himself for a second. Then he makes a move to walk away, so I place a hand on his arm to stop him.

'Oi, what are you laughing at?' I ask.

'Di told you it was me who told her?' he checks.

'Yes, well, no, technically she told Van, who told me.'

'Well, you might want to have a word with them both,' Matt says. 'One of them is lying to you.'

With that, he pulls his arm away from mine and walks off, leaving me standing here, wondering what the hell is going on.

I glance back over towards Vanessa. She's leaning back onto the railings casually. She has a glass of champagne in one hand, which she routinely sips from, but with her sunglasses still on and the smile she always wears in social situations, it's so hard to tell what's going on in that head of hers. Hmm. She has been acting a little bit funny. At some point, over the last few days, she's seemed so much more intense – the stag and hen party is an excellent example. Van is fun, but she threw that wild house party out of nowhere and had zero chill all night. The only way I can think to describe it is that Van has lost her cool. Everything she does, even when she's being a wild child, is just so effortless. These past few days it's been like she's trying too hard, but I just don't know why.

Van is the kind of person who you can tell all your secrets to and know that she will keep them no matter what, but it's not always a two-way street. She is completely unknowable. Her business is her business. Her heart is something she will deny exists, even if you tortured her, even if you cut out her actual heart and put it in her hand!

I could ask Di if she knew what was wrong with her but, more than anything, I don't want to ruin her wedding. Especially not when... oh, God.

I scan the room for Di as I think about her and expect to spot her posing for yet another photo from a delighted relative, but instead I catch her hurrying across the room, and she looks upset.

I head towards her, picking up the pace so that I can gain on her, which thankfully doesn't take long due to the number of people who are trying to flag her down to talk to her.

'Hey, hey,' I say. 'Are you OK? What's wrong?'

Di ushers me to the side of the room. Well, the wall of the cave.

'He knows,' she blurts. 'Oh my God, Peach, he knows.'

'Who knows what?' I ask her, knowing there are a few very different possible people who could know very different things.

'Why do I end up with my stupid mistake of an ex at my fucking wedding?' she rants. 'He knows about the baby – well, that's what he said. He says he's going to ruin the wedding, that he's going to tell everyone everything. He doesn't believe me that there isn't a baby. Someone must have told him.'

Van? She's the only other person who knows. I didn't tell anyone, and it obviously doesn't sound like Di has told anyone.

'Look, it's OK,' I reply. 'Obviously you're not pregnant.'

I nod towards the glass of champagne in her hand.

'People will just think he's bitter and making it up?' I offer. 'Why would anyone believe him?'

'Even if they didn't believe him, I don't want to lie to people

– I don't want to start my married life by lying to Charles. And I really, really don't want any drama at this wedding – I want it to be an amazing day I can remember for the rest of my life. I feel like the best-case scenario for me now is him kicking off and someone dragging him out by his tie. It's going to be so embarrassing.'

'Listen to me, I'm not going to let that happen, OK?'

'I don't want you saying anything to him,' she tells me. 'You'll get upset and you won't be able to help but kick off at him.'

'I won't say anything,' I promise her. 'I'll just keep an eye on things. You go to the loos and fix your make-up, then come back out here and I'll flank you and Charles. No one will get close.'

'Thank you,' she replies. She puffs air from her cheeks. 'Back in a few minutes.'

I scan the room for Alex and eventually spot him at the bar where he's throwing back a shot. He places his glass down, thanks the bartender, and then heads back into the heart of the crowd. I see him notice Di as she heads for the toilets. He speeds up to try to talk to her, so I begin hurrying over, but she's safely inside the sanctuary of the ladies' loos before Alex can get to her.

Alex lingers a moment or two before he gives up and starts to mingle. I watch him smiling and greeting people as he walks through the crowd. My heart sinks when he approaches Mum and Dad. Is he going to tell them? Alex leans towards my dad, as though he's about to tell him something. I'm relieved when he just gives him a hug, my mum a kiss, and then gets on his way, because I wouldn't have had time to stop him if I'd wanted to. Next he sidles up alongside my auntie and uncle, who are currently introducing themselves to Charles's mum and dad, and begins talking to them. It must only be small talk though, because everyone is smiling and having a good time.

I can't believe how stupid I was to think that, if I could just get Di and Charles down the aisle, that the wedding would be saved and everything would be fine. That was definitely one of the early levels of this game. We're clearly nowhere near the boss fight, but I can tell it's on the horizon.

There's something so nerve-wracking about watching Alex working the room, walking around, seemingly being normal as far as everyone else is concerned. I can see him looming around people, like this dark cloud, this time bomb just waiting to go off. He could open his mouth at any second and completely ruin everything.

Eventually, Alex approaches Van and his face turns into something a little more serious. I don't need to worry about him saying anything though because we're all being ushered to our seats so that we can eat. Oh, and I was so looking forward to this part. When we're all in our seats at least I won't have to worry about who is talking to who, because we'll all be confined to our tables, and being on the top table with Di and Charles, I can carefully monitor who tries to talk to them.

It's not the most fun way to spend a wedding though, is it?

35

Now that we're successfully through our meal and the speeches, Di seems a lot brighter. In fact, if you ask me, she's managed to push Alex out of her mind, at least for bursts of the last couple of hours. I wonder if he may have retreated a little because I've been watching him like a hawk and he's either a really good actor, or he's actually starting to enjoy himself.

But when the announcement comes that we can all finally leave our seats, mingle and dance, I gear myself up for working security detail again. If I can just keep Alex away from Di and Charles for the rest of the evening, then I will have done my job – the only real chief-bridesmaid duty I have: to make sure this wedding goes to plan without a hitch.

'Oh my God, let's dance,' Di says excitedly once the band starts playing. There had been talk about a surprise wedding band that Charles had booked without consulting Di, and he's chosen a good one. They're a cover band who perform popular hits, and when they open with Chesney Hawkes's 'The One and Only', you can tell it has made Di's day. Di has always been the kind of person who loves to dance, and she absolutely adores pop music – especially party hits.

'I'll catch you up in a couple of minutes,' Charles tells her. Kissing her before he'll let her out of his sight.

'Yeah, I'm just going to grab some more water and then I'm all over it too,' I reply.

Di and Van head off to the dance floor – they're the only two on there to start with, which is so like them. And as soon as I get another drink, I'll be joining them, although I might have to kick these heels off first – very gently, before I hide them somewhere safe, because I never would have thought I was the kind of girl who could fall in love with a pair of shoes but, in actual fact, I've just never been able to afford a pair expensive enough to love. I suppose, when they cost as much as it does to raise a child, you find it easier to care for them in a similar sort of way.

I make a move to head for the bar, but Charles stops me.

'Peach, just a sec,' he says.

I sit back down.

'Listen, while it's just us, I wanted to thank you, from the bottom of my heart, for making all of this happen.'

'You're welcome,' I tell him. 'I'm pretty sure I'd do anything for my sister.'

'She's lucky to have you,' he says. 'We both are. Thanks for keeping what happened in the past a secret from everyone.'

'Sometimes you have to keep things a secret to protect people,' I say with a shrug.

'Is that why you and Matt are pretending there's nothing going on between you?' he asks, with what he believes is a knowing smile. 'Because you're really overdoing it.'

'Oh, no, we're off again,' I tell him, very matter-of-factly. 'Our interactions, from start to finish, appear to have been a series of misunderstandings.'

'The two of you are clearly perfect for each other,' Charles says. 'And he must really like you, because Matt doesn't go in for this sort of thing lightly, and I get the feeling you don't either.'

'Hmm, I wonder whose fault that is?' I tease – God, I never thought I'd get to the stage where I was cracking jokes about what happened, much less with Charles himself. 'Listen, don't worry about it, I'm going to get a drink. Go and dance with your beautiful bride, enjoy yourselves, and I'll come and join you.'

'Cheers, sis,' he replies.

'OK, that's too soon, or too weird,' I say with a laugh. 'Probably just don't do it.'

'Got it,' he replies. 'Catch you in a bit.'

When I reach the bar, I order my drink and then turn around to look back at the dance floor. Di is having the time of her life. It makes me so happy to see my baby sister so happy. As crappy as I feel about my own romantic situation, it's hard to care when I'm basking in Di's happiness.

I notice Alex stand up from his seat and make a beeline for the top table. He's heading for Charles!

I get over there as fast as my heels will allow. By the time I'm there, Alex is giving Charles a handshake and a pat on the back.

'I just thought you should know—' Alex starts. I don't let him finish.

'Alex, can I borrow you?' I interrupt.

'Erm, yeah,' he replies. 'What, now?'

'Yeah,' I say. 'Just for a few minutes.'

'Looks like you're wanted, mate. Catch up with you later,' Charles tells him.

'This way,' I say, leading Alex over to the railings, next to the big drop down to the water below, where I'm having most of my important conversations, apparently. Perhaps I just like the idea of an exit route. 'Listen, you need to leave.'

'What? Why?' Alex frowns.

'She doesn't love you,' I tell him, cutting to the chase. Yes, I know that I promised Di I wouldn't say anything, but this is damage limitation. If I don't stop him, he's going to do something, so I'll take my chances trying to get through to him, even if tough love is the only card I have to play.

'Yes, she does,' he replies. 'She told me she did. Well, she told me she *could* – she said we could get there, one day. Anyway, how do you know? We said we were keeping it under wraps.'

'She told you she *could* love you one day?' I reply in disbelief.

'Yes. Like, eventually. If we took some time to date, get to know each other again, see where things went...'

'I find that really hard to believe,' I tell him. 'It's her wedding day. You need to get a grip. Would she really marry someone else if she did-slash-could love you?'

'Wait, are you talking about Di?' he says.

'Obviously,' I reply.

'Oh.' He thinks for a second. 'Ohhh.'

'Oh what?'

'Yeah, I'm not talking about Di. I'm sort of seeing someone else,' he confesses. 'But don't tell anyone.'

Does he really think I'm going to fall for that?

'Did you tell her about Canada?' I ask him.

'Peach, how many have you had?' he chuckles.

'Come on, you must have,' I say. 'It makes so much sense. Matt and I were talking about it in the bathroom that joins onto your bedroom, on the night of the party – you overheard us.'

Alex sighs.

'Are you really going to make me do this? Fine, OK, here it is,' he rambles, annoyed that I've backed him into a corner. 'I was with Vanessa that night, OK? She made me promise not to tell anyone until we knew where it was going, in case we upset anyone. I was with her that night, in one of the other rooms, because she said you were already in the room you share.'

'You and Vanessa?' I reply in disbelief.

'Yes,' he replies. 'Is that so hard to believe?'

It's like he's reading my mind.

'It's been a matter of *days*,' I point out.

'We've been getting together, any chance we can. And we have known each other for years,' he insists. 'Sure, it's early days, but we're just seeing what happens. She went a bit funny with me, for a bit. All that stuff she did at the party – totally to make me jealous, and it worked! The passion between us that night, oh my God.'

Alex's eyes roll into the back of his head.

'Let me stop you there,' I say quickly – I really don't need to hear that part. 'So, you're not interested in Di, and you weren't in your own room that night? You really did just come along for the free holiday?'

'No!' he replies firmly. 'And yes to the free holiday – who turns down a free holiday?'

No one, apparently. Still, things just aren't adding up. Di said her ex was hassling her. Begging her to get back with him. That he knew about the pregnancy scare. Why would she lie about all that?

And if it wasn't Matt who told Di about Canada, and it wasn't Alex, then who could it have been? I glance around the restaurant, looking for someone who could have something to gain by telling Di that Charles had been married before.

'You know, I think we were in Chris's room,' Alex says. 'So maybe he crashed in my room?'

As soon as Alex mentions Chris's name, I spot him, sitting at his table, slumped back in his chair. He's drinking whisky, and he's knocking it back. He's also glaring angrily and, when I follow his gaze, I can see what he's looking at: Di and Charles cuddled up on the dance floor, dancing to a beautiful, slowed-down, stripped-back cover of 'Toxic' by Britney Spears.

Suddenly everything clicks into place and it feels like the cave is closing in on me. Every part of the puzzle fits together perfectly and suddenly so, *so* much makes sense, but there's so much I can't get my head around too. Di and Chris?! My *sister* and my *ex*?!

'Sorry for accusing you,' I tell him quickly, trying to pretend everything is fine. 'I just got my wires crossed. I'll have a word with Van for you, if you like? I'll tell her to be normal.'

'Cheers,' he replies with a laugh. 'I do kind of like her weird though.'

'We all do,' I say. 'Sorry again.'

'That's OK,' he says. 'I was just about to tell Charles how happy I was for the pair of them. I'll have to wait until he tears himself away from his bride now.'

'Looking at them now, I reckon that will be after the honeymoon,' I joke, but suddenly it gets really hard to pretend I haven't just figured out exactly what's been going on. 'Hey, can you ask Chris if I can have a word with him, please?'

'Yeah, sure,' Alex replies. 'See you in a bit.'

I watch him wander over to Chris. He speaks into his ear before pointing me out. Chris throws back the last of his drink before heading over, as instructed, but the path he's taking is hardly a straight one. I feel motion sick just watching him.

'I don't want you back,' he tells me, making himself clear from the get-go.

'I know you don't,' I reply. 'You want Di. My *sister*.'

I can hardly say the words. I can't believe it.

'Yeah, yeah, all right,' he moans. 'Don't you start too. "Oh, she's my sister, we shouldn't have done it." Blah, blah, blah. She told you then?'

'She didn't need to,' I reply, swallowing down the lump in my throat. 'You overheard me and Matt talking about what Charles did in Canada?'

'Yeah,' he replies.

Wow. So Di must have lied about it being Matt who told her because she didn't want us connecting her to Chris.

'And you figured out I'd bought a pregnancy test, and that it was for Di,' I continue.

'You weren't very subtle about it,' he points out with a snort.

'So, what, the two of you slept together before she went on holiday?'

'Ding, ding, ding,' he replies kind of cruelly. 'Give this girl a medal.'

'How long were you together?' I ask.

'Well, just one night,' he replies. 'But it was a great night, and we left it at, saying when she got back from her holiday, she would call me. But she never called – and then Charles eventually called and I wound up here, and then it all felt like fate and I knew I needed to chase her.'

'Charles only invited you here to mess with me, you moron,' I tell him. 'And it's been far more effective than he could have anticipated.'

'When I realised Di thought she was pregnant—'

'Well, she isn't,' I inform him.

'Yeah, I figured that out when I saw her knocking back the drinks,' he replies.

Chris dials the bravado down a notch. I swear, it's almost as though he seems disappointed.

God, what a mess. If there's one thing I've learned this week, it's that the women in my family need to meet some new men, rather than simply sharing out the few we've got on the books already.

'Chris, what do you think is going to happen?' I ask him softly.

'I thought I could convince her to give things a shot with me,' he says confidently.

'And how's that working out for you?' I reply. 'Because, from where I'm standing, it looks like Di just married someone else, right in front of you.'

'I *know*,' he replies.

'Whatever you think you have with her – she doesn't feel the same. She just got married and look how happy she is. She isn't thinking about you. You just need to quit while you're ahead, and while no one knows.'

'What if I love her?' he says. 'What if I've always loved her?'

God, that hurts. That really, really hurts. You can be totally over someone, with no intentions of getting back together with them and feel absolutely at peace, but you only do that by isolating when things were good from when things went bad. But thinking back to when we were together and wondering if Chris was pining for my sister the whole time... Wondering if my sister was pining for him... Thinking about the two of them getting together and keeping it from me...

'If you do actually love her, you'll leave her alone,' I tell him. 'She's married, she's happy, she's not even thinking about you.'

'So, what do you suggest I do now, huh?' he asks.

'Go home,' I tell him. 'There's nothing you can do. Embarrassing her at her wedding won't make her love you – it will make her hate you. So please, just go home.'

Chris massages his temples. He must know I'm right.

'OK, fine, I'll leave,' he says. 'I know when I've lost.'

He's a few days behind schedule on that one but I'll let him have it. I just need him out of here. I can't even stand looking at him.

'I think staying here is just going to upset you,' I say. 'So maybe pack up and leave before people get back to the villa.'

'Fine,' he says. 'Fine, I'll go.'

'Thank you,' I tell him, but he doesn't reply. He just walks off.

That's Chris dealt with, now to deal with Di. I make my way over to her, onto the dance floor, and the second she sees me she takes me by the hands and starts dancing with me.

'Peach, it's P!nk,' she says excitedly as the band covers 'Who Knew'. 'We love this one! And Van requested 'Hotline Bling'. She's going to tell dad when it's on, so Charles can see his moves.'

'I'm legitimately so excited,' Charles tells me.

Their happiness is overwhelmingly contagious. It's hard not to feel something wonderful just by standing so close to them.

'Can I just borrow you for a minute, Di?' I say.

'Erm, yeah,' she replies. 'Is everything OK?'

I stop as we get to the edge of the dance floor.

'Just to let you know... Alex isn't going to be a problem,' I tell her. 'It seems like he's moved on to someone else.'

'Oh, OK,' she says.

She doesn't seem all that relieved, but of course she doesn't. She was never worried about Alex.

'Are you sure you're OK?' she asks. 'You don't seem yourself.'

'I'm fine,' I tell her. 'Just... you know. It's an emotional day.'

'You're so sweet,' she replies. 'Thank you so, so much for making this wedding happen. I genuinely don't think I've ever been happier.'

'You're welcome,' I reply.

Di grabs me and squeezes me tightly. I squeeze her back.

'Oh, by the way, Chris just came to say goodbye to me,' I add as she releases me. 'He said he had to fly back home tonight – I don't know if he had some kind of family emergency. I didn't want to pry. Anyway, he said to say sorry to you and Charles, but he had to go.'

'OK,' she says brightly. 'Never mind, hey? Coming to dance?'

'Go have fun,' I tell her. 'I'll be there in a bit.'

It's like I said earlier, sometimes you have to keep things a secret to protect people.

Di is my baby sister, I'd do anything for her, and this whole week has been about making sure today was her perfect wedding day. I love her and I'll always have her back, and if that means pretending I didn't find out about her one-night stand with my ex-boyfriend, then so be it. We've all made mistakes – we certainly all have at this wedding – and based on what Di said before when I thought we were talking about Alex instead of Chris, it's clear she thinks it was a huge mistake, so what's the point in calling her out about it? What would kicking off at her wedding achieve? At the end of the day, I will forgive her – I'm pretty sure I already have – and after everything I've been through to make sure this wedding goes ahead, I'm not about to be the person who ruins it.

I can't stay here though. I need to leave. I can't put on a brave face and pretend none of this happened. I need time, and space, to get past it, for everyone's sake.

I'm not exactly sure how I can leave in a hurry though, because we had to organise boats to get us here, but I'll find a way. The mood I'm in right now, I'd rather take my chances at swimming than stay here trying to keep this brave face on for another second...

36

I'm sitting on the boat dock, alone, far beneath the cave where the wedding party is still going strong. I can see the glow of the lights, I can hear the music and the happy guests. But down here, it's just me, with my fancy shoes on the floor next to me and my feet in the water below. It feels so lovely and cool, but otherwise I'm feeling pretty crappy.

Before I came down here, I put in a request for a boat, but they couldn't tell me how long it would take to get back and pick me up (I suppose I just missed the one Chris took, but I wouldn't have wanted to sit with him anyway), so here I am, thinking about things.

'Fancy some company?' I hear Van's voice call out.

She's making her way down the last few steps, carefully, with her shoes in one hand and a bottle of champagne in the other.

'Sit next to me at your own risk,' I call back. 'I know about Alex.'

'Oh,' is all she says. She doesn't retreat though. She plonks herself down next to me.

'Have a drink,' she says, passing me the bottle.

I take a swig.

'Did he tell you?' she asks softly.

'Nah, I figured it out,' I reply.

'Do you think Di will be upset?' she asks.

'No,' I reply confidently.

Well, she seems too loved-up, and with the Chris stuff being so fresh in her mind, I can't imagine her giving Van a speech about girl code anytime soon.

'I do quite like him,' she admits. 'I don't know why. I'm a bit embarrassed, to be honest, because I don't tend to like people.'

'I'm sure we could come up with a few million reasons between us,' I joke.

'Funny you should say that... Turns out he gave most of his money to charity!' she says in hushed tones, like it's something sordid. 'I have more money than him so, no, not that. I still like him anyway.'

'Well, I think it's great,' I tell her. 'I'm really happy for you, even if you're not.'

'What's going on with you?' she asks. 'You look like you've got the weight of the world on your shoulders.'

'I'm fine,' I tell her. 'Just ready to go home.'

My voice crackles on those last few words.

'As much as I'm sure you're enjoying living with your folks, I was wondering if you might be interested in sharing a place with me, when I move back to York?' she asks kind of casually. 'I don't fancy living on my own.'

'What, really?' I reply.

'Yeah, it will be great, like one of our old sleepovers, but much longer and with fewer Matthew McConaughey movies.'

I shoot her a look.

'I said less, not none, and only the ones before he became a serious actor,' she insists.

'Sounds perfect,' I tell her. 'Thank you.'

'We'll set the wheels in motion after the holiday,' she says. 'You know, I probably won't tell Di about Alex until after her honeymoon, at least.'

'Great idea,' I tell her. 'I think the rest of today just needs to tick along as smoothly as possible.'

'With that in mind, I have something for you,' she says, passing me the bottle again. 'Hang on to that, I'll go get it.'

'Erm, OK,' I say with a cautious chuckle.

'You just wait there,' she says as she disappears back up the steps.

I feel lighter, for knowing that Van is moving back to York, and better still now that she's invited me to move in with her. Well, I would have gone mad living with my parents for too long, and seeing as though I'm about to have a Di-shaped hole in my life, it will be so nice to have a friend – especially a friend like Vanessa.

I don't have to sit on my own for much longer before I hear Van approaching me again.

'Go on then, what have you got?' I ask.

'Er, I haven't got anything,' I hear Matt say.

'Oh, sorry, Van said she was... Did Van send you?'

'She told me you wanted to talk to me,' he says.

Ah, so that's what she had for me. I can't help but laugh quietly to myself.

'Yeah, I just wanted to talk,' I say, owning it.

'Were you leaving?' he asks as he takes a seat next to me.

'Yeah, I was just waiting for the next boat,' I reply.

'What? You can't leave yet,' he insists. 'The night is young, the party has hardly started – and Di will miss you.'

I shrug.

'I'll miss you,' he adds.

'Listen, I'm sorry I thought it was you who told Di about Canada. Someone I love and trust very much said that you told them, but they were lying, because they thought it was the best thing for everyone.'

'You disagree?' he prompts.

'I do, because it drove a wedge between us,' I tell him. 'Things were going so well.'

'It's just a bump in the road,' he replies.

'Yeah, but it's *another* bump in the road,' I say. 'We just haven't had a minute to figure things out before something else has thrown a spanner into the works. At this point, I can't tell if there's something real between us, or if this is just a whirlwind of a holiday romance that ends the second we get on that plane. It's just hard to see through all the bullshit – if we'd been given a fair shout, maybe we would have a better idea about how we were feeling right now. The run-up to this wedding has been such a rollercoaster.'

'But if we hadn't bumped into one another for this wedding, we never would have got back in touch,' he points out. 'So it's not all bad.'

'That's true,' I say with a sigh. 'I just wish we could wipe the slate clean. Try again, from the start, like *Groundhog Day*.'

Matt takes my face in his hands and pulls my lips onto his. He kisses me ever so gently for a few seconds before letting go again.

I may not be sure about a lot of things, but I can't deny everything that kiss makes me feel.

'It deeply concerns me how often you use that movie as a point of reference,' he whispers with a smile.

I laugh. I wasn't expecting him to say that.

'Look, come back to the party with me. We'll drink, we'll dance, we'll have fun – we won't worry about what we are or where we're going,' he says. 'We've gone a little off-track, but let's just go try to have a good time and see if we wander back in the right direction, OK?'

'OK,' I reply, not all that convincingly.

'I can tell you have no faith in the plan, but just stick with it,' he insists. 'I promise you, you'll know exactly where we stand and what you want by the time you get home.'

'Well, I can't argue with a promise,' I say. 'OK then, let's head back up.'

I find my enthusiasm for the rest of the evening, but I can't shake the feeling that things are not going to work out the way I want them to. But today isn't about me, it's about Di, and he's right, I should be there.

I just need to try to push the future out of my mind and try to have a good time and see where we end up, rather than worrying about it tonight. I just hope Matt is right, about things clicking into place, because right now I have no idea what's going to happen, and that doesn't seem like a good sign at all.

37

'Oh, can't you all stay?' Di asks, all emotional and teary-eyed. She looks to Charles, for his approval, but I get in there first.

'No way,' I insist. 'This is your honeymoon, remember? And anyway, you'll be heading to Hawaii in a couple of days.'

'I know, but I'm just going to miss you all so much,' she replies. 'We feel like a proper little family.'

'You know what? I feel like I understand why people on *Love Island* cry so much at the end of their journey now,' Lex chimes in.

'I understand why they cry so much during,' I add under my breath.

Chris had packed up and gone by the time we got back in from the wedding last night, and Van left for her flight back to LA a couple of hours ago. She says she's going to get her ducks in a row and move back to York as soon as possible, and I can't wait. Neither can Alex – he will not shut up about it – and given that I'm the only person who knows about them, I'm the only one he has to talk to about it, and he is *talking* about it.

Oh, and Ben left at the same time as Van, to catch his flight to... wherever he lives. I don't actually remember, if he ever even told me, but I suppose I was never actually all that interested in him. I guess I just stopped thinking about him.

So it's just me, Alex, Lex and Matt flying home together, just like we did on the way here. I wish I'd know then what I do now.

We're currently gathered by the dock on the island, waiting to board the boat that will take us back to the airport. It is such a warm, sunny day – the perfect kind, where the heat feels glorious and everything smells so good, but isn't it one of life's cruel jokes, that the last day of your holiday should be the hardest one to leave on?

I'm finding it difficult for a few reasons. Not just because southern Italy is a lot nicer in the summer than northern England, but because we're in the holiday bubble here, where nothing matters, and only we exist. Despite what Matt promised me last night – that I would know what I wanted and what we were doing before I got home – I feel no closer to knowing the answer to those questions, and once Matt and I are out of the holiday bubble that is keeping us close together, I worry that we'll just drift apart.

Di grabs me by the arm and pulls me to one side.

'I really can't thank you enough for everything you did yesterday,' she tells me again. She still doesn't know the half of it. 'For everything you've done over the past week, really. I was ready to let one little mistake ruin the rest of my life until you talked me out of it.'

'We all deserve a second chance,' I tell her.

'Well, I promise I'll never keep anything a secret from you again,' she reassures me. 'I'm so sorry that I did.'

I think Di saying this, with no idea that I know exactly what happened, is mostly for herself, rather than me. This is her way

of apologising to me and swearing not to make the same
mistake again, without actually confessing the truth to me. She
does really seem like she means it, and in a weird way, I appreciate the gesture. Hopefully now, we can just both forget about
it and put it behind us. I am still annoyed that she lied to me,
but otherwise, what's the point of rocking the boat over it?
Saying something yesterday would have ruined her wedding
and our relationship. And over what? A boy I broke up with
seven years ago, who I quickly decided I was better off without?
Nope. I thought Chris had ruined my life back then, but he
didn't, and I'm certainly not going to let him do the same now.

'Just focus on enjoying your honeymoon,' I tell her. 'It will
be back to reality soon.'

'Mind if I just muscle in here and say a proper goodbye to
my new sister-in-law?' Charles asks.

It has to be the biggest 180-flip of all time, but I genuinely
feel so warm towards him now.

'You take care of my baby sister,' I tell him as we hug.

'You don't need to worry about that,' he replies. 'You take
care of Matt for me. He's the closest thing I've got to a brother.'

'Sure,' I reply with a smile. We'll just leave it at that.

'Right, the boat is here, everyone on,' Lex says, suddenly the
boss.

We all say our goodbyes. We hug, we kiss, and then we get
on the boat. And then that's it. The holiday is over.

Just because of the order we boarded, Lex and Matt are
sitting together, and Alex and I are on the seats in front of them.

Alex twists around to talk to them.

'Do either of you mind if I sit with Peach on the flight
home?' he asks. 'I just have so much I want to talk to her about.'

'Knock yourself out,' Lex replies. I think she's a little
annoyed to have missed out on a holiday romance.

'Yeah, of course,' I hear Matt say.

Well, that's that then. We haven't had an opportunity to talk alone this morning, we're not sitting together on the boat, and now we're not going to get a chance to talk on the plane either.

All that leaves us with is our time together at the airport after we land, which doesn't exactly leave us with long enough for things to click into place, does it?

I'm desperately trying to think of something that can change between now and when we arrive back in England, a thought or a feeling that will let me know what the right thing to do is, but I just don't see it.

Perhaps this was just a holiday romance – albeit a rocky one – but it wasn't all bad. I got to see my sister get married. I stayed in an amazing villa on a stunning private island. I did have fun with Matt, I made peace/friends with Charles, and I did get to meet a rock star. Just because this one thing didn't work out, doesn't mean I don't have a lot to be happy about. I just need to focus on looking forwards. I'll be moving in with Van, which will be amazing, and I'm sure I can turn things around at work if I just knuckle down. Plus my parents are staying at the resort on San Valentino for a few days, so at least I'll have the house to myself, and buy myself a little time before the next Naked Wednesday comes around.

Yes, there's still a bit of me that hopes things will click into place, but if they don't, I'm going to try my best to stay positive. I'm just trying to keep a level head about it all because, as much as I would love a relationship with Matt, I feel like we've got more baggage than we just loaded onto this boat, and with only a few hours until we're home, perhaps this is where it all ends.

38

'... and when I told Vanessa about it, she called me a dork, because she said no one should be as interested in electric cars as I am.'

For our entire flight, Alex has talked about Vanessa non-stop. And I mean non-stop. He's barely stopped for air.

'She's just such an uber cool person – and it sounds like she always has been,' he continues. 'Even when she was at school, she was sporty, she was actually the best badminton player in her year, she—'

'Oh my God, Alex!' I snap. 'Buddy, you've got to stop. Van is my cousin. I already know all of this. Every last bit of it and so much more. You've got to stop talking about her.'

He laughs awkwardly.

'Sorry, I just *really* like her.'

'Yeah, well, you're in luck, because she likes you too,' I reply.

He's not only in luck, he's going to need it. Van can be a handful, but I think that might be one of the reasons he's so into her.

As we're told to fasten our seatbelts and prepare for landing, I look out of the window and, as the ground below us gets closer and closer, I feel any chance of a relationship with Matt getting further and further away.

I must have checked my room four times when I was packing to make sure I didn't leave anything behind, but I don't feel like anyone has truly invented a suitcase that can safely transport a holiday romance back to reality. I'd ask Alex to look into it, but I can't get him to stop talking about Van for long enough to listen.

We land safely and soundly, and making our way through the motions is a smooth process. Eventually, we each have our cases and it's time to say goodbye.

'Well, it's been fun,' Lex says, not entirely convincingly. It's not that I don't think she's had fun, I just don't think she credits any of us with having a hand in it. 'See you all at Christmas or whenever.'

She's off already, before I have a chance to say much more than a simple goodbye. Well, of all the crazy things that have happened during this holiday, Lex and I making friends is just a step too far.

'Come here,' Alex says, pulling me in for a hug.

He squeezes me so tightly my feet lift off the floor for a second.

'We're going to be seeing a lot more of each other,' he whispers into my ear, so excitedly his voice tickles my neck, making me squirm out of his grasp.

'Yeah, I'll see you around,' I tell him.

It's so funny to think that when he turned up at the airport, we were all so convinced he'd come to ruin the wedding. It turns out he really was just delighted to be invited and really fancied the holiday.

'Matt, my friend, come here,' Alex says before giving him a

hug. A super blokey one with pats on the back and macho throat clearing afterwards. 'See you around.'

'Yeah, great to meet you,' Matt tells him.

And then it's just us.

'Oh, before I go, I have something for you,' Matt tells me.

'Oh?'

I watch him rummage around inside his pocket and my heart jumps into my mouth, wondering what he's going to pull out, what he's going to say...

He hands me a roll of euros.

'Take this,' he says. 'For what happened at the hotel last week. For the wine incident.'

I'm so happy he quickly and meaningfully added that on at the end, but I'm disappointed that that's all he has to say.

'You don't have to,' I insist, holding the money out for him to take back.

'Honestly, I feel so guilty,' he replies. 'Take it, and message me your bank details, so I can send some more.'

'Thanks,' I reply, tucking the money into my bag.

Why did he have to bring up the money thing first? Now things feel even more awkward between us. Whatever he says next is going to have to be really, really good...

'OK, well, see you around,' he replies.

Matt pulls me close for a hug, but it's so still and uncomfortable, like whatever relationship we had between us is well and truly dead.

'Erm, yeah, see you later,' I reply.

And then he walks away. He grabs his suitcase, extends the handle, and then walks off, dragging it behind him, leaving me all alone.

Well, I guess that's that then. Matt did say that, by the time I was home, I'd know where I stood. I certainly know that now.

I'd best make my way home – my own way home, because there's no one around to pick me up from the airport, so I'll have to take a taxi.

I allow myself one last sigh before I pull myself together and get on my way.

It's another busy day at the airport, so I head as close to the main doors as possible and pull out my phone to book a taxi.

'Excuse me, did you say you were waiting for someone too?' a voice behind me asks. It sounds a lot like Matt, but that doesn't make any sense.

I turn around. It is Matt.

'What?' I say blankly.

'I was supposed to be picking up my mate,' he replies. 'He's lucky I love him – this quick favour isn't playing out all that quick.'

I cock my head. What is he doing?

'Are you picking someone up too?' he prompts. 'From the flight held up by the airport strike...'

Suddenly I realise.

'Sorry, yes, my sister,' I say through the biggest grin.

He's recreating the day we met.

'Last time I offer to do anyone a favour,' he replies. 'I could do with one myself though... have dinner with me?'

I'm speechless. All I can do is smile like a maniac. At least I'm being just as smooth as the day we met, which is not smooth at all.

'I'm staying at the hotel across the road and I'm booked in for dinner later – it's a whole thing, to do with my job, but I'll be eating alone. I'd love it if you fancied keeping me company? Dinner is on me.'

What were his words, when I told him he didn't have to pay for dinner the first time around?

'This isn't something weird, is it?' I ask. 'Because there's no such thing as a free dinner.'

'I'll explain everything when we get over there,' he replies. 'I hope you like oysters.'

'Is this actually happening?' I ask in a whisper, breaking character for just a second.

'Yes,' he whispers back. 'It's *Groundhog Day*.'

Well, I did say I wished we could wipe the slate clean and let go of all our baggage. It looks like Matt is making it happen. The *Groundhog Day*-te to (hopefully) end all *Groundhog Day*-tes.

It means so much to me, that he's put all this thought and effort into kicking off our second chance. If there is one thing I'm sure of after this past week, it's that everyone deserves a second chance. Anyone can be forgiven if they truly regret what they've done, and it's never too late to wipe the slate clean and start again. Your old baggage should never slow you down, and your past mistakes should never define you. The future is entirely what you make it, and who you make it with.

'But, before we head over there, can I ask, what's your name?' Matt says.

I laugh. I can't believe he's so committed to this. It might be the best thing anyone has ever done for me.

'I'm Peach,' I say. 'And it's lovely to meet you.'

'It's nice to meet you too,' he replies. 'I'm Matt.'

ACKNOWLEDGMENTS

Thanks so much to Nia my incredible editor, to Amanda, and everyone else at Boldwood HQ for their brilliant work.

Thank you to every single person who reads and reviews my books. I wouldn't be doing this without you. All of your wonderful feedback means the world to me.

Thank you to Darcy for being there for me. Huge thanks to the amazing Aud for all her love and encouragement. Thank you so much to Joey for all of his support and for always listening to me bang on about my weird ideas – I hope I'm as useful to your writing as you are to mine. Big thanks to James for providing as much IT support as he does moral support. Thank you so much to Kim, for always being my biggest fan, and for always getting me such amazing publication presents, and thank you to Pino for all his support over the years (including taxi services).

Finally huge thanks to my husband, Joe, for always being there for me. It has been such a strange, difficult year but having you by my side has made it so much easier.

MORE FROM PORTIA MACINTOSH

We hope you enjoyed reading *Life's a Beach*. If you did, please leave a review.

If you'd like to gift a copy, this book is also available as an ebook, digital audio download and audiobook CD.

Sign up to Portia MacIntosh's mailing list for news, competitions and updates on future books.

http://bit.ly/PortiaMacIntoshNewsletter

Discover more laugh-out-loud romantic comedies from Portia Macintosh:

ABOUT THE AUTHOR

Portia MacIntosh is a bestselling romantic comedy author of 15 novels, including *My Great Ex-Scape* and *Honeymoon For One*. Previously a music journalist, Portia writes hilarious stories, drawing on her real life experiences.

Visit Portia's website: https://portiamacintosh.com/

Follow Portia MacIntosh on social media here:

f facebook.com/portia.macintosh.3
twitter.com/PortiaMacIntosh
instagram.com/portiamacintoshauthor
BB bookbub.com/authors/portia-macintosh

ABOUT BOLDWOOD BOOKS

Boldwood Books is a fiction publishing company seeking out the best stories from around the world.

Find out more at www.boldwoodbooks.com

Sign up to the Book and Tonic newsletter for news, offers and competitions from Boldwood Books!

http://www.bit.ly/bookandtonic

We'd love to hear from you, follow us on social media:

 facebook.com/BookandTonic

twitter.com/BoldwoodBooks

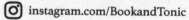 instagram.com/BookandTonic

CPSIA information can be obtained
at www.ICGtesting.com
Printed in the USA
LVHW041756061021
699709LV00010B/1821

9 781800 487543